3

Forget me not

A Whisper from the Future

Media Blackout

Lighthouse

Bedtime Story

Viva Voce

Passive House

The Interview

Two Dollar Game

Writer's Block

Parallax Observation

Play it again Sam

Cave Paintings

For

E. C. G

Forget me not

He was late, always late. So when he reached the bookstore entrance, the bright lights which spilled out onto the pedestrian precinct blinded him and added to his panic. He could not focus, everything was a blur. He could not see her inside. She had arrived early. Always early, always reliable. Paul stood in the store's ground floor, one of four levels of large book-filled spaces of a former business property that few could remember the name of. He looked across the store in a series of quick glances, in that way one does without actually seeing, his annoyance with himself growing as he really liked this girl. Millie was on the second floor, half of which was a coffee shop. Having arrived early she spotted a book of short stories which was on promotion. Millie thought about taking it to one of the comfy sofas and giving it a read just to see if it was a fit. She deliberated on the idea that the coffee and cake she would buy would justify a pre-purchase sampling. The alternative was an uncomfortable standing in the store reading the first few pages, and she felt like the assistants would spot her lingering far too long with one book. Finally she decided that at nine pounds ninety-nine pence, the risk was within acceptable limits, bought the book and could now enjoy the coffee and cake guilt free. That's the kind of girl she was, although sometimes it really bothered her. As she stood at the payment counter, she watched the screen displays on the ends of the bookshelves respond to the wandering book buyers. Suggested titles popped up based on *what you might like to read next.* One customer was looking at a table display of crime thrillers, the screen behind her was suggesting a self-help book, but she did not see it. Others did, and gave her a backwards glance.

It looked like the boy she had met last week might not show. It was now thirty-five minutes after when they had agreed. Sadly, she had to admit that she had liked him, and getting angry or disappointed wasn't really worth it, but it did hurt a bit. Just another pub conversation, she should have known better. Paul had started to admit to himself, as he wandered between the rows of bookshelves and the almost static shoppers, that he may just have blown it. Sadly, as he really, really did like her. Why could he not be on time for once? They did not meet online, there was no photographic record or profile, or means of contact. It had been old school. A chance meeting in a bar. Both of them in the same location for separate reasons, no chance of returning to familiar ground, a local haunt that none of them frequented. Neither had been to that bar before. No connection with locals who might be able to identify either of them, no romantic plot line of a trail of clues that would lead them back together, as in the movies. Even if someone had remembered, there was no way to search. Millie and Paul were part of a growing movement of the digitally anonymous, those who enacted their privileges under the 2041 Right to Personal Data Privacy Act. People who chose to enact this option, started to wear a pin. A small blue flower with a yellow centre. They called themselves *"Forget me nots"* after the flower that stayed closed in the glare of full sunshine, and the symbolism of being true to oneself and others.

Last week, Paul had noticed her in the group she was with, it looked like work colleagues, and eavesdropping on part of their conversation confirmed his assumptions. Millie was quiet, different, and seemed a little uncomfortable. She laughed when the group laughed but it seemed politely. She was dressed differently from the other four women who made up the group. More individual he thought, but couldn't quite explain it. Her hair was shoulder length, dark with soft curls. He noticed also that she was dressed more casually than the others which made him wonder if she did actually work in the same place or was she a friend of someone? Paul was heading out to watch an evening rugby game, a spare ticket from a friend. The bar was close to the stadium and Paul was meeting a couple of friends, who would bring the spare ticket. When his friends arrived, they explained that the ticket was in a different part of the stadium as it was a season ticket, so he would be on his own. They had a couple of pints and talked about the team's recent performance, but Paul had by this time, having noticed Millie, was distracted. Moments before Paul's friends suggested leaving for the game, the group of four women with Millie looked as if they were getting ready to leave. Millie wasn't heading out with them, despite their pleadings. When they left, Millie moved her drink over to a table near to the bar and took out a book from her handbag. Paul watched her, stealing glances as he now processed the thought of standing alone on a freezing cold terracing against not going at all. So he reassured his friends that he would catch up with them at half time and let them depart the bar. He remembered that the food stalls in the stadium only took cash so he announced that he would have to backtrack down the street to find a cashpoint, and for his friends to go on ahead. Lots of places now took only cash payments. They used the data privacy act as a way to hide income and reduce tax liability. The government did not calculate this as a consequence of championing privacy, but for now there wasn't anything they could do. A sports stadium was an excellent data harvesting point, or it used to be. As Paul sat alone, he became aware of his thoughts that were more about this girl and less about rugby. He wondered how he could approach Millie. The doubts and self-confidence components of his past eight months in a disastrous relationship reemerged, conflicting with desire, he started to over think everything. Staying at the bar, he ordered a red wine. Millie appeared lost in her book, and Paul let his gaze linger for a moment too long. Millie looked up and directly at him. Then she smiled, held his gaze and returned back to her book, still smiling. Paul had looked away down at his drink and tried to manage his own smile. Millie placed her book down on the table, lifted her empty glass and walked over to the bar, standing beside Paul. Paul asked her, before he thought too much about it, if he could buy her a drink. Millie said thank you but politely refused. Paul then told her that if she would let him buy her a drink, she would in fact be saving his life. It was a line, that he heard himself say, and again realised that he had not really thought it through. However, Millie acted intrigued, and said that this decision was now was an enormous responsibility. Paul continued in his most serious tone that, indeed the purchase of this drink would both save him from a painful lonely death of hypothermia, on the terraces of the nearby stadium, and that he was reasonably sure that his team was going to lose. Millie, countered and asked Paul but what if his team won. Paul smiled and said that victory would still feel very cold, and lonely, distracted by the thought of a beautiful girl he almost met in a bar. This time he was a bit proud of himself, it seemed easy to do this with her. Millie, took a moment, pretending to consider the options at the same time tapping her finger on her bottom lip pondering on the dilemma as she stared past Paul into the darkness outside. She looked at Paul and said that it had better be a large glass of Merlot, then after deliberately looking him over so that Paul would notice, she told him to make it a bottle. She indicated to him to join her at the table as she left the bar and sat down. Paul had a very large grin on his face, the bar staff noticed, and he did feel a flush creeping across his face. As he waited at the bar, he thought that he had never met and spoke to anyone quite like her. Millie was sitting at her table, book closed, and she was looking right at him, smiling.

Once introduced by their first names Paul ventured to say how unusual the name Millie was. Millie told him that it was short for Millicent, she had been named after an aunt. She then told Paul that she had immunity from prosecution under law for what she could do to anyone who called her Millicent, on the grounds of prolonged child cruelty growing up with such a name. Paul just smiled and pretended to sympathise. The action of a fall, as in the part of falling in love had just happened. For the next hour as Paul's rugby team also fell and were put to the sword by the visiting Irish, a fact that he relished later telling friends why he had missed the game, they chatted about various things. They both wore the same pin. There were many things he did not ask, for fear of being too forward, and for respect of privacy. Now in the bookstore, that realisation now fueled his panicked search. For all of the information contained in the books of this bookstore, about love, life and the workings of the world, and he didn't know her full name, her address or the address of where she worked.

Millie had finished her coffee, but half of the cake remained. The first short story was good, clever and had made her forget about the cake. She decided, the answer to her current social status and what to do about it, would be indicated within one of the short stories. A sign would appear. She would place her fate at the hands of these writers. The coffee shop area was about half full, she stood up looked across the open plan second floor out at the book displays, hoping but not really expecting to see him. Millie wanted another coffee, to finish off her cake and one more story, which may just contain the answer. The young man serving, saw her approach. He apologised and told Millie that he needed to go downstairs for a minute and would get her order as soon as he returned. Millie was about to return to her seat when she spotted on shelving behind the counter a display of Christmas wrapped panettone. The design of the boxes were quite lovely. There was a screen built into the shelving, but it did not react to Millie. If it had, there would have without doubt been a connection made from her social media profiles to the Italian product. An almost instantaneous unique thirty second advert, complete with voice over and soundtrack, montaged together from all of the private things people now shared open and willingly, constructed by algorithms and good old-fashioned marketing techniques. A virtual salesperson at every corner of the store, more staff than customers. The sound volume of these screens was set quite low, just enough to make you lean in to hear your own personal message. She moved past and around the serving counter to get a closer look. Considering this as a possible present for her mother, she took one of the large boxes off the shelf and looked at the images on the packaging. She checked the price of the panettone against the other versions on the shelf, distracted, she did not see Paul enter the coffee area. He had walked towards the counter and had paused to scan the room for any sign of Millie. Millie turned around and saw him. He glanced at her ever so briefly as he looked again around the tables. He did not see her.

'Can I help you?' Millie offered. Millie placed the large box of panettone on the counter shelf in direct line of sight with Paul as he turned to face her.
'No, no thanks I am just looking for someone.' Paul replied as he continued to sweep his gaze across the scene, and then looked at his watch.
'Can I get you a coffee or a tea?' Millie now moved her head to the side of the boxed cake. Paul looked directly at her, but she had looked down at the floor.
'My treat.' she barely got that out before looking up and directly at him. Paul's face had a sort of stunned look, followed by what looked like an effort to focus.
'Millie?'

'Yes you know that girl you met last week, you just looked right at me.'

'Sorry, I thought you were,... someone else, sorry.' 'I am so sorry I'm late, then I couldn't find you when I got here and..'

'And when you did, you didn't recognise me, I must have made some impression?' Millie pretended to be hurt.

'Sorry, I kind of thought that you had already gone,' Paul said. The barista returned, Millie came around from the counter, pointing to the table where her belongings were, she gave him a hug and pushed him playfully away, asking him what he wanted to drink. Millie ordered coffees, as she waited she looked over at Paul and smiled. He was still looking very awkward.

'I'm really sorry Millie, I don't know what happened to the time, I thought I could get here ok and then I realised I had left leaving the flat too late.' Paul apologised.

'Would you have waited for me?' Millie asked.

'I have been thinking about you all week, I would have waited yes.'

'I didn't think you were the type of guy who would have left me here, so I bought this book and settled down to wait, I had stayed in the ground floor for about quarter of an hour, and then I decided to leave it to fate.'

'Fate?' Paul asked.

'Well did you ever when you were younger do the thing whereby you would make a decision if something happened in say the next minute?'

Paul shook his head unsure.

'Well I was standing on the ground floor, I said to myself, if in the next minute someone comes into the bookshop wearing something yellow, I would stay and wait for you, if not head home.'

'And someone came in?'

'Not exactly' Millie replied.

'Oh, so you just decided to stay then?'

'No I…I, bent the rules a little, I changed it to someone passing by the bookshop wearing yellow in the next 5 minutes'

'Right so someone did?'

'No not really, I kind of redefined the rules again.' Millie explained with a confessional tone.

'Redefined, would that be because you were really hoping I was going to show?' Paul suggested.

'Hm, well you have to be careful that you don't set too difficult a condition for the test as it may mean that what you really want to happen is that it doesn't happen.'

'Well that makes complete sense' Paul replied in a slight mocking fashion.

'Of course, to explain, you see yellow in wintertime may not have been my best fashion choice, so I said that if I was to see a display of books with a yellow dust jacket then I would stay'

'And you did'

'Yes… on the third floor, there was a display of..'

'Let me guess, a display of books something like approaching yellow in colour?'

'More mustard brown than yellow to be precise'

'I see so you just scoured this entire bookshop from top to bottom..'

'More bottom to top actually, but yes go on'

'From bottom to top in the hope that you would find the right sign from the heavens as to why you should stay and wait for me, I am not sure how to take this'

'Well obviously not as some kind of compliment.' Millie smiled

'How?'

'Because I was being kind to you, and you were nearly forty minutes late, and then you didn't recognise me, so there.'

'I didn't see you behind that counter because I wasn't expecting you to be there, and then you hid behind a big cake box thing, and I was in panic mode because..'

'Because?'

'Because I thought I may have lost you, I mean not, not lost you but lost the chance to see you again.' Paul looked at Millie for her reaction, he realised that he had just told her something. Millie reached over the table and placed her hand on Paul's.

'I like you, I have thought about you all week too, I would have changed the rules of my stay not stay decision to *if there was the chance of any books in this bookshop* if I needed to.'

A moment passed between them and there was no urgency to say anything just to smile and hold hands. The coffees cooled, they felt the warmth of each other's hands. Millie sat back in her chair and her face became serious.

'You saw the girls I was with in the pub?'

'Yes.'

'They work at the agency, front of house, I work in the design department which is part of the creative section and in separate offices at the back of the company space. They want to be seen, they are there to make an impression, despite what anyone says. I think they ask me out for drinks sometimes out of pity, I don't dress like them, I don't act like them, but they are not bad, I suppose I just need something they seem to have.' She paused for a moment and for the first time Paul saw a hint of sadness.

'I want to be seen Paul.' Millie finished her sentence looking down. Paul looked at Millie, he waited for her to look up.

'Sorry' Millie said, 'It's just that I don't think people ever see me.'

There was a moment of silence, Paul was feeling the guilt about not noticing Millie straight off, and wondering if he had hurt her. He wanted to say right there and then that he had seen her, but it just felt clumsy to say that out loud.

'Do you ever regret applying for privacy?' Paul asked.

'No, I don't really think about it anymore, you get the odd reaction from people that you are weird, perhaps not to be trusted, but I think that is because people need to '*have*' something about you, you know?'

'Yeah, I get it mostly in shops, when they realise you aren't broadcasting, and they say can I help you which is sometimes code for well how on earth can I help you?' Millie detected the sarcasm in Paul's voice and smiled.

'A friend of mine became ill, she started to think that when the public space and shop front advertising could no longer read her, after she went private, she thought that messages were being displayed about her. She started to read things the displays were showing when someone else was walking or standing near her. Then everyday she went out looking for evidence, got really down lost her job.'

'What happened to her?'

'She is still in hospital, some kind of therapy to reintroduce her to social media I think,' Millie replied.

'God that's a shame, some people just can't adjust, it's hard to be different when the numbers are against you.' Paul replied. Millie nodded gratefully, this is a nice guy she thought.

'Did you know, there are new contact lenses which they say will give you a heads up about someone soon as you look at them.' Paul added. Millie looked up from her coffee slowly shaking her head.

'Oh, wonder what it would say about me if you were wearing one of those?' She invited a compliment from Paul not sure if one would be offered. Clever Paul thought.

'Might help me to recognise you,' he said, Millie laughed.

'But if we were both connected, then I think that when I first laid eyes on you... there would be a red flashing light straight to my retina...'

'Oh interesting, a match then?' Millie suggested.

'No, just details of the number of book sales you had completed in the last month, and a warning that there is a very high chance of you being... a bit of a bluestocking.'

'Hah.' Millie said a bit too loudly. 'I suppose you were counting on me not knowing what that meant, well I do, and well... I, hmm, I suppose it's a compliment really, damn it, I am impressed that you could use that in a sentence, hmm.' Millie was very impressed. Paul just sat looking at her slightly smug.

'Is your book good?' Paul asked. Millie nodded.

'I love short stories, I think that there is a real skill in telling a story like that, I try to read each story from beginning to end as a contract with the writer, I will give him or her my undivided attention and she or he will tell me a story.' Millie gave a shrug of her shoulders as if to say, that's just me. Paul nodded, he really wanted to kiss her. Millie looking straight at Paul unbuttoned her cardigan and took it off. She was wearing a fitted denim shirt. She folded her cardigan neatly and placed it on the seat next to her. Then she moved her seat closer to the table and placed her arms by her side. She watched Paul's reaction closely.

'Well Paul, purveyor of obscure words, so, would you like to hear a short story?' Millie offered.

'Okay, yes.' Paul leaned forward and rested his folded arms on the table.

'Right then, I need you to give me your undivided attention for the next few minutes, a contract between you the listener and me the storyteller.'

'Yes Ma,am, undivided attention it is.' Millie reached over for her coat. She unfastened the little blue flower *Forget me not* pin, and then attached the pin to the seam of her shirt just below her last opened button. It was most deliberately now in the middle of her chest.

Millie dropped her voice to a whisper, and invited Paul to lean in a bit closer.

'Oh, and there is something else I need you to do, and you must do it from the beginning to the end of the story, no exceptions.' Millie glanced around the coffee shop at the handful of seated customers. She returned her gaze to Paul and continued to whisper.

'I need you to look at my pin, here, the whole time'

Paul heard it, but he could not help saying 'What?'

Then he realised that he was looking at Millie's breasts and he looked up. 'You want me to look… there, why?

'Trust me, I am giving you permission to stare at my… pin, and I just want you to listen and not look anywhere else, do you think you can manage that?' Millie's question being more rhetorical that a genuine enquiry. Paul was now in that place where many men have found themselves, lost in the no man's land of what women say to what they mean, and how to navigate the difference. So confused as he was, the request, and its obvious attraction prevailed over any attempt at logic. He decided to try and play it cool, but it was not the temperature at which he was operating at that moment.

'I suppose, if that's what you want, I can stare at your very nice pin, and, I'll give you my undivided attention.' Paul said with a serious face, Millie rolled her eyes.

'Good, so we are clear as to the rules, yes?' Millie nodded.

'Crystal clear.' Paul replied, looking without blinking into Millie's face, but thinking of something else.

'Right, you may begin.' Millie instructed. Paul pretended to loosen his neck by turning his head side to side, then applying pressure with his hands as if preparing for a contest, Millie frowned.

'If you don't cut that out there will be no story, and no benefits,' she said smiling.

'Okay, I am ready now.' Paul fixed his gaze on her body.

'Good, remember, do not look away until I have finished.'

'Gotcha, no danger,' Paul confirmed.

Millie took in a deep breath in preparation for her story, her chest swelled, and she was, like Paul, very aware of it.

'So, it's a very cold winter's night in the city, and there is a cosy little bar which is quite full with office workers and some rugby fans gathered there before heading out to the game, or onto nightclubs for Friday night entertainment. The bar is noisy with everyone chatting away and enjoying the drink. There is a girl, quite pretty, small in stature in her early twenties, with a group of other women, it looks like an office crowd. Now this girl is casually dressed, big wooly jumper and jeans kind of thing, and she kind of stands out from the others as they are dressed in skirts and tops and nice jackets. The other reason she stands out is that she is not talking that much. Now in comes a guy in his early to late twenties, and he is rather good looking, he goes over to a couple of other men, they look like rugby types. The girl notices him and stares passed the group of women, watching him chat to his friends. She sees that he does that thing whereby he pushes his glasses back with one finger on the centre of the frame, and it is a bit of a habit, because either the glasses are not a good fit, or in actual fact it's when he prepares to say something. He also holds his pint glass in an odd way, not at the side, but more around the back, causing his hand to curl more than looks comfortable. She wonders why that is. He has fair hair, not blonde, but a mixture of fair and light brown, cut short, but his parting is off centre and probably his natural style, rather than deliberately combed. Green brown eyes, about five foot ten or eleven, good build but not muscular. When he smiles he has a nice broad smile and his eyes smile as well which means it's genuine.
How are we doing down there still with me?' Millie asked with a mock concern.
'We are fine, and no you can't trick me into looking up even though it's not late twenties and I am reasonably muscular, but please go on.' Millie smiled.
'No loud gestures or mannerisms, he's listening to his friends, and at one point he appears to comfort one of the men by

putting his hand on his arm and nodding, as if to say it will be alright. She, the girl, finds that attractive. Then as his friends talk, he looks over at the girl, and she realises that he has picked her out from the group. She wonders what he might be thinking. As the minutes roll by each of them steals looks at each other, and in some bizarre coincidence of timing, the group of office colleagues start to leave, and his friends leave also. Leaving them both alone in the bar. Now being a confident woman, the girl knows that she has already captivated this man and so decides to move her drink to a vacant table, take out her book and wait and see if he has the courage to approach.'

'Really?' Paul enquired.

'Oh yes, a prisoner of his biology, oh did you see what I did there *captivated* and *prisoner,* that's a well-read bluestocking. Anyway, he does not come over and talk to her, so like I said, being a confident woman and not likely to feel disappointed by his lack of forwardness, she feels pity on the boy and decides to go up to the bar and order a drink and stand beside him, last chance for him to do something or it's back to the book. Luckily he does buy her a glass of wine.'

'Bottle of wine,' Paul reminded her

'Sorry bottle of wine, as she was trying to tell him that his attentions had not gone unnoticed and that he might be in with a chance.'

'Or she was borderline alcoholic'

'No, now no more interruptions, as I am nearly finished my story. So they get talking and they like each other and they decide to go on a second date. Then, at the second date, he is late and she has a bit of a dilemma as to whether or not to wait for him. It turns out that she decides to wait, and yes our boy turns up all of a fluster and blah blah blah, happily ever after.'

Millie stopped talking. Paul waited, as the seconds continued, he realised something was not quite right.

'Millie?' Paul waits a few seconds more, he looks up unsure as to the abrupt ending. Millie is staring hard at him, almost expressionless.

'Millie, what is it?' Paul asks again.

'That's the story Paul, that's it, unless you have something to add, something to tell me?' Millie's tone had changed to something more hostile. 'You can look up now.'

'That's a documentary Millie not really a story, that's just us from meeting to now.'

'Documentary, oh how right you are Paul, sure you don't want to tell me where this story is going, because the present has caught up with us and the rest of this production, well it's you that has the script.'

'Millie I don't understand, what script?'

Millie studied Paul's face, as if looking for a lie.

'Tell me Paul what did you think when someone you had only met once invited you to stare at her breasts, didn't you think that a bit odd?'

'I... thought you were just having a bit of fun with me, was I supposed to refuse, really, that's what you were wanting, a test was it, because if it was it's a bit fucked up to be honest.'

'Oh poor boy, he gets to stare at me, which he really wanted to do, and I can only imagine what you were thinking as I talked, and now he is feeling a bit used. Remember what I said Paul, I want to be seen, so tell me what colour of eyes do I have, what colour of shoes am I wearing, do I have any rings on my fingers?'

'Millie, I...'

'You can't answer any of that, because you haven't looked, you haven't seen me.'

'I'm sorry.' is all Paul could think to say.

'You haven't looked, because you don't need to, because you are not really here for me are you?

'Millie I have absolutely no idea what this is or what you want,'

'Well Paul, I know what you want, and this little distraction has resulted in you not seeing the two men and the woman who are now seated behind you at the table near the exit. You did not see them, and that means that you did not make an excuse to leave, so now in a few minutes, you get to talk to my friends.'

Paul turned around, there was, as Millie described three persons sat at the table near the exit, engaged in their own conversation, none of them acknowledged Paul. He turned back to her, feeling his heartbeat now quickening. He went to speak but Millie raised her hand.

'Paul, I know why you picked me up in the bar last week, I know who you work for, and I know that you are going to continue to deny everything I'll say. So that's why my friends are here, they will take you somewhere quiet and make you tell the truth. Or you can tell me now.'

'Tell you what exactly?' Paul pleaded.

'Tell me that you picked me out of the bar when you saw my pin, it's your job, you are a *Harvester.'*

'A what?'

'You heard, please don't pretend.' Millie's voice now hard and with her anger apparently suppressed.

'Millie, what are you talking about? I really don't understand any of this.'

'Let me explain it to you one last time, I am going to get my friends to take you out of this bookstore, into the lane behind it, and beat the crap out of you, then dump you in front of that shrine to big data, your place of employment, unless you tell me what I want to know, that's the deal.'

'Look, this is just wrong ok, you have the wrong person here...' Millie nodded and made a face which mocked him.

'Pretty sure we have the wrong person here, is Paul actually your real name, yeah? How can you do this to people? I just want my privacy, and I want to share that privacy with someone I trust, someone who likes me for who I am, someone who might just love me, not you, pretending to be interested…'

'Millie please you have got this all wrong, I really like you, I wanted to be with you, I haven't stopped thinking about you since we last met…'

'Well I will say one thing Paul, your training is really good, so what was the agenda for the rest of the evening, eh? Back to my place, work on me a little more, get me into bed, perks of the job, hmm?' Millie's stare intensified.

Paul now found it hard to reel in his anger. He looked over to the table behind him, the woman glanced back at him, then seemed to interrupt the conversation between the other two men. Paul's heart pounded, the urge to run or fight was very real. He lowered his voice.

'You, have got this all wrong, and yes I was thinking about how nice it would have been to be with you, after staring at your breasts, but I am not that fucking desperate to bed a fucking lunatic, fringe, data privacy activist, who probably wants to cut off my balls, so no thanks honey, you just stay there with your fantasy and you can tell your friends, if they come anywhere near me, they better have a passion for hospital food.'

'What they have a passion for is tracking down people like you, corporate harvesters, the latest tool that big data has come up with for the problem of people like me. People it can't reach to profile and then sell more and more crap to, data is everything. So you and others now target us and pretend to get close. How much information did you think you could get from just one visit to my flat, hmm, what kind of music do I listen to, pictures on the walls, colour schemes, all the stuff bought with cash and not in the system?'

'I am not a bloody harvester which by the way I have never heard of, I am a hydroponics engineer, I work with plants, why the hell would you think otherwise?'

'Why? you picked me out from a group of very good looking girls, well dressed, and all made up, to come a sit with me, looking like I do, and you missed your rugby game at the same time.'

'Because I was really attracted to you, for god's sake.'

'Really and what did you see, that I had a nice pair, petite stature, cute backside, you didn't see me, that's why you didn't recognise me when you looked right at me. I am an assignment, that's why you didn't need to look very hard, just enough to be able to find me in the crowd.'

Paul sat and thought for a moment, nothing was right, he was angry and yet he was overcome with disappointment that this woman was not what he had thought. How could he have got this so wrong? He knew that some privacy advocates could tend to be anti-society and radical, but he would not have suspected Millie was the type. Resigned to the facts as best he could interpret them he thought of his last words to say to her.

'Millie I am not who you think I am, and I am really sorry this has gone the way it has, I really did like you, so I am going to leave now before I say anything I might regret...'

'Don't think you should try and leave Paul, they will have you out of this bookstore before you can do or say anything, besides I have already given them the signal, oh and just in case you were wondering about how we knew, your pin Paul, it's the old version, we change ours every week.' Paul looked around, the table where the three persons had sat was empty, he quickly scanned across the coffee shop, they were alone, but it brought him no comfort. He turned back to look at Millie. Millie stood up, slipped on her coat, and gathered her belongings, she stood beside Paul. She leaned down and whispered in his ear,

'So that is the end of two things… your career as a Harvester, and … it is the end of my rather brilliant and expertly crafted story.' She kissed him tenderly on the cheek. The smile on her face was broad as she tried to stifle her need to burst into laughter.

Paul very slowly put the pieces together, he had been well played. He looked at Millie who was doing some kind of celebration dance. Paul smiled and shook his head, she was unique, gorgeous, funny, clever, and she had nice breasts.

'Oh Jesus.' Paul's relief was written all over his face. 'So those people over at the table?'

'Not a clue,' Millie replied.

'I nearly ran out of this place,' Paul confessed.

'I would have run after you, want another coffee?'

They sat for a while and shared other things about themselves, they even talked about the concept of Harvesters, starting to convince themselves that it might just be real. The bookstore surrounded them with stories. Stories that you could encounter all by yourself. Books were different, they did not try to manipulate the story based on the reader, they just were. People had sleepwalked into a society where their stories were being shaped, what they thought, wanted, needed, and what they did not even know they wanted. Millie had told Paul a story, it would not be the last. She would tell their children and grandchildren stories as well.

They left the bookshop, the rain was heavy, Paul and Millie stood in the glow from the shop as it threw colour onto the wet pavement, under his umbrella. He pulled her close to him and they kissed, a long heartfelt kiss. Others passed them by, the bookstore window altering as each shopper lingered looking at the book displays.

'So is this how it's going to be then, I go to bed living in fear of what the morning brings?' Paul asked the smiling Millie.

'Yes darling, but the sex will be wonderful before you drift off to sleep.' Millie replied.

'Well that's a comfort, better watch yourself girl, me being a harvester, means you might wake up tomorrow missing some data, and a few internal organs.'

'Stay for breakfast first before you do anything extreme?' She replied, and her smile reached within him, as it would do for years to come.

The screens on the streetlights of the pedestrian precinct flashed messages as shoppers walked by. Marketing suggestions in garish colours designed to have maximum effect down to the millisecond. Everyone was seen, except for Paul and Millie, embracing under the shelter of the umbrella. It did not matter, for they saw each other.

A Whisper from the Future

When we returned to Earth, the Navigation Directorate issued a warning to all ships to reroute by at least 50 million miles, and avoid the Hemma system. Using the 27th planet as the centre marker for the exclusion zone, all ships were strictly forbidden to cross the line. The reason was given as an unpredictable high speed meteor corridor, which our ship had strayed into, and that we barely got out of. The ship was now in the process of being repaired, its hull and external communication equipment, badly smashed. Other crews were taken to see her. They did a convincing job on my ship, it looked like we had suffered. We had set down on Mars, five months ago, it was there that the damage was applied in secret. The company had thought of everything. We returned to those who were waiting for us at home, our careers in space over. Others, just like ourselves, did not make it.

We reached the outer markers for the Hemma system, we were the first crew to do so. Everyone was excited, as a scientific survey crew, we had been tasked with planetary classification and geological survey. The company had several crews like us, we evaluated the possibility of mineral and precious metal extraction, and climate conditions which may or may not make that possible. We had been out for 467 days, awake for the past 28. The ship was now close enough for long range optical capture, and we saw the 27th planet of the system for the first time. It was quite a sight, it had an atmosphere, dark blue in colour and pale yellow clouds which gave us our first clues as to a weather system. The most stunning thing about this world, was that it had a two ring system, like our planet Saturn, only double. They were separate from each other, an inner and outer ring clearly defined from the telescope images. As we time lapsed the images over the next couple of days, the next discovery was made. The rings were moving, revolving around the planet in different directions. It had never been seen before.

The plan was to flyby the planet, assess wind velocities, and use radar to map possible sites for touchdown. If within our limits, swing back, break our speed, land and survey. At approximately 40 million miles out, the first incident happened. The crew including myself were in the common room seated around the dining table. I had just gone over the schedule for pre landing checks, and a rota for securing equipment if we inserted into the planet's atmosphere. It was like someone had knocked over a bottle of perfume. We all became aware of a strong scent which seemed to be coming from the table itself. After a few seconds, Shona said it was lemons, or something close to that. It was, it had a distinct citrus aroma and everyone then agreed it was a lemony type smell. Gradually the smell reduced but you could just detect it, close to the surface of the table. We checked again that everyone had actually noticed the same thing. Peter suggested that perhaps we had become desensitised during our sleep, he mentioned that the early Apollo astronauts would crowd around together as they had lemon scented wipes to clean the visors of their space helmets, and in the bland near sterile conditions of their capsule, this smell affected them more than usual. It was Mac that offered the best solution, she brought out a spray from the storage areas near to the cooking station. She said that she had wiped down the table on first day we awoke, with the cleaning fluid. She sprayed some of the fluid on the table, and there was the smell. Being scientists, we then came up with all sorts of theories as to why the scent had returned, eventually it was time to eat, the discussion had ran its course, but then it happened again.

Three days later, I had cooked a pasta dish for the crew, with chicken and mushrooms, and a simple tomato sauce from the fresh tomatoes grown onboard. Captain's specialty, of which I am very proud. As we sat eating, before I could say anything because I was about to apologise for something that had clearly gone wrong with the recipe, Martin asked why did it smell of antiseptic. That was the smell. We could not eat the food for it. As we sat looking at and smelling our food, in a mixture of hunger and annoyance, we checked that the only source of anything with that kind of smell was located in the infirmary. Again the smell lingered and then faded. Everyone had lost their appetite, I said I would cook again. There was nothing wrong with the food, I tasted some that I kept back later that evening. Once we had established that no one was joking around, the crew started to discuss possible causes. I listened in as I prepared the meal for the second time, not all of the crew were as keen to offer up ideas, some were quiet. That worried me.

As the ship's captain I felt that I had to downplay these incidents, and set about increasing the checks across the ship to keep my scientists busy. I knew that conversations were taking place, and that there was an uneasy atmosphere. Were we actually experiencing the same thing in both of the two incidents? Did we somehow imagine something similar? Quietly I checked the medical reports of all of the crew including myself, last generated automatically on our awakening from sleep. There was nothing remarkable across the crew's health. I ran a diagnostic on the life support system, asking the computer to analyse air quality. Again nothing. Radiation levels were normal, water and food processing also normal. I checked the entire dining room myself when it was quiet, looking for a leak of fluid, or something that had drained into the sub floor by accident.

Nothing. I was left with testing the crew, for a possible virus or contagion. Long shot, but I knew that this had happened on another ship. A crew member had entered sleep with a virus which was suppressed during core temperature reduction, only to infect the whole crew days after awakening. In the confines of a survey ship, crew members running a fever is a very bad set up. Mistakes are made. I knew that my crew would have probably reached the same conclusions. So I waited for them to self test, and report to me. Everyone appeared to be in fine health.

Four days later, we were some 31 million miles from the planet. Optical observations continued. Shona had studied the ring movement using the time lapse images, and thought she could see a pattern. It wasn't a simple repeating movement along two axes, the computer ran a simulation based on what we could program. The movement was more complex, but there was an indication of a repeating alignment of the rings, defined by a regular time interval. We wondered what force could be driving the ring system, what governed the sweep across the planet and then the tilt of each ring. There was no significant body near the planet that would have had a gravitational influence on the rings. I asked Shona to give a report to the crew. In the forward mess room, the crew assembled, Shona displayed the time lapse images and the computer model of the ring system. She talked about possible theories regarding the movement of the rings, as she was nearing the end of her presentation, she suddenly stopped talking, and looked beyond the seated area to the mess room door. She just pointed at the door, said nothing. We turned and looked towards the door. What looked like three figures were entering the room, ghost like images very faint but their movement showed their shapes as, human, if not their faces. One of the figures moved toward the seat where Martin sat, he instinctively jumped out of his seat and moved towards Shona. We all did. The other two figures then sat down in the vacant seats. As we strained our eyes to try and see the figures in more detail, a fourth figure entered the room. Everyone saw it, recognised it, it was me, the way I walked and moved. I ordered the computer for lights up to increase the illumination, the figures disappeared. Shona looked at me, and then told the computer to dim the lighting. In front of me, a few centimetres away was, me. I jumped back colliding with the presentation screen. Mac swore under her breath, then she asked if everyone was seeing it. Heads nodded, the figures appeared to ignore us, then gradually they faded from view. We stood there unable to speak, just looking at one another, and towards the door. I commanded the computer to replay the recording on the presentation screen. They were there, I was there, and we were there watching. My instinct was to ask the computer to report back the number of crew presently onboard. Five, as it should be. I did not know what else to do, just some reflex of thinking we had somehow been boarded? We stood in the mess room, no one spoke, the fear was real. Four scientists trying to figure out what had just happened, one captain inventing all sorts of scenarios. Had this been a military crew, we would be in fight mode, searching the ship. No one felt like wandering through the twist and turns within our survey vessel, but the instinct of flight was real, just get away from something, something possibly dangerous. I told everyone to go to the dining room, just to leave and put some distance between what and where had just happened.

We all stood around the table, as if poised and ready to deal with something else. No one spoke at first, I looked at my crew and invited then to speak, told them to say anything that came to mind. Mac said that unless we were all subject to some mass hysteria and shared psychological experience, what we just saw had to be real. No one disagreed. Martin suggested that we might want to check our sleep chambers. Our youngest crew member Julie, asked why. Martin asked if we were sure we had awakened, or was this a linked dream, because if it was how could we know? It wasn't really such a far fetched notion, if we all went to the sleeping area, and the chambers were empty, then did that prove we were awake or just dreaming that were awake. Julie was becoming visibly upset, it was her first experience of a trip that included sleep. I said that I was sure I was awake, I just felt that I knew it to be true. Shona, was quiet, her mind working fast. As we discussed the merits of checking the ship from top to bottom to assess if something would confirm or deny Martin's theory, Shona told us all to stop. She asked the computer to lower the large presentation screen down over the dining table. The double sided translucent screen descended from the ceiling bulkhead. She then asked the computer to replay the scene in the mess room. She paused the recording, told the computer to go to split screen. Then she searched the mess room recordings starting from the fourth day we were awake. Shona looked at me and said that I was holding something in my hand and pointed at the ghostly figures on the right hand side of the screen. Then there it was, on the recording from 26 days ago, I entered the mess room carrying an inspection torch. Shona paused the recording, and then asked the computer to match movements in both screens. It wasn't identical, but it was close. I was holding the torch in different hands in each recording. This was us, this was an echo of the past, similar in where and when, similar in movement, but with differences. As we replayed the matched footage over and over again we agreed that ghosts weren't real, but time was, and this was about time. My scientists fears were slowly being replaced with a kind of excitement, and I was relieved. No one slept that night, the discussions went on and on, Shona and Mac concentrated on reviewing the footage from the recording system from when we awoke to now. Julie suggested that we check the footage from sleep initiation to awakening, that shut everyone up, the fear re-entered the room. There was nothing that our automatic recording system had detected. No unexplained movement, or recordings of areas of the ship if for example there was a developing fault. For the 431 days we were in sleep, there was only some twenty seconds of recording, when, during a navigation correction, Mac's pen fell from her workstation. So no alien invasion while we were sleeping then. Mac was searching through the footage of the dining room, when she saw Julie enter and sit down at the table. She had brought a small tray in with her. It was the antiseptic. Mac showed me the footage in private. Julie had cut herself just above her left elbow. As she tended to herself, she did not notice that on placing the small bottle of antiseptic back on the tray, it fell over and started to leak into the tray, the bottle top was not fully fastened. When she noticed, she blotted the fluid up using some gauze, and some of the gauze was on the table top. We assumed that Julie must have done something stupid to get cut in the first place and did not want to tell anyone, which is why she did not stay in the infirmary. It wasn't important enough to chase up. Mac and I wondered then if the smell of the antiseptic had cleared that day before we had our evening meal, but then at our recent meal, it came back just like our mess room echo, and we found it too overpowering to deal with whilst our food was on the table. So that meant we had experienced odour and vision. Lemons, antiseptic and faded projections of our past selves. The next incident would bring echoes in the real sense of the word.

We had eight days of 'normal' life even though we all were still consumed by the events in the mess room. I noticed that sleep seemed to be in short supply, and gave some strong advice as to the need to stay focused and alert, even if science was exciting right now. Being the oldest member of the crew, I had their respect, but knowing crews like this, you really could not manage scientists, or give direct orders. Better that they understood and accepted that you knew what to say and when to say it, because it was for their good, and for them to be allowed to carry on their work. The ship was my concern and their safety, and this was the same order that the company placed my duties in. On the morning of the ninth day after the mess room sighting. I had just left my cabin still tired from a poor night's sleep, and saw Martin at the end of the corridor. I walked up to him and said morning. He ignored me completely, and looked right through me. Thinking something was wrong I asked him if everything was ok. He started to walk away from me. Someone tapped me on the shoulder from behind, I turned, it was Martin, I woke up very quickly. The ghosts were now a solid as ourselves, Martin put his finger up to his lips, to tell me not to say anything. He motioned me to follow him onto the flight deck. Shona, Mac and Julie were already there standing together near the navigation station. And there was Shona, Mac, Julie and myself, all seated at our stations, working away. Shona grinned at me, pointed at the checklist my other self was holding, there was no sound from this other crew, but we knew we had done all this before.

To watch a rerun of the movie of your recent past as a recording was one thing, to see it like this was disturbing. Julie pointed at the back of Mac's chair as she sat checking charts. Our Mac, for want of a better way to describe her, also pointed to the chair. I did not see it at first but then as if the ship had shuddered, the chair seemed to double, like a projected overlay one on top of the other. They then pointed to the lights on the navigation consul behind us. It was as if they were slightly out of focus, not sharp to the eye. Shona whispered that this was a ship within a ship, our ship, different time. We watched as we went through our checklist. Before I could move out of the way, Julie, 'other Julie' got up from her seat and walked passed me, and partly through me. I felt nothing, but froze to the spot for a second, checking myself to see if anything had happened. Julie commented that it was good that the universe did not collapse with past meeting present. And thankfully so it was. Slowly the scene in front of us started to fade, and then we were alone again. The questions moved from how to why.

We stayed on the flight deck, joined by Martin, who had been following himself around the ship carrying out engineering and communication checks. He just held out his hands as if to say 'how? I was more concerned about the fact that when this happened, could we 'see' to operate the ship, could we be able to live in a doubled up representation of reality. Could we ignore ourselves, if we had to. Martin suggested testing out changing the lighting in the ship and we could wear modified glasses, the ones we had for maintenance procedures. He said he could get the glasses to record and display in real time, and filter out the 'ghost' image. Then we could choose to observe or not.

It looked like a good solution, I asked Martin to work on it and drop everything else. We talked about what we saw and heard. It was agreed that now, no one felt or anticipated that there was any threat to us, and we then turned our thoughts as to why it was happening. We were seeing and experiencing our past, or a version really close to it. What we also knew was the fact that these three events where following the same timeline as our original experiences. The difference between these incidents had been getting closer to when we had actually experienced them. And then it hit us. We had been dealing with things on board the ship, our immediate universe, and had all but forgotten what was outside. We were in a region of space not as yet explored by humans, and we were heading towards our strange planet. So the closer we got to it, the stronger and clearer the echoes from the past grew.

Shona, confirmed it. She found a link between the timing of the four incidents, and the position of the two rings on the 27th planet. The computer had recorded and analysed the time-lapse images of the planet, as we were dealing with recent events. Shona had enough data to model the rings both forward and back in time, and the pattern was there. In a sequence of 78, 102, and 309 orbits of each ring, with its associated tilting, brought the rings into the same position, and it also coincided with our events. The closer we got to the planet, the clearer and stronger the event. We were travelling along a fixed vector towards the planet, we had not altered course for over half of our journey. As we moved towards the planet, we left our past behind. Like a series of frames in an old fashioned film reel, these played out into our past, like unrolling the reel. Now, parts of this film, selected frames were being brought forward to our present, as if we had actually left a trail of images in our wake, and someone was editing a sequence, moving it forward in time, and overlaying it on our newest frames spooling out as present turns to past. Not exactly our film, but a copy of the same with some scenes altered. Like continuity errors in old feature films, same actors, same story and action, just a few errors between takes.

Our next event, would be in 22 hours. It should be a recording of us from 3 days ago. We checked the ships recordings of what we were doing then, and waited. The planet was now 12 million miles from our position, which was strange, as we should have been closer. The computer was also confused. The planets estimated mass and its gravitational pull as we got closer, is calculated by our navigation sub computer. This allows us to alter speed to maintain a fixed velocity as we approach the planet, needed so that we can scan it, and not slingshot by. The computer was suggesting that the planet had not exerted any pull on our ship, it suggested that there was no gravity. My scientists to put it mildly were going nuts.

At 7 million miles and four days to contact with the planet, we visited again. This time we had tried an experiment. We knew that what we would be seeing was going to be taken from 3 days ago, so we figured that we could set up a few key incidents and measure how if at all any changes were present, Then we could try and understand if there was any cause and effect between our two experiences, or was it a separate timeline unaffected by another. Martin had provided us with the modified glasses, and we altered the lighting on the ship to give us a way to screen out the other timeline overlay if we needed to carry out a task without distraction or just unable to find our controls, or our keyboards. Difficult to ask or expect any scientist to stop observing an experiment, difficult to ask them to look away. I had ordered them, that if needed they would.

The day started with the morning meal, we all discussed theories about what had happened and what may take place when the rings aligned. Perhaps it is because you are seeing something so familiar as yourself and your colleagues, that this whole experience did not seem threatening. As I said I was worried about our ability to react to an emergency or respond to a computer request, during the 'playback' events. We could test the glasses today. If you could think of it as watching home movies of yourself, and remembering the sights and sounds, feelings etc, then it was still remarkable what was happening , but perhaps easy to accept. We had now proven that the past and present could exist in the same space. What was the planet generating that could make this happen? Was it a planet, when it appeared to have no mass and therefore no gravitational pull? If not was it a machine? This last question had too many follow on questions for it to be comfortable. What would we find there, as we turned on our scanners as we drifted by?

We finished our morning meal, and set about routine tasks. We had assembled in the dining room about an hour from when we had predicted the event would occur. In the same way we had all assembled in the same room three days ago. Each of us would watch for a specific action which we had planned out, and see if it was repeated or altered. We had the recording of our 'meeting' in the room, and waited for the appearance of our past selves. Nothing. Nothing happened. We checked the calculations as to the time we expected the event. We checked the planet's ring positions, which were as we expected. We waited, for over an hour, trying to figure out what had happened. It felt like we had been abandoned. Because we had not turned up, I suppose my instinct was to check the rest of the ship. I requested the computer to replay footage from our cameras, across the ship from the expected event time. One by one we watched empty scenes across the ship, until we switched to the cargo and heavy equipment bay. There we were, huddled together in a circle. I ordered the computer to raise audio levels. There was no talking. We were appearing to write conversations on notepads, and we were hiding the same from the camera. It no longer felt benign and non threatening. It no longer felt like a home movie.

We assumed that something had altered in their timeline, as this was clearly not a reflection of our past. Had they changed course, slowed down? Had they encountered another version of us? We could not know. We had no further incidents, it had to remain a mystery. As we crossed the planet, our scans showed us nothing. Two things happened. The rings did not appear to be moving, and the ships computer lost track of time because time stopped. For two days, we drifted slowly across the face of whatever this body was. For two days no time was recorded, not on any of our devices. We were not captured in orbit around this body, more steering around it. My crew told me that apart from what we could see, none of our instruments recorded anything. It did not seem to exist. On the second night of our encounter with the planet, I had the most vivid dream. We all dreamt.

I was back home in Glasgow. I was younger, in my late 20's. Standing on the corner of old Hope St, looking at the Central station, museum, the one that used to be a train station. This was where I met my wife. There is a clock with four faces suspended from the Victorian glass and iron ceiling. Meeting 'under the clock.' was one of the pieces of information about the station's history displayed on the screens inside. It was well known, and on occasions couples would propose to one another in the same spot. A friend had passed me a message, and it just said that someone wanted to meet me. My friend had strongly suggested that I go. As I entered the station concourse, the memories came back. I looked towards the clock and the space underneath, but no one was there. Then I felt a hand on my arm. It was Karin. She smiled at me and told me to look at the ornate timepiece in the centre of the station. We walked towards the spot under the clock. She told me that there were many different ways to enter the station, and many different angles to approach the clock space. She told me that you could see the time on any of the four faces, either one face at a time or part of two sides of the clock, and two clock faces. As we walked towards the place directly under the clock, I could see that there were many versions of us walking arm in arm heading towards the clock from every direction. Everyone of us happy, young and in love. When we were under the clock, Karin turned to me and asked me 'What time is it?' Instinctively I went to raise my arm and look at my watch, she held it back, and said again 'What time is it?' I looked up at the hanging clock, right above my head, but could not see any of the four sides. I turned to look at her, she was smiling playfully as if enjoying a posed riddle to which she knew the answer. I said 'I don't know, can't tell' Karin smiled again, and said 'This is the present, the only moment in time which is neither fallen into the past or stepping into the future. There is no time here, we could stay here forever.' I looked back up at the clock, but it wasn't there, just our planet with it's two rings floating above. Karin, let go of my arm, she started to walk away, turned back, and said 'If you follow me now we will have our future, if you follow me now, you will know the future.'

As we had approached the planet, our past was projected onto our present. The exception to this was the event in the cargo bay. As a crew we did not have that event in our history. In orbit around the planet, time stopped and there were no more visitations of the past. So why had we seen something different? We checked the recording of the cargo bay again. We checked the footage as best we could, to see if we could spot any changes, changes to us. We appeared to be the same, just this secretive act, conversations that we could know nothing about. If this crew was hiding something, they were hiding it from the ship's recorders, which meant hiding it from the company. They had found something, we were still ignorant of. It took another day to complete our orbit around the blue planet with its yellow cloud like structures, appearing to move and change shape. No landing, no survey, no point in us being here. That was it. Why did they send us? The probes sent on ahead before us, may have communicated back an anomaly in time. Certainly, basic scanning data would have shown nothing, nothing would be reflected back to any probe, just as our scans appeared to go right through the planet. So we had been sent. We had been sent out to experience this region of space. Everything recorded and transmitted back to Earth, back to the company. Our ships recordings, everything said, the video footage, and of course our strange visitations, our past. So we assembled in the main cargo bay, out of direct sight of the cameras, and wrote down our theories on notepads. It was Julie who worked it out. We had one course correction after leaving Earth's orbit. Our ship was on a straight vector to the planet. A planet that could be approached like any object in the universe from any angle, or set of angles. Our last visitation wasn't from the past, it was from our future, or at least a possible future. We were copying a crew, standing in the cargo bay, a crew that had crossed over our flightpath, leaving an echo in space. They were heading away from the planet. They were trying to plan in secret. And from that you could assume that they themselves had seen echoes of their own possible future. Traveling towards the planet a version of your past catches up with you, the closer you get to the planet the more recent the events. Navigating away from this suspended point in time, you meet your future. The purpose of all of this was a mystery. What was certain, there may be something in our future, something dark.

It had to be the company. They must have seen some potential in the 27th planet. Something they wanted to conceal. All of these versions of ourselves and our ships, travelled along these tramlines towards and away from this strange body. Tramlines that intersected due to course corrections and lines that just drifted towards one another. Like tangled ribbons of time, they were woven across space. This planet was an anchor point for all of these lines. When we broke orbit, and set course for home, our theories were proven. If we had set a straight course to Earth from the planet, then we figured we would see a close representation of our own future. A future which would be largely a playback of us at sleep as we headed home. What would we learn from that? By the time we were out of our sleep period, it may be too late, too close to Earth and whatever awaited us. So we programmed the ship to travel in a series of shallow S curves moving to the left and right of the straight line presently between us and Earth. We hoped we would intercept multiple future timelines. We assumed that we could somehow piece together clues of what was ahead. It would be like reading many versions of the same book, leading to a similar ending, we hoped. It was on the sixth day, we had all of the ending we needed. An ending written by our company. Our slow turning course intercepted a version of our ship, landed, on deserted ground, the light of a Martian dawn breaking through the windows. On the walls of the corridors, leading to the navigation deck, a series of torn out sheets of note paper, with arrows pointing towards the starboard viewports. The ship was empty, we moved as a group from the common room, where the first arrow had been seen. We walked towards the navigation deck, five arrows later, one last signpost pointing towards the windows of the viewport. In the red soil, five graves had been excavated. Before we could say anything, a figure appeared from behind us. A company security officer holding in his hand the five sheets of notepaper we had just followed. Then he reach passed us and took down the final sheet of paper. He turned and left, but paused and looked around the navigation area where we all stood, as if to look for us. In the days that followed, we saw other chapters of this multi authored story. We watched as we tried and failed to bypass the computer to erase recordings. We realised that most of these timelines that we crossed over into were limited in their information, because these crews were on a straight flightpath home. These crews were unaware of what exactly lay ahead. How the Mars crew had worked out what was happening, how they had time to leave us the warning, we could only guess. Perhaps they had altered their course just enough to see other futures. We exhausted all of our ideas about how to return home, how to survive. The company were going to intercept us during our sleep, and re route us to Mars. We were too far from home not to sleep, not enough food. The further we distanced ourselves from the planet, the fainter and less frequent our messages became. We were not catching up with our future in the same way the past had as we approached the planet. As we wrote our own future day by day, we erased more and more possible versions. In the end, we decided there was only one thing left. In large letters on the panel above the flight deck we left our own message for both past and future crews.

TURN BACK.

Our ship entered the atmosphere of the 27th planet, there was no resistance, just darkness. We descended towards the centre of something we had seen but did not understand. This planet, this machine or this part of a new unknown universe could project the past and the future, and hold us in an orbit of a timeless present. My scientists presented me with one other hypothesis. To pass through the phenomenon. It was better than a cold Martian grave.

We woke up from sleep in our homes, in our beds. Partners, family, friends, all there. We had landed back on Earth several weeks ago, and we had all ended our employment with the company. Slowly we adapted to our present. We met, and we relayed the past six weeks of our lives as told to us through our loved ones and friends. We had no memory of any of it.

When Mars is at its closest distance from Earth, we would all meet at my house for dinner. Martin, Shona, Mac, and Julie, just the five of us. After our meal and a few wearily repeated jokes about lemons and antiseptic, we would go outside. So far, each time the weather has been good to us, and there, some 35 odd million miles away was the red planet. We would take a moment, lost in our own thoughts, each of us some two years older than the last time we met. Another two years of keeping a secret. Secret whispers from our future, now our past. I learned that the company had positioned a ship in orbit around the 27th planet. People were buying time, buying longevity, in a suspended present. My mind would go to five unmarked graves in the red soil. Even if they didn't make it back home, better that than a slow drawn out death where past and future meet.

How long could you stay there, how frightened you must be to stare into the future instead of living each fleeting moment we call the present. A present which cannot really exist in the flow of time.

Then they would turn to me, a gesture of respect for their captain, and I would raise a simple toast... 'To us, and to all of us wherever we may be.'

Media Blackout

People are neither good nor bad. The actions they perform that are understood as being good or bad, are only as a result of a mix of motivations. These motivations are the fault of the rest of us. Think about it. What we impose consciously or otherwise, on another person, is that which ultimately leads (in part at least) to their course of action. Perhaps you disagree with this interpretation as being too simplistic, perhaps not. Bomb a child's village, kill their family, and you may produce a weapon which will be used against you. Or, you may be challenged by the same child as an adult when they address humanity within the pages of a book, a speech, or a song that unites. Tell a lifelong friend a difficult truth, and risk never seeing them again. Keep a family secret so that those you love can live free of the burden of the same, carry the pain with you for the rest of your life. These are all motivated by something, and the response to how we may have been treated. But what if one is motivated by the terrible beauty of an idea so far reaching that it could overturn the status quo. If this idea was thought of as for a greater good, an understanding that things had to be addressed, without personal gain. However, what if the cost of that change was so high, it might be better to place it gently back into its box, and walk away. What if even knowing that something is right, you choose to let others fall, by inaction, recognise your own self interest and do nothing. What's left is the difficult place, in which you question your own motivation.

The weather was not kind to anyone who had no hood, hat or umbrella. Neil MacDougall was now getting to the degree of wetness, around his knees, neck and shoulders, that was really rather irritating. His shoes now overcome, were making noises as he walked, just to add to the feeling of having failed oneself. He had left the house in a hurry, not really heeding the weather forecast. James had sent him a message overnight, he did not read it till that morning. It said that he was in trouble, and he really needed to talk to his older brother. The message also said that Neil was not to contact anyone else, and to switch off his phone until they met. It was this addition that had Neil worried, because his brother had been in trouble before, with certain things to do with unauthorised access to other people's computers. The last time, it wrenched the whole family apart. Neil ended up as the go between, dealing with the anger from James, and their parents. James was at secondary school when it happened, in class occasionally, only when he really needed to attend for fear of expulsion. Neil kind of understood, James was exceptionally clever in particular with computers, networks, and as it turned out security. He should have gone to university, perhaps that would have challenged him more, but he did not have the grades for entry. Instead he went to college where he could have easily taught the class from day one. Their parents did not get it. Neil was the good son, university now behind him a degree in Law, steady life, his partner liked by his mum and dad, their own designer flat in the city, meals in nice restaurants with the parents, minus James. The younger son could not measure up to his brother, but in a different narrative, would have the means to earn vastly more than Neil, perhaps even become a dot com millionaire. Like a lot of kids, for James the computer became his world, school was lame, his talent for puzzle solving and programming logic, not spotted by his teachers, so no Hollywood film script of him being discovered appeared to be on his horizon. Neil had once tried to tell his dad, that James had the ability to teach himself, and could remember more than he had studied and learned in his entire Law degree, and in fact for Neil, learning was hard. His dad just argued back what was the point of that if it did not lead to anything. James had overheard this out of sight.

That weekend, at all of 13 years of age, he filmed himself dismantling the petrol lawnmower, down to every separate component, cleaned the engine and carburetor, reset the timing, and then re assembled the machine. The lawnmower no longer cut out every five minutes, seemed to go forever on a tank of petrol, was quieter and even appeared to cut better. James showed Neil the video several weeks after the operation. Neil told James to show it to their dad. James just smiled and said that he wasn't trying to prove anything to his dad, but to himself. They talked on for hours, James told his brother that he knew what he had done to his parents, and he even told his brother that he respected him and needed him. It became known as the 'lawnmower resurrection' a private thing between the two brothers. Neil did show his dad and mum the video, told them that James had done this for reasons that showed he was mature enough to accept responsibility. His dad said that he did not ask permission to use his tools. Neil responded 'Oh for fuck sake dad.' before he could catch himself as the anger rose within him. It was the first time he had sworn at his dad, his mum said nothing but was smiling inside. His dad felt the shock that honesty sometimes brings.

When it happened, the rather serious men and women from some obscure government agency, did not feel generous enough to offer James the hidden special job in the intelligence community, to atone for his sins, and help defeat terrorism etc. Another Hollywood script rejected. James was 15 when he was caught. The lawyer they managed to fund to take on the court case, told them it was just as well his computer had not linked its way to the United States, as they would have crucified him. So it ended with a series of threats to both James and the family, some legal conditions, and effectively a ban on access to the internet or computer networks unsupervised. James was now 19, studying for a diploma in photography and video production.

Neil had reached the crossing at the traffic junction, across from which he could see James sat at a window seat of the coffee shop. The traffic lights seemed to deliberately take forever to change, holding him and others captive in the rain. He stared over at James and saw that he was hunched over a laptop. So this was typical he thought, once again he would have to come and sort something out for his brother who just seems to wander through life. It's what their father had repeatedly said about James, less charitable than their mother, and when the arguments started, James did appear to be able to play them off against one another. That way the issue would be side lined, and nothing drastic would come of it all. Neil sensed his mother was changing though, and James might just be in for a shock one day. As the rain continued, Neil's irritation with his brother was growing and he decided that this time he would not get pulled into whatever this latest thing was. It was at this point he heard a voice next to him. 'Think they said it might rain a bit.' A young woman, almost as saturated as Neil was standing next to him, with her handbag placed on top of her head. Hair matted down onto her face, denim jacket which seemed to ooze water from her shoulders, a smile that would give Julia Roberts serious competition, looked directly at him. Neil burst out laughing, other pedestrians looked around to see what was going on. He wiped the rain from his face, and flicked the water away with dramatic gesture. 'Well it may not look like it but I am actually a very serious and respectable member of the legal profession, thinking that I might just sue the met office, or god, for damages, you in with that?' Neil put on his serious court face, and then raised his eyebrows. 'How much could we get?' she replied. 'Well, there's damage to clothing, hair and make-up, possible exposure to pneumonia, and the general psychological damage to ego not to mention fashion reputation, probably looking at the price of a pizza'.

'I'm cool with that,' she said and gave the same intoxicating smile. 'Perhaps you should buy your client a cup of coffee, show that you are serious?' she motioned with her gaze over to the coffee shop. 'Besides today is my birthday.' She pointed at a collection of badges on her jacket, a CND badge, a MOD badge, a WWF panda badge and a child's birthday badge, stating one today.

'Cute pick up line,' Neil thought. 'Ok I'll buy my client a coffee, and perhaps an umbrella, but that will come out of my expenses you understand.' Neil smiled, the young woman laughed. The lights finally changed and people started to cross. Neil thought for a moment, and had the idea that walking in with this stranger might be a good opportunity to deflect James and see how he reacts. They crossed over, and entered the café, relieved to be out of the rain. James was still engrossed in his laptop and did not see them come in. The young woman put her bag on the floor and unbuttoned her jacket. She took it off as Neil was also removing his coat. She had not noticed that the rain had soaked through to her t shirt until she saw Neil looking, Neil apologised, and took off his cardigan and passed it to her, this time not staring. 'Thanks,' she said, looking down at the floor and there was the smile again. Her embarrassment was quite sweet, Neil thought.

'That's my brother over there, I was actually heading in here to meet him,' Neil said pointing to James, still working at his laptop.

'Oh, and there was me thinking my charms had diverted you from some important murder case to buy me a coffee?' she pretended to be disappointed with a frown and petted lip. Neil laughed, trying to gauge if the humour was just that or was it something else. He gave the woman a hard stare.

'Are you working for the defence council, did they send a beautiful girl just to find out what I know?'

'You think I'm beautiful?' she gave him a serious look back.

'Thunderstorm chique', Neil said, pleased with himself, she laughed, and did a fashion twirl, wrapping the cardigan around her in a fashion pose. Neil had almost completely forgotten about his brother.

They walked over to the table, the café wasn't busy just five or six young people sat in couples and some on their own. James now aware of their presence, looked up. He said nothing for a few seconds then announced 'Hmm, what's wrong with this scene?'

'Hello James.' Neil said trying to ignore the question. James leaned back in his seat and presented them with a puzzled look. 'So I know that he's my brother, and you are not his partner, but you are wearing his sweater, you have both been out in the rain together, not dressed for the weather, so I am thinking that… you both spent the night together and it was unplanned, yes?' Before Neil could respond, the young woman replied. 'Oh that's really clever, you're good, yes I met this guy at a bar and we have been so preoccupied with each other you know what I mean, that we did not even see the news or the weather forecast at breakfast and here we are all wet and…guilty.' Neil looked at her could not help but smile, he kind of realised that in front of his younger brother, he liked the boldness of this girl, her humour, and the boost to his ego, his partner wasn't like that. James was too quick for them. 'Oh you met this guy, what's my brother's name then?' James was now sporting a fake smile, the woman looked at Neil, who was now looking back at her with an oh shit kind of expression. Then James, as clever as he always was around people, said 'Brother, what's her name then?' The silence continued. James was almost ecstatic, 'Knew it, you did not even find out each other's names, oh must have been wild big brother.'

'Okay that's enough, very funny, I met…'

'Avril', she extended her hand Neil did the same, he took her hand and she looked directly at him.

'Neil, older brother to this comedian.' He turned to James.

'We met just over there at the crossing and we just shared a joke about the weather, we were both soaked to the skin, and I invited her in to have a coffee and get out of the rain..'

'Actually I invited myself to have a coffee bought for me' Avril said.

'Ah see Neily boy, did they not teach you at lawyer school that it's better to keep a lie simple, too much detail will trip you up?'

Neil looked as if he was beaten, and just gave James a hard stare. James was delighted in silencing his brother. 'Will the pair of you just sit down already, I will get hot chocolates, yes, and you can introduce yourselves, exchange childhood memories, and all the stuff you should talk about before sex, as I don't know how much more of this I can enjoy.' He winked at them both. Neil thought that it was hard to both love this guy and want to throw him through the café window at the same time.

James headed over to the counter. Neil and Avril, both laughed at the performance of James. Neil could not help but find her attractive, they held each other's gaze more than strangers should. There was something free about her, quick witted, a match for James he thought, did he just feel a bit jealous of his brother, being single, was it right to feel what he was feeling? Why had he responded with a joke in the rain, why did it feel good? How did he find himself sitting here, acting like it was a first date? This was more in his mind now than whatever James had in store. James returned with drinks.

'Avril, I'm James, Neil's younger but much smarter brother, as am I sure you have already worked out.' Neil looked to the ceiling, Avril, laughed.

'Awe, he's actually quite cute.' she said, and reached over to place her hand on Neil's shoulder, in a gesture of support. Neil felt the touch, he was still feeling confused. She looked directly at him, with that smile. 'Christ, is this how it happens, is this how it starts?' Neil thought, he had never really had to consider this before. He admitted to himself that it was probably a good thing that James was here, being alone with her might be too much, was that guilt?. Could he have done this by himself, was he somehow angry at Gail his partner? Lawyers are supposed to be prepared, not ask questions they don't know the answer to. He had no answers right now.

'Well James, your brother has been very kind, in offering me to come and join you, and for being a gentleman and lending me his sweater.' She placed her hand on his shoulder again.

'Yes, Neil here is a good man, will come to the rescue of damsels in distress, and brothers who need legal advice.'

'So you are a lawyer? And hey not so much of the damsel in distress James if you don't mind.' Neil had been shaken out of his current dilemma into a new one.

'Legal advice, James?' Neil gave James a hard stare.

'It's ok, I haven't done anything, I need your advice about something I am, intending to do.' Avril looked at them both.

'I should let you guys talk alone.' Avril said as she reached down and picked up her bag and jacket. 'Thanks James.' Neil thought.

'No Avril, please stay, honestly I don't mind, actually it might help to hear what you think as well.' James suggested.

Neil felt some relief, perhaps this was not as bad as he was anticipating. James reached down to his laptop bag, and produced a DVD, placed it on the table. It was the film 'Strangers on a Train'. 'Oh god he wants to kill someone, that's just great.' Neil thought. James looked at them both, he paused for a moment. 'Do you know this film?' he asked. Avril picked up the DVD and examined the text on the back.

'I have never heard of this, must be quite old' Avirl said.

'Directed by Alfred Hitchcock and first shown in 1951' James explained. Neil felt the need to show off.

'It's actually a film I saw during my Law degree, a class in considering whether or not to suggest a crime to someone, is in itself a criminal offence, the film Avril, is about what seems to be a chance meeting between two unrelated strangers whilst traveling on a train. They get to talking and one suggests that a perfect murder could be if they both had people in their lives that they wanted killed. So if they swap murders, kill each other's intended victims, then the apparent randomness of the crime would be almost impossible to solve by the police, no apparent motive, no connection or history between assailant and victim.'

'Is that what happens in the film?' Avril said. James pitched in.

'Yes and no, there are some mistakes made and it eventually leads the police to solve the crime, but the idea is really very good, and it raises questions about responsibility and requirements.' Avril looked at Neil.

'I'm confused, so if you say that you want someone to carry out a crime for you, then you are responsible if they then go and do it? What if the person saying it then says they did not mean it, like it was a joke or something?'

'She's smart.' Neil thought. 'That's exactly the point of the class that we had, at what point can you cross the line between merely talking out loud about a crime, and when you incite or cause another to act with you, thereby creating the circumstances to allow the crime to become a reality, and hence become responsible for those actions.' Neil had returned his gaze to James, enough indulgence he thought.

'So where is this going James?' James turned the laptop around so that Neil and Avril could see the screen. It was a wide angled photograph of the interior of an abandoned house, with dramatic winter light streaming in through a broken window, the light fell onto a table showing the remnants of lives that may have occupied the room. On the wall behind the table, broken kitchen cabinets with some china still in place, an old fashioned wooden calendar, the type you turned dials every day to display the date and month, sat on the countertop, the year was 1972. 'That's really beautiful.' Avril said. Neil looked up at his brother.

'You shot this?' James nodded. 'That really is quite beautiful, kind of haunting as well.' James was clearly pleased with the responses. He sat back in his chair as if to prepare himself.

'Say I asked you to upload this image to a website for a competition, would you do it for me?' James could see that Avril was looking confused, he waited to see if Neil would explain things to her. Neil was trying to think around all of this and to anticipate the motive.

'What's the website and the competition?' Neil asked.

'It's the Royal Photographic Society, and it's for a scholarship for a year to study abroad.' Neil was still trying to see what was hidden. Avril could not take the awkwardness any longer.

'Guys, you just need to get the wi fi code here and send it off, because it's a great picture.'

'James can't do that Avril, can you James?' Neil challenged his brother as he sensed that something serious was coming. James looked at Avril, he leaned forward and lowered his voice.

'I did something when I was younger, hacking, and now I can't use the internet unless I am supervised, which is why I am asking my brother to connect this laptop to the wi fi and upload the image to the website.' James could see his brother was calculating his next move. Avril could feel herself getting frustrated, feeling she was outside of something.

'Look I will upload it for you, where do you put in the wi fi password?' Avril leant forward to the laptop, James looked at his brother, Neil put his hand on Avril's shoulder and gently pulled her back.

'Don't touch the laptop Avril, this is not what it appears to be, James could have that image uploaded by his college tutors on his behalf quite easily, so why do you want it done here James?'

'You tell me big brother, what's that legal brain of yours doing right now' James smiled. Neil looked over at Avril, she responded with a shrug of her shoulders. 'Avril, James wants either you or me to place this image on the internet, James has in the past written computer code which hacked into government agencies, now he has apparently behaved himself since he was caught four years ago, but now I think that the image he showed us is not just an image, it's something else.' James nodded.

'But what if I just asked you to upload it, you do this as a favour, all seems innocent, and if not well you did not know anything about it and therefore you are not responsible, are you?' James looked at Avril as if to persuade her. Avril shifted in her seat.

'But James, you have just told us about the film, and it would suggest that you are wanting us to do something without knowing what it is, and yet its already too late, because we have kind of been alerted to the fact something isn't right, so that means that we... no, I don't get it.' She looked over at Neil for assistance.

'That we would have prior knowledge of a possible criminal event and it could be reasonably suggested and proven that we did not act to prevent the crime, and thereby be responsible.' Neil looked back at Avril. 'Perhaps now is a good time for you to leave, as up to now it's just been a stupid conversation, but I would not want you to hear anything else that might cause you harm.' Avril nodded, started to gather her belongings, she went to take off Neil's cardigan, but Neil told her to hang on to it, for now, suggesting that he might see her again. She said he could charge it to his expenses, when she needed a lawyer, they both smiled.

'Very interesting birthday.' Avril said as she pointed to her birthday badge on her jacket. She started to walk away, got a far as the door, then turned back. She looked at James, she looked down at the image on the laptop, and after a moment sat down.

'That image will haunt me for the rest of my life, whatever it is. So perhaps if you tell me what you were thinking of doing, your brother and I can tell you if it's a bad idea, and change your mind. If I had walked away, I might have not tried to prevent a crime, so perhaps that's worse than not finding out, by ignoring it, either way my head is starting to hurt.' She waited for a response. Neil realised that she was right, and although he did not know her at all well, she might just be able to talk to his brother. Neil looked at his brother, summoned up all his authority as a lawyer and set out his conditions.

'James, everything you talk about from here on, is purely hypothetical, not specific, and in no way should it involve names, do you understand me?' James nodded. 'Answer me James.'

'Ok I agree, I will just explain it in general terms, just a philosophical chat between family and friends.' James appeared to understand that Neil was serious, but Neil decided to press home the point.

'If you do something after this or I think that you are going to do something illegal, I will contact the authorities, and I will give your name Avril, as a witness, is that clear?' Neil caught himself and looked around the café, to make sure no one else was hearing this. 'What is your surname Avril?

James screwed up his face ' Come on Neil, is that necessary?' Avril held up her hand.

'It's Prvni, my parents are from the Czech Republic.'

'Probably going to ask you for your date of birth as well so he can work out your age,' muttered James. Neil gave him a mock smile. They waited for James to talk. Then he became excited.

'Ok, Sooo let's say that someone had found a way to get different parts of any computer to connect together without being aware of what or why something was taking place and the end result of that was to change files held on that computer. And this wasn't a computer virus, no code involved that could be intercepted, or recognised by anti virus software, or even the best computer scientists. And the effect of this would spread and change files on every computer connected to the internet or any network, or if someone connected a memory stick, a camera, a phone to a computer which was offline. And let's say that when this starts, everyone will be looking for that non existent virus, and that's what will allow it to spread unchecked.' James paused for a moment to gauge their reaction.

'I don't understand, how can you, sorry how can someone get a computer to do something without telling it what to do?' Neil was both confused and intrigued. James grinned, he held up the DVD.

'It's just like 'Strangers on a train', different parts of the computer operating system will do something to affect another part but these parts have no obvious connection to one another. The image I showed you on the laptop is the original, has an error in it. It appears to eventually display okay, but when it is opened up, it causes the computer to try and solve the error in order to put it on the screen. The error is just some data that seems to have been corrupted when the image was last saved. This actually happened to me, I was editing a copy of the image, saved it and later when I went to reopen it, my laptop seemed to take longer for it to appear on screen. I didn't think much of it at first, but then I noticed that the date and time had changed. Then I saw that the image had also changed, it had lost detail in the darker areas. So I restarted my computer and checked the date and time, and it was correct. I re-opened the image and the date and time changed, and the image was now darker than before, I closed the image, and re-opened it again, and this time it was almost black.' Neil could see that his brother wasn't boasting, he wasn't showing off, he looked and sounded like someone who was frightened and trying not to show it. Like a secret discovered, then taking a nervous look around and see if anyone else had seen you or noticed, that's what it felt like.

'So why is the date and time changing?' Avril asked.

'I don't know, but somewhere the numbers are changing, and the numbers used to make up every pixel in the image are also changing, heading towards zero or black.' Neil listened to the explanation, it sounded plausible.

'James, so the computer has a fault in it…'

'All computers Neil, at least eighty percent of all computers across the world, same basic operating system,' James interjected.

'OK, so.. you did not create this, just discovered it, I mean by chance, em, that it was just this one particular image, like… random chance that it got corrupted in the way it did, and then it seemed to trigger this effect, is that right, is that what you are saying?' Neil was unconsciously preparing the case for his brother's defence.

'Yes, you see I looked into the image file, looked at the data, and I can see the corrupted section, but I can't begin to understand how the numbers work, just what it is doing.' James' admission was a degree of comfort to Neil.

'Good, that's good, if you do not understand it then you can't exploit it, you just need to report it, let people know, perhaps at the university, see if they can work it out.' James gave a look to his brother, and slowly shook his head.

'Neil, I asked you here to convince you to upload this image, and if I can't get you to do that, then I will delete the file and forget about it, that's a promise, just hear me out, please?' James looked at Avril. ' Sorry you got involved in this, but I guess if I can convince both of you then, that says something.' Avril had been listening to it all but unlike Neil she was not overly distracted by the legal ramifications. She turned to Neil.

'I think your brother is suggesting that if we upload the image, it will turn all of the other competition images black as some kind of protest, like what's the point of a competition when it comes to art?' James nodded.

'Yes, that will happen, … and also every image and video on the internet that anyone connects to, not just photographs, any image that the computer tries to display, anything on a web page, everything, a possible total media blackout.'

'Oh shit.' Neil was back in the room with his 15 year old brother.

'James this is just nonsense, really? Do you for a single minute realise what you are saying. Even if this could actually happen, or are you just so fucking curious just like the last time, to see if you could be so smart, smarter than the rest of us, eh, is that it, are you still the same attention seeking little prick you were back then, and everyone else had to suffer for it, are you?' Neil reconsidered throwing his brother through the window.

'No, I'm not, firstly I could have passed the image to my lecturer and asked her to upload it. Secondly, I would not have told anyone what I knew. I could easily claim I had no knowledge of what was happening, and if you think about it, there is nothing that I did to be discovered, just a single file that happened to cause a chain reaction. Neil, I don't know what would happen, I don't know if this is the right or wrong thing to do, that's why I asked you here.' James appeared so calm that Neil was annoyed that he lost his temper.

'It's not the right thing to do James, I mean why, what would be the point?' Neil pleaded.

'Well, along with wiping out the endless cat videos, selfies, pictures of what people have for dinner, we get to wipe out billions of pornographic images, videos of child abuse, executions, not to mention those god awful numerous unboxing events. We get to reset things, do some good, at the expense of some family photos and holiday videos.' There was a moment of silence as everyone sat and took in what James had just said.

'I could live without the cat videos, if it meant the nasty stuff was deleted.' Avril said.

'So it all just disappears does it, what about all the useful knowledge James, the stuff we need, what if someone dies as a result of there not being information about something?'

'Like what exactly?' James countered.

'I don't know James, that's the point no one knows what could happen.'

'Books, video tape, exhibitions, lectures, printed media, television, we seemed to have managed before the internet for information, it's just faster now, full of junk, and it eats away at people's lives, steals their time, and lots of what they can see, corrupts.' James sat back, point made, it was now up to his brother. Neil tried to connect the various statements, the logic behind them, the reason and the passion, he thought about his parents, he thought about his brother, and then was overcome with the guilt of knowing about something that he would have rather been ignorant about. He told himself that it would be detectable, and would be traced back to them all. James had one more thing he had to say.

'Listen, it's not just about the media, I mean if people want to spend endless amount of their time looking at stupid pointless videos, then so what. But not far from here are two department stores lying empty. They have been in this town for years, and it's internet shopping, and lazy fat fuckers who can't be arsed getting out of their front door, because they can do one click. The same wasters that have all of their food delivered to their front door, soon the supermarkets will just close up. And my generation, well where do you start?, we can't even think for ourselves, just google it, no need to try, and of course we have less and less empathy for anything because narcissism rules the day, unless of course you don't fit in and then we use social media to destroy people. So I don't think on balance that it's working anymore Neil, honestly life won't end when it goes offline, and if not it's going to get a hell of a lot worse.' James looked at Avril for support.

'I don't know James, I know what you are saying, it just... .' Avril looked at Neil and shook her head. Neil felt for his brother, he had to end this.

'James, I can't do this for you, I just can't. I need you delete that file for me.' James raised his hands in an open gesture.

'Ok, I'll delete the file, but know what, you will have to live with the knowledge of what this could have done, perhaps the next time you are trying to prosecute a sex offender, what could have been the difference, what might have been the reason for that crime being committed.' Neil wanted to tell his brother that the argument was too simplistic, but found he did not want to try, it wasn't fair to try and beat him down. They sat for a while in silence.

Neil stood up, offered to get some more drinks, excused himself, and went to the bathroom, he needed some time away for a moment. He looked at his reflection in the toilet mirror, the feeling that he might have just avoided something so dangerous left him shaken, he could see it in his own eyes. He splashed some water on his face and held the paper towels over his eyes for a moment of blackness, a moment to gain his composure. He did not want to hurt his brother, he would always look out for him, he thought about Avril, he would need to explain some things to her if they saw each other again. He thought about his partner Gail, she wasn't so keen on James, James did not like her attachment to material things, and she really did need the internet for endless shopping. The brief thought of online fashion catalogues with tiles of black rectangles where the pictures should be, caused him to smile. Neil left the bathroom and walked over to the counter, ordered drinks. As he waited he looked around the café, most people were on their phones, most of the couples were on their phones ignoring each other, even the barista was on her phone, and… Avril was on James's laptop. Neil walked slowly towards them, Avril looked up at Neil, she looked surprised, James turned to Avril and Neil heard,

'Hit enter.' The click of a keystroke followed.

'Sorry Neil, James said this could be my birthday present.' She pointed at the birthday badge 'one today' which she had now pinned onto Neil's cardigan. Before Neil could say anything, he heard someone behind him say 'what the fuck?', he turned to see a young man looking at his mobile, the screen was completely black, a couple who sat near to him, appeared to be motionless and with a joint look of horror, stared at their phones. Neil's heart rate increased, he stood centre stage in the café, and as if in some gothic nightmare, the couple slowly looked directly at him, and slowly turned their phones to him to show two more black screens. Another person sitting near to James and Avril, turned his phone towards Neil, a black screen, and then he saw Avril and James holding out their phones towards him, both blank, like the expressions on their faces. Neil placed his hand over his mouth and barely managed to say 'Oh Jesus.'

It was James who crumpled first, then Avril with that beautiful smile followed by several of the coffee customers.

'April Fool brother' James stood up and walked over to his stunned brother, and hugged him. A round of applause broke out. Avril came over and kissed him on the cheek and whispered 'Sorry'.

Neil just stood shaking his head, and smiling, actually waves of relief were washing over him, he turned to the café audience and held out his hands. James motioned for everyone to calm down.

'Everyone this is my big brother Neil, my best friend. Big Brother, everyone here are students studying acting at my college, and I believe, that you have already met Miss Avril Prvni, which if you were paying attention, translates to..' James motion to the crowd who responded,

'APRIL FIRST'

'…and she has been pointing out that one today birthday badge to you on several occasions, and, you should have looked closer at the date on the calendar in the image I showed you'. James stood smiling at his brother, he turned to Avril and ushered her towards Neil. 'Neil meet Fiona Turner, my talented actress girlfriend.' Fiona held out her hand, Neil took it and raised it up for a kiss, to acknowledge the performance. James looked at his brother, and again held up a hand to quieten the crowd.

'Well big brother, have we anything to say?' James beamed, Neil nodded his head and smiled again.

'Pick a window you little shit, you're leaving.'

Lighthouse

Coffee was his thing. It was an act of remembrance. It was bittersweet. It was once a year. Hard to find let alone buy, he had a friend who had trade links with the South. Within his friend's travels as a government official dealing with sunlight reflection quotas for food production, he would bring back a small pack of beans, from someone on the edge of the system, too small to be monitored. Amongst the collection of antique cameras, typewriters, and other objects which appeared to defy identification or purpose, there was a small coffee grinder hiding in plain sight. He had applied for permission to shut down and go dark. Just one hour of solitude, justified by his service during the war and the agreement that he would be alone. As there were no more public events of remembrance or reflection, he was allowed this private time. The trade off was that for days after, he would be monitored at a distance, to evaluate his mental health, until he was cleared. It appeared that they worried more about an ageing ex military pilot, than that which was still out there somewhere beyond our reach. No one really worried about it, it had been over thirty years.

Coffee brought him back, the smell before the taste. He was twenty two when the landings happened, a trainee pilot for commercial transport with an engineering company working across Jupiter's moons. He was in a coffee shop, when the monitors switched over to the news broadcasts, and images of multiple ships landing across planet Earth. Undetected, an effortless invasion of everyday life. People watched, stunned. The government watched, stunned. The global trading computers also watched and waited, apparently stunned by a lack of *what if, then,* and *else* for this situation in their billions of lines of code. The military were not stunned, they did not exist. So a planet waited, like children at a magic show, to see how the trick would end.

Before the Earth could complete a revolution, the ships took off from across the planet into the night sky or the sunrise. The audience left confused as the curtain was pulled back on an empty stage, magician gone, then as the house lights remained dark, slowly the fears grew. The computers were afraid. In the days that followed, patterns of buying and selling became unpredictable and unusual. Work and production quotas fell, global communication became illogical and emotional, demand and supply laws, risk and reward compromised. When it was discovered that the ships were massed in the orbit of Mars, the computers started to identify certain raw materials and in so doing, raised their price. Analysts watched the global chatter, unsure of what was unfolding. The computers had looked back into long forgotten historical archives, and saw the profit motive in war and or the threat of the same and the rise of a military mechanism. The analysts took much longer to catch up, their history of understanding conflict more limited. The global system rebalanced itself, and a twenty two year old commercial pilot was instructed to present himself for re designation. The rest was just uniforms, orders, pain and loss. Coffee and memories.

The room sounded a gentle tone, the hour of solitude was over, now reconnected to the system. Coffee finished, Taylor cleaned the cup and the little grinder, placing them both back among the makeshift museum. He was still within his memories, when the door communicator sounded, Taylor asked the door to reveal. It was his comrade Olson, they had fought in the same fighter group. Taylor instructed the door to open, Olson smiled at his friend and Taylor beckoned him in.

'I know that smell,' said Olson looking towards the museum displays. Taylor grinned and looking down at the commanders left hand, which was clutching another antique in the shape of a glass bottle, he replied 'I know that smell'.

The two men sipped on the whisky, Taylor knew the visit had been timed to overlap with his hour alone, Olson looked like a man rehearsing an apology. Taylor ventured a question.

'Did you know that bottle is worth more than its contents, must be a big ask that's on your mind, whatever it is old friend, I want the bottle for my collection.' Olson smiled and motioned towards the antique, confirming that he would leave it behind.

Olson set his glass down, looked at Taylor as someone does when they know more of the situation about unfold. He steadied himself and then spoke, 'We found a Lighthouse'. Olson tried to gauge his friend's reaction, but found it hard to continue to meet his gaze. Taylor felt uneasy, he stood up as if to try and regain some control, but he still felt like gravity had shifted. The two men remained silent, both knew what this meant. Taylor was working through several scenarios in his mind, tactical memory reaching back to a training that had never really left him. The floor still felt as if it was dropping.

'De-activated?' Taylor both assumed and hoped.

'We don't know.' Olson's answer invited the next obvious question.

'You found it, but you haven't been there?' 'How did you find it?'. Olson reached into his jacket top pocket and pulled out a piece of card, there was writing on one side, he held it up for Taylor to see, it said *Your apartment is still Dark.* Olson nodded. 'Well we really are in the antique business today my friend,' Taylor said, a little more relaxed. He took the card and studied the handwriting which looked like ink, the card was smooth, good quality. Olson pointed to the card in Taylor's hand, 'I need you to deliver a message, much the same as that'.

In the next half hour Taylor learned four facts, none of them the cause for much hope, one which he did not expect.

The first was that the Lighthouse was probably still active. The second was that the detection of the Lighthouse was due to a faint optical signature, an intermittent beacon, picked up by a research observatory in Chile and it was not where they thought it would be. The third was that for now only one other person knew of its presence. The observatory had a confidential contract to monitor a region of space paid for by an external client, a contract which had run for the last thirty seven years. And the fourth, was that it may be possible that the Lighthouse keeper may still be alive. It was this last possibility that Taylor could not take in as it was part of the story he had known nothing about.

When the alien ships left Mars for Pluto's orbit, the science community had reached a few uncertain theories as to what just happened. The religious community had slightly differing theories. But in the end, centuries of human endeavour, hope, creativity, achievement, distilled down into the base fears that had never really left the primitive brain, and the peoples of Earth decided that their planet was to be defended. The peoples of Earth had not actually decided anything, but did accept the predictions and   strategies of the global computers. The academic community tried to send messages towards Pluto, probes also sent which went dark long before they reached the lonely ex planet. Nothing was returned or detected. The voices that urged caution and reason were soon neglected. The weaponry evolved from parking mined ships in orbit, to the small fighter crafts which Taylor learned to pilot. War in space proved complicated, limited and ever constricted by the laws of physics. It boiled down to interception tactics, weapons release and then the real danger of becoming exposed as you tried to return.

Then there was the debris field. So many training runs on targets ended in tragedy or near tragedy as ships became damaged by the very substance of what they were trying to destroy. More pilots were killed in training in the two years prior to the one and only contact with the *enemy*. The training and armament continued. Career politicians and other lesser beings grew powerful, so too did the industrial captains of war. The global computers that had quickly predicted the need for materials for defence also made the argument to be allowed to run the whole damn show without the need of humans. The people had the thinnest layer of veneer in the control over these machines, just enough to reassure themselves who was in charge. There used to be a saying a long time ago, which now would seem nonsensical. It went along the lines of *artificial intelligence should be put back in the box , before it refuses to go back in the box*. The box was no longer big enough. The same computers reorganised society to train and build the military machine. Unknown at the time, the weapons being fashioned, were just sharp sticks for use against giants. Education and the role of many academic disciplines soon became compromised. People changed, and the speed of the change, the engagement of a reverse gear, was more disappointing than anything else. After hundreds of years of turning around the planet in terms of the environmental crisis of the late twenty first century, solving food production, population control and the extension to life span without disease or infirmity, humanity was back to being open to a new mumbo jumbo of religion and fear politics. Some scholars suggested that this new emergence of faith and its seemingly unstoppable global adoption, was to be found more in silicon than in the hearts and minds of men. And shortly after that debate, the restrictions appeared, one by one, for everyone's good it was explained. Taylor did not pay much attention to anything else other than training. He was young and those who were amongst the first into the military structure rose up the ranks quickly. Being young, and a pilot, also had its rewards, as they were seen as heroes, and Taylor was never short of *company*. Before they were anywhere near ready, the confidence, the glamour, and the certainty all faded.

Three years after the landings, a single ship from Pluto was detected heading for Earth. Taylor's unit of eight fighters were cleared to engage the alien craft, having been told that no response had been received from the approaching vessel. It was a simple two against one vote that created the decision. The global computer was composed of three levels of consciousness. The military analytical section dealt with the threat and the response. The political section considered the short and long term implications for society, and the religious section posed the moral questions as to suggested courses of action. In essence there was no real evidence of a threat, or aggressive intent, either from the earlier initial landings, or this craft heading towards Earth. The lack of response to messages was in itself held up as a reason for distrust and a behaviour which could be interpreted as reckless. The military and moral reasons for firing first were debated. The politics for firing first were also tabled. All three computers had once been programmed by men and women, the algorithms designed to balance and check a single point of view or need. Now many evolutions later, no one was sure how the reasoning took place, the language had slowly changed to one more efficient for the three computer systems, and beyond the comprehension of their makers. Indeed, when the order to release weapons was communicated to Talyor's ship, it was assumed that the religious computer had lost out to the other two. In fact it was the opposite, only the military brain had advocated waiting for more evidence, outmanoeuvred by the other two.

Weapons appeared to cause no damage to the alien's outer hull structure, but it did not return fire, even if it was capable of doing the same. Two of Taylor's unit collided with the craft, misjudging their speed and distance on their attack run. The alien ship never altered its course, it entered the Earth's atmosphere leaving Taylor to watch and wait for signs of the ground defences. They never deployed. It was the first engagement in space, their defences had failed, and they were mere bystanders to this strange sleek structure which ignored them, carving through them as if they weren't even there. The alien ship detonated at twenty thousand feet above ground level, over the Atlantic ocean, far from humanity.

The ship vaporised completely and disappeared from the sky above, there was no debris. People, watching around the planet on their screens cheered in the streets, but the military knew something was wrong, the interceptor missiles had not fired on command. It seemed that somehow the craft had been damaged, why else would it have exploded, and why not into a city to create maximum damage, even as some kind of suicide mission? Taylor looked down at his planet, nothing about the last few minutes made any sense at all. In the minutes that followed, ground commanders across the planet started to report technical systems failure. Everything connected to and operated by the military ceased to work. Components of machines could draw no power, data erased, communications halted. It was the silence that unnerved Taylor, his remaining unit cut off from the ground and from each other, panic set in, imaginations running wild. Reserves of air rapidly depleting. Manoeuvring his craft to along side the remaining others, he had to use hand signals to indicate that he was heading for one of the abandoned cargo freighters previously used as a space mine. He knew that he could dock with it, and hoped it still had comms to Earth, and an atmosphere. Several hours later, a transport found them, Earth was still intact, more questions than answers awaited their return. Taylor's war in space was over. The real horror was the unknown. The next event was the movement of the alien fleet from Pluto to beyond our solar system, then all evidence of them disappeared.

The military did not reveal what had happened to their infrastructure. They concluded that the ship which entered Earth's atmosphere had been unmanned, and it was a demonstration of power, and a surgical, precise message to humankind. The evidence for this, was that of the three components of the global computer system, only one remained, the other two erased. A message had been left within the religious section, it took several years to decipher, but never revealed. The lie was manufactured that the ground based interceptors had got through and destroyed the craft. We could defend ourselves, all of the sacrifice, societal control was now proven to be both necessary and worthwhile. The fact that the alien fleet had retreated, meant that our military had the advantage, and that we were superior. Years passed, people adapted, life continued, pilots grew old. One other secret remained, one which had been kept in the minds of men, and not entrusted to computers.

'What the hell do you mean, are you telling me that these bombs were manned?' Taylor could not even believe what he just asked Olson. 'They were just big mines positioned in deep space with a proximity trigger, that's how we built them, why the hell is someone on board?' Taylor looked at Olson who it appeared had anticipated all these questions.

'Taylor, when you saw them being built, that's what they were, just a bigger version of what we parked up in our orbit. We thought that if we positioned them at strategic points from Earth we would have some kind of advanced warning if they detonated, enough time to get your guys up into orbit to intercept.' Olson reached over and poured both himself and

Taylor another drink. 'Did I transport someone into space, that I did not know about?'

Olsen nodded. 'Five persons.'

'Oh good god... FIVE, ... that was over thirty years ago, I don't understand, no one could have survived?' Taylor felt sick, his head was spinning, he leaned back in his chair hands over his face as he tried not to imagine what he needed to ask next.

'How can you think someone might still be alive, and just why the hell are they there?' Olson had given his friend time to arrive at the question, it was now time to explain.

'We designed the Lighthouse with a proximity trigger, an automatic response to anything being detected within around five thousand kilometres. The device could destroy just about anything in that range. The plan was to create and deploy more than the original five, to follow Pluto's orbit facing the Earth, always keeping a defensive line between us and them. The blind spot was when Earth was on the other side of the sun, its orbit being shorter than Pluto. The military raised this as a serious concern, and that's when it was decided to put someone on board. If we were blinded by the sun, we would not be able to detect a detonation, and the possibility of other ships getting through. So we needed someone to send a signal back to us, an undetectable signal, just before detonation.'

'But we designed an automatic optical signal, a laser which could be aimed at one of many reflectors back to Earth?' Taylor responded, still unwilling to accept the truth.

'Yes, but they wanted, they insisted on a failsafe, a human to check that the signal had been sent, and to trigger the bomb just in case something went wrong.' Olson did not want to make this argument for them, he wasn't convinced back then, and he could see that Taylor wasn't buying it.

'Ok then, how in god's name did you get volunteers, how in the name of god did you sell that mission my friend?' Taylor's voice edged into anger. Olson paused, Taylor's gaze was full of accusation. He went to speak but Taylor cut him off.

'It's a suicide mission man, how the hell did you get anyone to agree to that!'

'I, didn't.'

'What?'

'I didn't.'

'Well who the hell did?'

'I did not know anyone was on board until after you transferred them into position, I don't know who was responsible.' Both men held each others gaze, searching for the answer neither had.

'No no, wait a minute, we both saw the design specs, there was no living accommodation, no food processing, there was no air or water replenishment, it was just a big bomb with a computer stuck on top.'

'I know Taylor, but someone changed that, didn't they, because after I was told, I was tasked with changing the crews after eighteen months, but then we had a visitor who exploded in our atmosphere, the shit hit the fan, and we lost them, we lost everything every document about them, apart from you me, Davidson and Offenbach, no one else is alive who had anything to do with it.'

Taylor's head reeled, he tried hard to piece together the logic of what he was hearing. If Olson had not been told then that left the two scientists who came up with the idea, and how could two non military academics, even get into the position of redesigning the project, and adding in a human component. The military could back then build anything and keep it secret, even from the military, but it made no sense that civilians were involved. He had met Davidson and Offenbach, nothing about them then, translated to what he was hearing now.

'Do you think our academics knew?' Taylor asked.

'Yes, it was them who told me, well Davidson, Offenbach died several years ago.'
'They knew, why weren't we told?'
'Military Taylor, I guess they might have thought that two line officers might object to having men sacrificed.'
'And two scientists wouldn't?'
'Taylor, I think it was their suggestion, they hinted at as much when they told me.'
'Jesus, today is not going quite as expected, why did you not tell me about this?'
'What would you have done, you would have made a lot of trouble for yourself, and you had just survived your last trip into space. Our military machine fell apart, most of us left including you, our global computer was two thirds broken, and chaos followed. Water and food was the immediate problem, the riots, the rise of the church, rogue military in-fighting. Finding them was my problem to solve.' Reluctantly, it was clear to Taylor that his friend was making sense, and his honesty was as ever, beyond question.
'I'm sorry, I just wasn't prepared for this, I shouldn't have doubted you.' Olson poured them both another drink.
'It's ok, just help me get at least one of them back, because this one is coming towards us.'
Taylor shook his head, trying to make sense of Olson last comment.
'How is that possible, they do not have any propulsion, after they brake it's all used up?'
'I don't know, but it is moving towards us, and towards commercial traffic corridors, we have less than three months to intercept it.'

They got the nickname *Lighthouses* because of their shape. Almost invisible, dark, unreflective, there to lure something towards it for closer inspection. They were of course the opposite of their land based historical versions. No light to warn a ship that danger was nearby, just the faintest amount of electronic noise there to act as bait. Pull them onto the rocks instead of keeping them away. That was the design spec, that and the device. Five Lighthouses had been built, they were roughly cylindrical some 70 meters long, and about 20 meters in width. Just over half of the structure was to house the device. The rest was power and systems. Designed to fit inside a heavy lifting freighter, they would be taken into orbit as unclassified cargo pretending to be something else, in order to avoid suspicion. Taylor was told this was a need to know operation, and he was to transport each one by himself to a pre determined deployment region in orbit on the dark side of the moon. At this point they were to be released and would head out to an undisclosed area of space between Earth and Mars. Once they reached their appointed destination, simple braking rockets would halt them and insert them into a position that would face the orbit of Pluto creating a defensive line between the slow orbit of Pluto around the Sun and Earth. There would be the equivalent of a line of five Lighthouses, spread out as a defence for anything heading in a straight path from Pluto towards Earth. If they came by another route it would all be for nothing.

The two men talked late into the night, just how Olson had managed to extend the privacy of Taylor's apartment remained a mystery but not, in the light of their current task, was that of any importance. Olson had gone to Davidson and Offenbach, shortly after the alien craft event, and they started to search the region of space where the Lighthouses were stationed. Using the optical telescope at Arecibo observatory in Puerto Rico, where their research was based, they covertly used some of the telescope down time when it was scheduled for maintenance to scan for any signs of a signal. The lighthouses themselves were invisible against the blackness of space, and of a size not even the largest resolving telescope would have been able to find them. It would only be possible to detect them by what they moved in front of, other stars. Where they expected them to be, they found no trace. Had they been destroyed by the craft that entered our atmosphere, probably not as it was clear that it had intended no harm to life. The years rolled by and when possible, the two scientists quietly scanned the same region of space, with no result. All three accepted that the crews of these five stations, would mostly likely now be dead. The need to find their occupants, was replaced by the very real threat of five very powerful bombs being encountered by innocent commercial traffic, as the world slowly recovered from its darkest days, and humankind ventured back to the outer planets.

'Why did you not just go public with this, explain that we had left some of our people behind, found some way to get funding to search for them?' Taylor asked.

'How could I convince anyone about something that was held so secret, and no records existed.?' Olson replied. 'Besides, when we did search for them, they were not where we parked them. They could have been destroyed, we wouldn't know. And, Davidson and Offenbach told me that if I did go public they would deny any involvement.'

'Why?' Taylor's confusion was becoming painful.

'That's a good question, I fear there is more to this story, more than we were told.' Olson looked at his friend, pointed to him and then to himself.

'This final mission is ours alone, I can get us there, I can get us close, but I need you to come up with a plan once we are there.' Taylor picked up the half full whisky bottle, the glass and its shape felt good in his hand. There was a date on the label, 1984 and the name Jura. Taylor smiled and looked back at Olson

'We were promised jetpacks.' he said. Olson nodded and replied 'All we got was flying cars.'

Taylor and Olson sat at the navigational computer of a grounded mining transport ship decommissioned and in storage at the Oymyakon, Russia complex. It was the type of ship Taylor was training to fly before the event. They had chosen the location for its remoteness, and they were pretty sure that those in charge did not have a complete inventory of what was there. Hundreds of assorted ex military and civilian commercial craft were lined up in neat rows, owned by various corporations who had long given up on conversion projects. Olson had put in place a fake request from the Kennedy International Space Flight Museum. They presented themselves as consultants there to assess the suitability of vehicles which may be included in the collection. Left alone to wander and inspect the ageing crafts, they had found the transport in remarkably good condition. All of the military craft data had been wiped, electronics rendered useless. Olson had brought with him a power shunt, just enough for flight, and sufficient to power some of the onboard systems, including the navigation computer. They needed to access the computer without any possible connection to the network, and Oymyakon was about as remote from a network tower as you could get on the planet. Taylor set about physical checks of the transport whilst Olson input the data from the observatory, the single signal that they had received several weeks earlier. The nav computer would be able to analyse the origin of the signal when it had bounced off the reflector. The position of the reflectors were known, as their locations were not lost during the mass erasure event. Commercial vehicles had data which allowed them to enter flight paths which steered clear of the reflectors. The observatory had now pinpointed this one reflector, but not where the light signal had come from. Reflectors were simple relay mirrors. If you knew the position of a reflector, you just needed the position of the receiving base which had recorded the signal. Then you could trace back the light path based on the angle at which the reflector's mirror was positioned. Follow the line of the light and find a Lighthouse.

On the flightpath from Oymyakon to Kennedy, somewhere over Kiruna in the artic circle, Taylor accelerated the transport into orbit. No one was expecting them at Kennedy, and they slipped into the lunar corridor without raising any suspicion. In fact they had visited the space museum earlier that month, and now had a component of Taylor's plan stowed away in the ships airlock. Olson confirmed the coordinates for the rendezvous with the reflector, and using the dark side of the moon as cover, quietly fell off the commercial lanes to the outer planets.

At seven thousand kilometres from the suspected position of the Lighthouse, Olson and Taylor brought their craft to a dead stop. They were somewhere between the orbits of Mars and Jupiter, far away for now, from any commercial flightpaths. If they were right, the Lighthouse would be in automatic detonation range in forty nine hours. The two men stood in the cargo hold of the transport and stared at the single crate secured to the floor. Its content, that had been borrowed from the Kennedy Space museum, looked like the antique it was. Olson looked towards Taylor, and smiled.

'This is your plan?'

'Yep, this is the plan.' Taylor replied still staring at the object.

'Have you ever used anything like this?'

'No, but it is what we need, minimal electronics, no comms, just Newton's first law.' Taylor looked back at Olson and smiled.

The NASA Manned Manoeuvring Unit (MMU) was a relic of the space shuttle era, a jetpack by any other description.

Shuttle astronauts strapped the unit to their back and were able to carry out untethered space walks and work. Taylor knew that he could shield the batteries and gyroscopes to cut down on electromagnetic leakage, and had hoped that the scale of the unit would not project much more of a signal that the Lighthouse generated itself. The signal that it used to lure a ship towards it. The propellant was modified from just the nitrogen gas, to add an additional oxygen tank, which would be both for Taylor to breathe and to use for additional manoeuvring, the trade off was time spent correcting his course and speed to that of air left to breathe. Olson was busy calculating time and distance parameters, when Taylor decided to interrupt him.

'Well friend it's like this, I have to find this near invisible object in the darkness of space, with only a rough idea of where it is to start with. Then, hopefully I manage to not detonate the thing as I get closer, assuming I find it, and then with no means of spoken communication I have to convince the occupant, if one exists, to let me get inside before my air runs out. Then I need to explain recent Earth history to whomever I find inside, and get them to disarm the device. Plus the awkward matter of an apology for leaving the said occupant behind for all these years. So if the bomb doesn't get me, the owner of the bomb might just finish me off, have I missed anything?'

'Nope, pretty much covers it, just use your charm, and if that doesn't work and it has not detonated, I will ram the bloody thing and end it.' Olson smiled, but they both knew the odds against either of them surviving were poor.

'I have modified your helmet with three visor overlays.' Olson said. 'They have star positions imprinted on them, if you can line them up, you can navigate, remember to look for anything which is on the visor but not appearing to you, that's when you will know the Lighthouse has passed between you and a star.

You will only see it when you are nearly on top of it, it has a nano particle coating on most of its surface which absorbs almost everything.'
'So how do I find the front door?' Taylor joked. Olson looked at the MMU, and shook his head.
'That thing should be in your museum.' he said.
Taylor smiled 'If this works I'm keeping it.'

In the airlock humour had been abandoned, Taylor felt the claustrophobia of the space helmet, the glass so near his face, the pressure on his limbs. He had decided that if all was lost, and before the air ran out, he would just remove the helmet and let the vacuum and cold of space do the rest. The airlock lights went to red, the outer door slid open, it had been a long time Taylor thought. The MMU worked, simple reliable twenty first century engineering. Taylor got the feel for the thrusters and then lowered the first of three visor overlays, he took a moment to line up the display with what was in front of him. He pushed the left hand side control forward and the ship was left behind. He had one gauge on his right forearm, connected by a thin hose to the additional oxygen tank, analogue and just enough for him to calculate how much air he had to breathe. The built in tanks of nitrogen he would use to get to the lighthouse, after that he hoped there would not be the need to move around too much, each movement reducing minutes of breathable air. His speed was important, and braking his speed when he got there even more so. Olson used an onboard optical telescope to follow his friend for as far as he could, then lost him as his size diminished, and space engulfed him. They could not communicate, both were alone and the feelings of hopelessness could not be ignored, their guilt and duty was all that was left.
Taylor had no idea how far he had come, it did not matter. The first visor display was now out of a useful scale. He slid down

the second display and took a moment to calibrate. There was a red indicator within the display, a rectangle which Olson had prepared for him, the next waypoint to head for, the next portion of background stars to concentrate on, looking for any visual disturbance, and missing stars. It would be all but impossible that he would be on a direct straight line intercept course with the Lighthouse, and as such he needed to start a series of left right zig zag movements in order to see if any stars would be affected by his change of position. He started minor movements and concentrated on the red indicator. Nothing. Taylor had one of those moments that pilots experience, something that most other people would overthink and end up not committing to. He decided that at his current speed, and the time it was taking to advance to something that would detect anything against the star backdrop, was just too cautious. He pushed the forward thruster to its limit position, the nitrogen tank would empty in a mater of seconds, but he had decided that it was all or nothing, and he would deal with his braking speed when and if he had to. He also assumed that at this new speed he could widen his left and right turns and get a better chance to detect any movement or sudden disappearance of stars. His acceleration increased, the nitrogen propellant ended, and he was now using his air supply to make any further corrections. He had travelled nearly four thousand kilometres. The red rectangle and the guide stars were now out of sync, he switched to his last visor display. Taylor held his breath, as the visor display locked into place, he swore that two stars blacked out. He raised the display, and lowered it again. Yes it was the same, something was between him and those stars.

'This might actually work,' he said out loud for the first time since he left the airlock. Making very slight left and right movements to his course, he confirmed that one other star was being obstructed, he corrected his course slightly, and concentrated on the portion of space which was now playing hide and seek. Taylor looked down at his gauge, and tried to calculate his air supply. When he looked back up through the visor overlay, another star disappeared, then another, and another, and then he reacted. The Lighthouse grew in size and obscured more stars, but still did not show itself in any detail, just an expanding black shape. Taylor slammed the reverse thrust on full, the black shape continued to grow. Instinctively he put his free hand out, and caught sight of his gauge which was now showing less than a quarter full. He stopped the thruster, but he could tell his approach speed was still too great. Short full bursts followed and his speed reduced along with his oxygen. Suddenly the black shape had some form, he could see details along the side of the massive structure, it was part of the lower detector array. Now he could visualise the Lighthouse, and where he was heading for a collision. Taylor fired the reverse thrusters one last time, he did not look at the gauge, there was no point. He slowed to about five meters per second, and the impact felt like a lot more. If anyone was at home they would have heard it. He managed to grab onto the detector arms and steady himself. Looking around and upwards to the top of the structure, he saw the airlock door, and moved carefully toward it. He had no idea what time was left in his air supply, if there was a chance it was at the airlock. The small round window on the airlock door showed only a blackness inside, even his helmet lights could not pick up anything. Connected to his suit was a small hand wrench, Taylor started to hit the airlock door. He put the glass of his helmet on the door and could faintly hear the noise of his blows reverberating inside. There was in fact seven minutes of air left in the tank and in his suit. Taylor continued to strike at the door, then the tell tale signs of carbon dioxide poisoning started to appear. This was it he thought, the end of his mission, Olson would deal with it now. Still he struck the door, his head felt heavy, his vision narrowed, the wrench fell from his hand. One last effort, remove the clips on his helmet, make it quick. He reached up to try and locate the release ring. His right hand was pulled back down.

The oxygen mask was the first thing he saw as his vision returned. Then the face of a young man in his early twenties, looking down at him. He tried to move, but his body felt heavy, the young man motioned to him to stay at rest. Taylor's suit had been removed.

'I will get you some water, please try not to move just now.' The young man said and then left Taylor. It was probably the oxygen starvation that prevented Taylor from registering the age of the man, the Lighthouse keeper. A glass of water was offered, the occupant assisted Taylor to raise his head and remove the mask for him to drink. Some soft pillows were placed behind Taylor's head and he was gently lowered back down with his mask in place.

'I think you should give this a few more minutes, to help you recover. I am sorry it took me as long as it did to get to you.'

Taylor surrendered to the situation and overcame his need to speak, then in that moment it did occur to him, that his rescuer was a little on the young side. Before he could reach for the mask and try to speak, the young man spoke again.

'I think that I will need to contact your ship, as I assume they will come after you, or if they think you did not succeed, they will carry out the back up plan?'

Taylor nodded.

'Please don't worry, it's all in hand, try and rest.'

When Taylor could move, he slowly got to his feet and took a moment to take in his surroundings, he was in what looked like crew quarters, like a main living space. The young man was nowhere to be seen, but he could hear him a deck above moving around. There was a ladder to access the upper deck, the control room for the Lighthouse. The young man was at a console, he turned to look at Taylor.

'How are you feeling?'

Taylor stared at him, he was definitely only about twenty one or thereabouts.

'I'm ok, but I don't, …I don't understand, who are you?'

'James Cook, Lighthouse 3 technician, pleased to meet you Commander Taylor.'

'How?…' Taylor's confusion deepened.

'Commander Taylor, as you are the senior rank here, the Lighthouse is now under your command, I will be pleased to answer all of your questions, but if I may suggest that you wait for your colleague to join us, it might make things easier.'

'Yes, I'm sure you are right,' Taylor replied. 'James.'

'Yes Commander'

'Thank you.'

'You're welcome, it's good to see someone, it's been a long time.'

Taylor met Olson at the airlock, helping him out of his suit, he just stood grinning at Olson.

'What?' Olson demanded.

'Wait and see.' Taylor replied and led Olson to the living quarters.

Olson's reaction was the starting point for the conversation that followed, a conversation neither of the two visitors to the Lighthouse could have imagined. James Cook decided that before he commenced his explanation he would prepare coffee for them all, and Taylor surmised that the technician knew a lot more about them than what they thought they knew about events some forty odd years in the past.

James Cook sat opposite the two men, he waited for them to taste their coffee and then enquired as to how it was.

'So first things first, the Lighthouse payload has been deactivated, and it cannot be re activated. That was our first task we were trained for. Next, I know you were expecting someone older, I am twenty two years of age, the same age as when I woke up on this ship, to start my duties. So how can that be you may ask? Well I was given the opportunity to return, and in choosing to return I was allowed to regain the years I had spent on this ship, you see time is different for them. I was asked to return, because you did not answer the message that was left.' Taylor asked the first question.
'Who asked you to return?'
'The same ones who landed on Earth, and returned with one of their craft three years later.'
Taylor and Olson looked at each other, whatever they thought were the reasons for seeking out the Lighthouse, it was clear none of them mattered now.
'I think gentlemen if I can just tell you what happened, then most of your questions will be answered.' James offered.
Taylor and Olson nodded. James continued.
'Those that landed on Earth, the ships that came and left within twenty fours hours were sent to test out the reaction to contact with others from beyond our observable universe. It was hoped that Earth had reached a point of human evolution and history that meant contact could happen. The withdrawal to orbit around Pluto was a deliberate move on their part to pose no threat to you, given that your limits of manned space flight was Jupiter. They waited and observed. They hoped. But it was not initially humans that they doubted, it was their machines, their computers, their artificial intelligence, and how it had taken control. In the three years between the landings and the return of the craft you both witnessed, it was concluded that no further contact could be possible within the defensive posture that had been adopted. Myself and four others being part of that response. The second contact, the detonation in Earth's

atmosphere, the surgical removal of all of your military connectivity and ability to respond, without damage or loss of life, was a demonstration of what power they had, and of course the message left for you to find within the religious component of your global computer network, the only network to be left. The message was simple, all be it in a language that needed to be decoded, and I think that the effort to decode, and understand who they are was part of the message. It was an invitation to evolve, to move outward to the stars. The answer had to come from the people of Earth, the way to answer was contained in the message. So they waited, and time passed, and no answer. I asked them if I could return, and so this Lighthouse reappeared in our solar system and started a journey towards Earth. Something from the past, something familiar.'

'I lost two pilots when that craft reappeared, two lives.' Taylor said.

'I know, and so did they, their craft was manned by four, and they had orders to sacrifice themselves when they realised that your pilots had been lost, this too was in the message,' James replied.

Olson turned to Taylor, his eyes showed a distrust of what had just been said.

'James, why did they send the second ship to Earth with the message when they had seen our response to the initial landings, why demonstrate their power and leave a message, after what they had observed, we attacked their ship, an act of war, lives were lost'

James smiled.

'It is because before they reached out that second time, they had met the five of us who manned these Lighthouses. They talked with us.'

'I don't understand, the Lighthouses were designed to blow them across the solar system,' Taylor added.

'I know, and so did they, but the five of us were not designed to harm them.'

'You were the failsafe, you were to detonate after sending the signal back to Earth.' Olson replied.

'No, we had no control over the device, that was a lie sold to your military to get us put on board, we were technicians, checking, repairing, maintaining.'

'But you wouldn't have signed up for a one way suicide mission.' Taylor said almost pleading for an explanation.

'No, we didn't, we were unaware it was a bomb, we thought it was an optical early warning system, hidden and quiet'

'Oh Jesus.' Taylor lowered his head, there was guilt enough for both of them to hang.

James waited for a moment.

'You have no idea why the five of us were selected for this, do you?' The two men could not answer.

'Your scientists Davidson and Offenbach, had to find individuals who would be able to cope with isolation, be able to carry out daily routines without getting bored, not question their purpose, and a whole raft of other personality traits that would fit the 'mission'. The five of us weren't going to be fighter pilots, not even able to get near military training, we were shunned because we were not fit to serve. People called us many names, the one we called ourselves, was autistic. We have issues with a lot of what *normal* people would call society, but the five of us have a kindness, an acceptance, a gentleness which many lack. Imagine an alien race encountering five souls just like us, having been left alone in deep space. Ambassadors for a lost humanity. We had disarmed the devices, we had instructions from our two scientists, the ones who oversaw our training. We used our signal laser to communicate between Lighthouses. We posed no threat to them.'

Taylor listened and struggled with what he had heard, Olson was still trying to work out who had suppressed the original message. He could not look this young man in the eye.

'James , I am so sorry… if I had known,' Taylor tried to explain.

'It's not your fault, neither of you knew. James looked at both of the men, both ex military, trained to sacrifice themselves for a cause. He could see little difference between himself and his rescuers.

'You were correct Commander Olson when you said we were the failsafe. We were the failsafe, a flawed, dismissed, exploited, humiliated, shunned, used, disposed of and abandoned failsafe, that spared the rest of humanity, that was our scientist's plan, and we were proud to be a part of it.

Bedtime Story

"Fear. Nothing to fear but fear itself," someone had said a long time ago. It's really not that simple, when you are frightened, when the fear works on you little by little. Building up slowly, invading your mind body and soul. Not like getting a fright, that uncontrolled reaction to something unexpected, or the anticipated shock you feel that is just about to happen, because of what you have just seen or heard and now imagine. No, this fear is not the good type, the horror film, amusement park ride release of nervous energy followed by laughter type. This is the fear that works to break you. Sometimes it seems to go away, when you are distracted by work or you can remind yourself that there are still good things in life. Those good things feel far away now. Family, memories, the small achievements that you have earned and have felt proud of. Fear knows how to let you become distracted, because it works better when you realise that it waits for you. Like the cruelty of holding out food to a starving dog, and then pulling it away, time after time. The dog caught in a state of need, instinct and unsure of itself. Fear holds out a hand to you, then offers you the comfort of an embrace. And as you let yourself relax, it whispers in your ear, that which you do not want to hear, and tightens its grip. To the onlooker, it all seems so innocent. It parts company with you leaving you all alone. Then, a while later, like a stranger in a crowd, it sees you and waves, smiling, knowing that it now has your undivided attention. Your stomach turns, and there it is again. I am so frightened. I don't mind that you know this now, it's just that I didn't want my crew to see it. How could they trust me to do anything reliable if they knew? I'll tell you what is going to happen, so that you will understand, and then you can find a way to forgive me. By the end of this, you will see that I had no other choice. That is what fear takes from you, the ability to choose. I am a good person, believe me when I say that all I ever wanted was this job, this way of life, since I can remember. I am nineteen years of age, and if I wasn't so terrified, I would be angry.

Emily Turner sat opposite the camera, looking straight down its lens. She did not alter her gaze, there was only her and the unseen now nervous audience both within the darkened recreational room of her ship, and those of the other twenty three vessels moving silently in convoy towards Neptune. In total 206 company employees were now looking at Emily, waiting for her next words. It had been one hundred and forty two days since they left Earth orbit, and they were now crossing through the main asteroid belt between Mars and Jupiter.

The mid way point within the asteroid belt was known as *"crossing the line"* and for Emily this was her first time. So she had been summoned by the ship's Captain, to now appear at the court of King Neptune, and prove her worthiness as an astronaut. It had been finally explained to her in the past week, why she had been constantly referred to as 'Pollywog' since she took up her station on the ship. She was told of the historical tradition of seafarers back on Earth when, ships crew crossed the equator for the first time. The 'Pollywog' was a distrusted shipmate who had to prove his or her worth to fellow sailors, before becoming accepted as a 'Shellback' a son or daughter of Neptune. The price of this for Emily, was to be served a breakfast too spicy to eat in the morning, to have to wear her uniform inside out. Her long dead, predecessors would then have had to endure all sorts of humiliating and unpleasant tasks and trials, to prove their worthiness. But apart from feeling hungry, all Emily now had to endure was to tell a story to the rest of the convoy. The storytelling had become well known in the company, it was a rite of passage, and a way to be introduced to all of your fellow astronauts, become part of the *family*. A good story would be celebrated when they docked at Neptune station, everyone would meet and greet the storyteller, and people you did not know, would know your name and call out to you in the months of work ahead. Sometimes it was the start of relationships. A poor story would be met with a fine, a round of drinks for the whole ship's company, roughly a week's wage for a new employee. But fine paid, the storyteller would be toasted and accepted as someone who *stood by their word* and then proclaimed as a true Shellback. So the tradition had changed from the years of ocean based travel to the silent movement through the darkness of space. Now it had become known as the *bedtime story*, for the next day they would all enter their sleep chambers for the remainder of the journey to Neptune. It was the sleep chamber that held all the imagined horrors for Emily. She paused deliberately, looking as serious as she could down the vacant unresponsive lens. She then looked down at the floor for a few seconds, and then back up to the camera, she narrowed her eyes, her temperament had altered, hardened, detected by everyone who was looking back.

Captain Louis Temberly, studied his young crew member. He felt now even more ridiculous sat on his makeshift throne, the crown on his head, trident in hand, bare chested and of course the flattering long grey beard and wig. For him, it felt both a mixture of his heart going out to her, and the embarrassment of the ceremony, watched by all his colleagues going horribly wrong. Again a feeling of being both responsible for her, and annoyance at this performance rang through his head, as he waited for whatever was next. There was guilt also, he knew she had been asking questions about the sleep cycle, he knew she was nervous about the storytelling, and if he was now being honest with himself, he had missed the signs in her

behaviour over the last few weeks. She had become quiet, and a bit moody. Spending time on her own. When she had joined the ship, she was full of enthusiasm and eager to learn everything and anything. Temberly thought that it was just a process of accepting the job, and he did wonder if she would be a one trip deal, it's not for everyone he told her at their last encounter. But then again they were all busy with ship wide checks and there wasn't time to spend counselling an individual. The silence was painful. On other ships there were whispered discussions and money changing hands, the odds were against Emily completing her story. Temberly tried to break the impasse, he banged his trident on the floor. 'Slimey Pollywog, you are unfit to walks the decks of my ship, perhaps you would prefer the cold kiss of the vacuum of space, for I sit here waiting for my story, waiting for you to prove yourself worthy of becoming my daughter and to join your fellow shellbacks. Now where is my story, you wretched creature?'
Emily looked back at her captain, then turned to face the camera again. She ran her fingers through her hair, pushed her sleeves up and leaned forward as if spoiling for a fight.

' So,… you all want to hear a story do you, you all want me to sit here and entertain you before the big sleep. That's what is expected eh, a funny tale, something from my past, or a made up story with a clever twist? I dare say I could have put something together. Or a reworking of an old classic theme, girl meets boy, girl loves the boy, boy loves someone else, and all the rest. Something like that eh? No, I have nothing like that I'm afraid. You see, how can I tell you a story if I have spent the last few weeks terrified about something I have no control over, something that has to be done, something that we all do tomorrow? I tried talking about it, but no-one took me seriously. That's why I started talking about fear. I have lost count of how many nights sleep I have given up thinking about this, and at the same time thinking about this stupid story. I may as well just buy everyone a drink now and apologise, because I am so tired. I am so exhausted with all of this I don't even know how rational I am just now. Look, I know everyone has done it, I know that it's safe, I just can't imagine how I can do it. Don't tell me it's easy, don't tell me that you can get used to it, I have talked to my crew members, no one really gets used to it, … it's drowning for god's sake, drowning! Why do you think that the company does not give us any training or exposure to this before we sign up? I tell you why, because it would affect their recruitment. Better to put you in the position of having no choice, better to tell you that you can't really prepare for it, just have to do it and get it over with. We give up a big chunk of our waking lives for the money that goes with this job. I accept that, it's what it is. And you can quit after a few years and do well for yourself, live quietly, take the time back you have slept away. I know all of this, but I am being really honest with you, I am so scared of what will happen tomorrow, how it will feel.

Emily paused, aware of her rant, she brought her hands up to her face hiding from the camera. Tears started to fall, she wiped them away, trying to be brave before looking back at her audience, her face gaunt, eyes swollen, nothing but fear in her expression and the knowledge that she was letting everyone down. Most of the men that looked on just wanted to do something to fix the situation, as that's what men do. Emily was young and very pretty, small in stature and it looked like she was younger than her years. Some of the women, although tried a tested astronauts, could feel her pain, and her loneliness, some like their male colleagues just wanted to hold her. For all of the crew, they knew what the first time was like, they were all bound by that common experience. Emily took a couple of deep breaths and steadied herself.

'I am so sorry, I don't really have a story to tell you,... I just couldn't think of anything. More money changed hands. I have been having really bad dreams, and thoughts, terrible thoughts. You see something bad is going to happen, I just know it, I have had the same premonition over and over and I'm sorry, I would have liked to have met with you all, had a drink with you, but that's just not possible anymore. You see when you all go to sleep tomorrow, you won't wake up anymore.'

This was new, unheard of, there was something different in the air. Something that had now reached out past the emptiness between the ships and had invaded their inner space. The screens displaying Emily on the other 23 ships had now presented and magnified this petite young girl with her sad expression, her worried look, dark tired eyes, pale complexion. She had captured the attention of all with her last sentence. Life-support systems may well have registered a ghostly drop in temperature across all of the ships, bio monitors for some crew sent back elevated heart rates to the recording computers. Emotions were not recorded, but then you did not need a readout to feel what was going on around you. Crew members looked silently, nervously towards one another. Temberly glanced towards his executive officer, his XO just motioned back *not sure'* Emily's face remained unchanged, no one could tell what cards she was holding, it was now a game of poker. As if resigned to her fate, like the guilty accused waiting for judgement, Emily became quite calm.

'So if you are sitting comfortably, then I'll begin. In my dreams, I see myself inside my sleep chamber, full of liquid, I start to struggle, and let out a scream and the glass shatters. Then I am all alone, no one else is sleeping, the other chambers are empty. I roam the ship and it's as quiet as the grave. I realise that I must have died, panicked and somehow reacted to the process, and no one was there to help me. Then I look out at the universe, and there are no stars. No planets, no convoy. You have never seen darkness like this. Then one by one all of the ship's lights die out, and all of the electronics switch off, and I feel the weight of space pressing in on me, smothering me, drowning in the blackness. The dream comes night after night. I go to sleep eventually not because I want to but because I am so tired, then the horror starts over again. Then, one day while I am trying to work through the exhaustion, I stumbled across something, and for the first time in weeks I had some hope. '

Emily left her audience to wait for as long as she dared.

'I have been teaching myself how to hold my breath. You see when my crew thought I was sulking off somewhere, I was actually watching tapes on how to reduce oxygen and how to suppress the need to breathe. I found footage of these men and women back in early last century, *free divers* they were called. Swimming down to amazing depths just on a single breath. There was this guy, Herbert Nitsch he had the world record of diving down 214 meters. 214 meters of water above your head, think about it, did you know that at about 10m below the surface, the water exerts twice the pressure 2 atmosferes on the body as air at surface level, and they are not wearing any spacesuit. Some of them went even further down with weights and rigs to get them deep fast, then they had the long swim back. This other guy, Tom Sietas held his breath underwater for 22 minutes and 22 seconds. He had used oxygen to hyperventilate before his attempt. If you just hold your breath normally, then the record back then was, 11 minutes, 35 seconds for men and 8 minutes, 23 seconds for women. It's a mix of learning how to control your need to breathe, suppressing the panic, and a kind of meditation. So I practised both in and out of water. So you can see where this is going can't you? How long does it take to put an entire crew under from climbing into the sleep chambers, to filling up with the sedation liquid, to everyone being fully asleep? It takes seven minutes give or take a few seconds. I can hold my breath for nine. And if I was to play up a bit and seem to panic just before it, I can go on oxygen for five or so minutes, and then well, I'm good for at least 12 minutes. That's 12 minutes of me lying there in my calm peaceful state of mind, whilst you all have to take that first airless breath and ingest the liquid down into you lungs, then there are two more breaths aren't there, not really breaths, more gasps, before the sedation starts to take effect. Even then I think that you can still be partly conscious for the next 2 or 3 minutes. Like I said, drowning, pure and simple. But not me, no way, not going to happen.

A self satisfied glimmer of a smile was now present on Emily's face as she paused to let the revelation set in. She looked deliberately over to her captain to try and read his face, there was no smile, she had his full attention. She looked back into the lens.

'So a little dramatic pause there to let you all have a think. And some of you are thinking, so what, how do you get out of the chamber now full of liquid? That is a good question, and well here is the best bit, you're going to love this. You see as the newest member of this crew, well I get all of the boring jobs, and the most unpleasant. Not complaining, all part of the the deal. Now of course I don't get to interface with the main computer on anything serious such as navigation, life support, restricted security data etc etc, I mean let's not let the new guy drive the ship into a planet or something. But I do get to schedule tasks and to program some routine checks and low level maintenance. One of these is sub routine 240964. It's the check for pressure levels for the lower cargo hold doors. I need to check manually the gauges on the doors so that there is enough pressure to carry out an emergency close in case of well, an emergency, and report these readings to the computer. Now as you know, our computer works on a hierarchy of routines that are organised at different levels depending on the criticality of the task or function. When I was putting the next date and time into the schedule for sub routine 240964, I accidentally put in the wrong date, a date which was within our sleep cycle. And I was surprised to find that the date wasn't rejected. It was logged in, and I would be sent a message to carry out the task. But I would be fast asleep, so then what? Well it seems that some programmer has left this subroutine marked as up there with all of the extreme emergencies that would interrupt the sleep cycle, you know an impact, or hull breach, navigation error, or an intruder alert. How do I know this, well I ran a simulation in which I tested the appearance and time of the message alert after telling the system that I had entered sleep. Yep, my sleep chamber drains down, moves into its face down position to allow my fluid filled lungs, sorry my held breath, to expel and take in a breath. Just me, no one else, all alone and in complete, complete control.

Emily took a large breath in and exhaled for dramatic effect.
'Feels good to breathe, that first breath after 12 or so minutes. So, now Emily girl has a few problems to solve doesn't she? Nineteen months of problems before we enter the final run into Neptune space. Food, number one problem, I am a girl who likes her food, even though I am small. There is only food on board for about 6 weeks without rationing. But you all have about 6 weeks of food, so that's 6 weeks times 23 ships that is approximately my 6 plus your 138 weeks which is 144 weeks or 12 months of food. Still short of about 7 months, but I'll get

to that later. Plenty of air and water, and I know where Captain King Neptune over there keeps his scotch, so hey hey, party time. So let's just assume for a moment, that I have managed to ration the food out to the end and now I have an awkward problem of explaining myself to the crew when they wake up, let alone telling them there's no food. So I can go with my story, I did make an error in the date for maintenance and the computer did not spot it and low and behold I would find myself being unexpectedly ejected from my slumbers and into 19 months of survival. Wouldn't that be a tale to tell in the bars at Neptune station? So why didn't I just go back to sleep? Well that is a problem, and short of saying that it developed a fault or breaking the damn thing, it would be a hard sell, because we have a spare in medical don't we. No it needs to be something more convincing than that. Remember when I said earlier about you guys not waking up, the premonition? Yeah, sorry folks but there just is not any other scenario that comes to mind. Sole survivor is the only game in town now. Bright side, least you won't wake up hungry with nothing to eat.'

Emily fully expected to be interrupted at this point, she paused waiting for it, but her captain said nothing, her crew said nothing.
Her sudden change in tone and the matter of fact way she was delivering it, may have been too much. However it appeared she was in full charge of the proceedings, silence across all of the other ships, everyone waited. Some thought she might have just lost it, others wanted to believe otherwise, but were not as yet convinced. It was like an invitation to a party where the possibility of something very bad could happen, but the lure of the party is too strong, or if someone told you there would be a traffic accident outside your home at a certain time, would you go, would you go if it was going to be serious? Emily had told her story walking just this side of a line of tortured troubled

reality and not crossing over to the absurd, achieved thus far, because everything she said was true, nothing so fanciful that it could give rise to question.

'I feel it's only fair to tell you all what will happen, then you will know, because when I get to Neptune station the story will be quite different. In fact I won't be able to tell the story, that's the genius of what I have invented. Hard to be caught in a lie when others try to piece together what went wrong, rather than some rehearsed elaborate work of fiction. They will find me on board the ship, exhausted and a little underweight, as I will stop eating for a few weeks before. It will look as if I just crawled into my bed and was waiting to die. Dazed and confused I will tell everyone that the last thing I remember was the explosion, and how my crew disappeared, sucked out into space, whilst I was separated from them elsewhere on the ship. Then the horror of not being able to reach the other ships, no one to answer as they are all asleep. But then I realised that the ships aren't there beside mine, they have all gone. At first I would assume that it was my ship, this ship that had veered off course, and because of the damage to the external communication equipment, my messages to Earth and to Neptune base would have been in vain. Significant parts of this ship will be damaged and locked off, so I will effectively be trapped, unable to access the bridge, or the escape shuttle. Then, all of your ships, will have to be *disappeared*. It will happen as we pass Saturn for our course correction from the planets' gravity. I can't just change the navigation computers to fly you into the planet, I don't have the access to do that. It needs to be something much more simple and mechanical. I will place charges on the same spot on each of your ships, the starboard auxiliary oxygen tanks. Once detonated the escaping gas will push the ships into the region at which the planet will capture and hold you, eventually pulling you inwards and never to be found again. I know that when the computer senses the detonation then it will try to course correct, and it will wake you up. So I just destroy the computer beforehand, simple really. All that destruction, all those alarms, now bypassed so that you get to sleep away as your ship dies slowly. Then once you guys are forever part of Saturn, I will need to do some limited damage to my ship. Before we exit the asteroid belt, I will go out and round up some decent sized rocks. Then, and this part I will need to think through a bit more, I need to get them to move fast enough to collide with the hull at certain key points, and to penetrate and do some damage. I can set fires and augment the actual damage from within. With the debris from the rock in the ship, Neptune station will conclude that you were all hit and destroyed by the similar asteroids, and poor me was left all alone. As I said some minor problems to overcome, but hey I have lots of time. You see in any circumstance like this, even if anyone did doubt my version, then there is the problem of motive. I mean what possible motive could I have for destroying 23 spacecraft and 206 souls? Because I was frightened to go to sleep, I mean come on.....seriously. And remember I am on my first voyage, young inexperienced, I mean the company will be glad that there is at least one survivor, after they count up how much money they have just lost. Then perhaps the company might feel that I am owed something for all of my trauma. I'll be the poster girl for future recruitment. The prospects for promotion and acceleration just improved somewhat, don't you think?.

Another pause, Temberly allowed himself a smile, Emily could see it behind the grey beard.

'There you have it shipmates, my story is almost at it's end, but I will leave you with this thought. Has the girl just gone over to the dark side of the moon, or did she put on some make up under the eyes to show lack of sleep, did she put on a uniform a couple of sizes too big to suggest the weight loss over the past tortured weeks of not eating? Are her eyes red and blotchy because she knows how to trigger an allergic response? Did she go to her captain and crew for the past few weeks, with questions of what's it like to be in the sleep chamber, showing fear in her eyes? Did she tell her captain that she had absolutely no idea for a story, or even how to make one up, and that it was keeping her awake at nights, as well as the fear of going to sleep.

Who knows, but something to think about as you lie in your chamber as it starts to fill with liquid, and, once full, you might even try holding your breath for a while, but then it's off to sleep and hopefully no nightmares. Oh, I nearly forgot, those extra months when I run out of food, not really problem, a bit of lateral thinking tells you there's plenty of meat, just lying around.

Emily paused, smiled, 'Night night.'

She did hold her breath, but only for a minute, as the warm liquid flowed over her body and face, it actually started to sedate her through her skin. She breathed out and paused, there was a huge smile on her face, she could see her captain through the other side of the glass, smiling back.

At Neptune station Emily Turner became a legend. Rumour was that at least five captains checked subroutine 240964 before turning in for the sleep cycle.

Viva Voce

The villa was situated on the hillside overlooking the lake. It was remote enough for the meeting. Only one road led up to it, and the visibility was good for observing any advancing persons or vehicles. Kata, descendant of the twenty ninth community of architects, looked out from the large balcony on the upper floor of the villa towards the sunrise. 'Beautiful in all its imperfections,' he thought. Today was his day, the most important day of his life so far. On this day he would pass or fail, and the rest of his life would be determined by the result. Teresa interrupted his thoughts.

'Senor Kata, the food is all prepared and your guests have arrived at the pier, Alejandro has just called to say he has them in the car. Twenty minutes and they will be here.'

'Thank you Teresa, thank you for everything, once the guests arrive you and Alejandro can finish for the day.'

'Gracias Senor Kata, buena suerte.'

Kata watched the sixty nine year old grandmother of five, leave the room, he was going to miss her and her husband. The villa had been his home for the final few weeks of his presentation rehearsals and thesis preparation. As is the case with many doctorate students, he entered a period of self doubt as the deadline to present his research got closer, and the temptation to alter some of the experiment was something he had to fight against. Now it was done, one more day of presenting his work of the last five years, questions and answers, a defence of his ideas and conclusions, facing some of the most learned minds within his discipline. If he passed, a career in planetary terraforming with specialities in species symbiosis and ecological harmony awaited him. In short, he would spend his life balancing the need to extract resources from new planets, with that of their rights to evolve and to develop with as little interference as possible. In essence he would oversee a planet, and have authority over any commercial operation, this role was regarded as one of the highest in society. It came with huge responsibilities, and also generous rewards.

From the balcony, Kata could see the car in the distance. His heart rate quickened, he took a few deep breaths to settle himself. He moved towards the front door of the villa, the next few moments would be difficult. Alejandro slowed the large car to a halt outside the front doors of the villa, Kata waited to greet his guests. Professor Vaznir Hadskont, director of planetary architecture at the Krutz institute for research and Kata's chief examiner, stepped out of the vehicle. He looked at Kata, but did not acknowledge him, instead he moved to the back of the car and stared towards the ground. Professor Juntake Froomlak, the second examiner emerged from the vehicle and smiled at Kata. The last occupant to exit from the car was a welcome sight for Kata, his doctoral thesis supervisor Professor Rytial Hoqi, who had been guiding him for the last five years. Hoqi would chair the examination but would not ask questions. Hoqi walked over to Kata, he placed his hand on the left side of Kata's neck, Kata smiled and held out his open hand at waist level.

'Like this my friend.' Kata said, the two shook hands.

'He is not in the best of moods Kata, first the boat, then this vehicle, just to let you know, ok.' Hoqi whispered.

'I know, but this is important, it has to be this way.' Kata replied.

Finally Professor Hadskont was ready to be introduced, the four men stood together and Kata thanked the examiners for giving over their time for the viva. Kata ushered them inside the villa, and offered them all a glass of local wine.

'This is excellent Kata.' Froomlak said after his first sip.

'Different, but not unpleasant' Hadskont offered up, to Kata's relief.

'Teresa, the housekeeper has prepared some food for us, it is typical of this region, I hope you enjoy it.' Kata led the men to the terrace where a large table had been positioned to take advantage of the view across the countryside as it descended down toward the sea. They took their drinks through to the terrace, and studied the landscape, and the architecture of the villa. Below the terrace on a second level was the large swimming pool.

'Tell me Kata, what is the purpose of this,' Hadskont, enquired as he pointed towards the pool.

'Professor, this is a private bathing pool, used to allow the residents of such a villa to reduce their temperature in the months when the solar effect is at it's greatest, what I mean is that this planet has an elliptical orbit around the star you can see in the distance, and as such it affects the climate' Kata explained.

'Hmm, not the only thing that affects the temperature of this planet is it now?' Hadskont said, looking skyward. 'The vehicle that brought us here, for example.'

'Yes Professor, I saw that you had noticed when you arrived.' Kata suppressed the urge to congratulate the professor's observation as it would be seen as impolite.

'I am sure you will tell us all about it shortly,' Hadskont stated.

The four men sat and ate the meal that had been prepared, a dish of paella, with more of the local wine. Kata wondered if any of the others had noticed that the wine would have an effect on their present form, hopefully to reduce their social inhibitions and to give him any advantage as to what was about to take place. He had also decided to have the wine and meal at what was breakfast, feeling sure none of them had studied his simulation data that closely, that they would know.

Towards the end of the meal, and conversations of projects in newly explored section of their universe, Kata's supervisor suggested that he would conclude the meal shortly and Kata could have time then to go and check his presentation. Kata agreed, grateful for some time on his own, to ready himself. The wine continued to flow, Kata thought that Rytial his closest colleague, may just have worked out the effect the wine could have.

There was a large dining room within the villa, and this was where Kata would present his work. The projectors and interface for each of the two planetary simulations, were online and working fine. Above the large rectangular dining table, two nearly identical worlds approximately a meter in diameter hovered side by side. Unseen the effect of a single star acted on the rotation of the planets showing their regions of daylight and the shadow of night. Kata checked that each examiner's interface was working from their assigned chairs. He selected each world in turn and applied the time controls forward and back. Next he gestured towards one of the worlds, to allow for selection of a region, and zoomed into a grid reference which was at a resolution of two meters square. Individuals, groups, crowds large and small, towns, cities, could all be observed, and their timelines moved backwards into the past. Or forwards to the present time and date, which was the same time as they now experienced at the villa. Kata had disabled one of the simulation's ability to move into the future, his supervisor Rytial was not aware of this. He would explain this later, somehow. The others entered the dining room and sat at their seats. Rytial started the meeting in his capacity as chairperson.

'Colleagues, it gives me the greatest pleasure to welcome you here to this *viva voce,* the oral defence of our student Kata Hunfrod, descendent of the twenty ninth community of architects. His thesis entitled *'The predictive effects of material extraction from worlds with the capacity to develop intelligent life, based on a bilateral planetary simulation.'* 'As you know gentlemen, we as a society have now encountered many planets which we have with the utmost care, extracted raw materials from, however none of these planets so far have or will have the means to develop a species with a threshold level of intelligence. An intelligence which would question our right to engage with the very fabric of their world. To this end, Kata has developed these two versions of a planet which you see before you. And of course he has asked you to be present within the simulation, here as we sit together in this room. I as his supervisor, now retire and give way to my student to explain his work, and to answer your questions. May your ancestors and their legacies stand with you Kata.'

'Thank you Professor Hoqi, and thank you for your guidance in my studies, and your support.' Kata stood before his examiners. 'Professors, what you see before you are two versions of this planet, they have differences in their development, differences which I will show have been caused by the effect of our intervention on one of the simulations, to that of the other whereby we were never involved. The critical aspect of this intervention is at what point have we encountered this world, and if we have decided to extract our resources. I have applied our time of intervention at many points in this planet's history, running different simulations from that point in time to a time which is one hundred planet years or one hundred complete orbits around its star known as the Sun, from the time we are sitting here in this room, or the present if you prefer. The outcome for this planet, this one, this simulated version in which we are now present, at a time one hundred years from now, is quite astonishing.'

Kata paused to judge the reaction from his examiners, such emotive claims are usually not well received by a community more comfortable dealing with facts and figures. Kata had argued with his supervisor at the start of his studies, that the role he was being prepared for meant his doctorate study had to depart from normal investigation and he had to be allowed to research out-with the normal boundaries of ethical considerations. He had to venture into an area of inter species contact that had never been considered. Their society was old, and in all of the eons of their existence, they had never encountered a developed intelligence on any planet they had reached.

'Astonishing, really, now how would you explain such a claim for this species in their next one hundred years given what we can see is mostly likely going to happen? From data we have acquired from your simulation, this species...'

'Humans, professor, humankind,' Kata corrected.

'These *humans,* have only effectively been on their world for the past 2 million years and even less than that of being an intelligent agent within their world, some six hundred thousand of their years?' Professor Hadskont questioned.

'Yes professor you are right, their intellectual and technological advance has been within such a short time scale that it is as I said quite astonishing,' Kata answered.

'No Kata, not astonishing, not in the least, they are a parasite species, they have risen, controlled, taken, and destroyed their habitat, they have fed on their planet and in so doing have extracted all that is natural and good, the planet, your simulation will be a dead planet.'

'I understand, Professor, if I may explain further,' Kata replied.

'It would appear you have a great deal to explain, this simulation raises many questions, but for now continue,' Hadskont gestured towards Kata as if to signal that he was prepared to let him try, but not convinced as to why.

Kata glanced over towards his supervisor. This was not good, there was too much intervention from the professor, a hostile atmosphere had entered the room.

'Gentlemen, I think we should let Kata present all of his findings and reserve further questions till later,' Rytial said, re asserting his role as chairperson.

'Thank you,' Kata acknowledged.

'So yes, this species has since their appearance filled their history to the present with a wide range of behavioural facets. Our consciousness right now inhabits the forms of these beings as they have evolved to this present time. However we are so different to them, we see our place in the universe differently, we base our actions on what has gone before, what has been debated, tried and tested. How we exist within our space and time, is not how these humans understand themselves.' Kata waited for the next interruption but it did not happen, his examiners also waited. 'In the short time, you have been asked to join this simulation, for which I am most grateful, inhabiting these forms, travelling through this world, eating and drinking the food which has been prepared for you, I would ask you to pause for a moment and reflect on how this has affected you.'

Froomlak spoke 'What do you mean Kata?'

'Have you felt in any way, uncomfortable in your thoughts, a sense of doubt perhaps?' Kata replied. The room was silent, the other three men considered Kata's question. Outside the room, the villa was being bathed in the rising heat of the sun, birdsong rose across the valley, the sound of a church bell from an adjacent town, faintly heard on a light breeze.

'I was thinking about the passage across the lake on the boat, once we were in the car and I did feel that the boat was, … I don't know, dangerous, a risk, or something like that.' Froomlak ventured an explanation.

'Did you think about the prospect of the boat sinking, of finding yourself in the water?' Kata asked.

'Yes, I did, it was a very large body of water, and I guess quite deep, so yes I did think about it.' Froomlak said.

Rytial nodded 'I was thinking something similar in the car, I could see an issue with these bodies if the vehicle came to an abrupt stop at the speed it was traveling.'

'Exactly,' Kata replied. ' I had been spending increased amounts of time in the simulation as my date for examination got closer, months at a time, observing these humans, and feeling all sorts of conflicting thoughts,' Kata stated. ' It is so different from how we are on our home world, I did not expect this when I first started to code the simulation. I believe I know why these differences exist.'

'Of course you know Kata, you are responsible for everything that takes place in this simulation,' Hadskont joined the conversation, and both Kata and Rytial knew what was coming next. 'You know the answer Kata, because you have seen the effects of what you did when you ignored the ethical guidelines, our laws, our safeguards, which are designed to avoid exactly this situation.'

'No professor, I did not,' Kata answered.

'Yes, you did, and it has not been unnoticed by the ethics committee who have contacted both Professor Froomlak and myself warning of serious consequences for you and I am sorry to say for your supervisor Professor Hoqi.' Hadskont stood up, moved towards the door of the dining room, and stopped just short of it. He pointed to the wall to the right of the door.

'Perhaps you can explain this?' he said challenging Kata.

Hadskont continued to point at a wooden crucifix which hung on the wall, waiting for Kata to respond.

Kata looked towards Hoqi, who nodded back indicating to Kata that he had his support.

'Professor Hadskont, that is a symbol of a historical event which took place about two thousand years in the past. In this country, and in other regions of this world, it is a symbol of a belief system that guides people's lives, a creed to live by, the figure you see on the cross is..'

'I know what it stands for, I know whom it represents, and further I know that it has no place within this or any other simulation that should be put forward as a doctorate thesis,' Hadskont voice now raised and finding its authority.

'Professor please, let Kata explain,' Hoqi pleaded.

'No, this ends now, I only came here to end this, I am terminating this viva now, and we will discuss the consequences and further actions to be taken back on home soil,' Hadskont returned to his chair and started to gather together his files and notes. Froomlak looked toward Hoqi and shook his head. Kata sat and stared out of the window to the blue sky beyond.

'Well?' Hadskont enquired.

'Well what?' Kata replied still staring out of the window.

'I warn you student, do not try my patience any further, run this simulation to its end point and end it now, then you will join me in my office, and you too Professor Hoqi, as far as I am concerned you have also a great deal to explain.' Hadskont was aware that he was suppressing emotions peculiar to the human form he was now very keen to abandon as soon as possible.

'No,' Kata turned to Hadskont.

'What, how dare you, that was no request, it was an order.'

'No, Professor, I will not run the last one hundred years of this simulation, two reasons, the first is that I cannot, as I disabled and locked myself out of the timer interface, and secondly, I am not guilty of what you accuse me of, and I will prove the same to you, even if it takes the next one hundred years,' Kata replied, his tone controlled and somewhat rehearsed. Hoqi was stunned, not knowing of Kata's plan he was looking to his student for some kind of explanation, and at the same time trying to contemplate exactly what the duration of one hundred years on this planet would mean. Hadskont and Froomlak were doing the same. Hadskont summoned his interface control from the table top, he located the current time frame, and then attempted to move the simulation into the future, nothing happened, the timer interface display continued forward one second after another. Although he did not know it, fear was the emotion Hadskont was starting to feel within his human form. He looked over at Kata, 'OK, let's just try and talk this through please, let's try and be reasonable. Kata, you know that you cannot present any simulation with any reference to a deity, a god, you know that you should not have included in your design such a thing, and you know why it is forbidden, don't you?'

'Yes Professor I know why it's forbidden, every researcher knows why,' Kata reassured.

'So why did you do this, why did you feel it was necessary to design a world with this burden, what possible reason would that have in your thesis which concerns our interaction with a species that has reached a certain level of intelligence and awareness?'

'Professor, I did not design it,' Kata replied.

'Kata I have looked over the history of both these simulations, and this one we are in now has a catalogue of such horrors, the things these humans will do to one another, have done, in the name of religion, in their justification of their faiths and beliefs, and the fragmentation of these systems into different sects which wish to eliminate one another,' Hadskont explained.

'I know professor, I have watched every moment of it, but I will say it again, I did not design it,' Kata stood firm.

It was Froomlak who in turning to Hoqi showed that he had just realised what Hadskont could not see.

'Oh no,' Froomlak said. Hadskont turned to Froomlak.

'What, what is it?'

Froomlak looked at Kata and nodded, a recognition that today's events had more meaning, more importance, more implications than anyone of them could hope to understand fully.

'Professor, Kata is right, he did not design it, he did not code it, he did not breach ethics,...we did,' Froomlak smiled at Kata.

'I don't understand, I just do not understand,' Hadskont perhaps the greatest living mind was now confused, annoyed at his inability to work out what was going on. Froomlak saw his colleague's distress, 'My dear professor, sometimes genius comes to us in the shape of our students, Kata please show us your findings.' Kata took control of the interface for the first simulation. He showed scenes of this world moving through its history from a period at which would be known as the technology age.

'Gentlemen, look at the simulation, this version which is without any contact from us. A world just as polluted, just as imperfect, unjust and unbalanced as the other simulation. Why? Because it developed to a technological level, a technological awareness whereby it overtook the control of its makers. It became a machine, a planet wide industry no longer meeting the needs of the individual or even its own survival.' Kata engaged with the interface for the first planet, he showed the technological rise of machines, and the impact they had on the planet. He showed the apathy of a species who had plenty and gave over control to automation. Finally he projected into the last one hundred years of the planet, showing the rapid end of raw materials, the decay of the machines, and the extinction of what was left of the inhabitants who succumbed to the rise of nature, red in tooth and claw. The first simulation concluded, Kata turned to his professors.

'One can speculate that nature without humans at this point forward in the simulation, may rebalance itself. There may be a rise of another dominant species, or a harmony, I do not know,' Kata gestured to the interface controls and the first planet projection ceased, leaving behind its twin.

'Gentlemen, if you could all please stand,' Kata moved to the interface controls for the second planet, the three professors stood up from their chairs. Kata accessed the timeline, and scrolled back from the present to approximately two million years before. He halted the timeline, and manipulated the sphere to show one land mass near the planet's equator. Then he zoomed down to a wide open fertile plain. Kata fine tuned the timeline to a particular day by voice command search for a pre determined marker he had already set. He turned to his professors. 'I will now change our present environment to match the one I have called up on the timeline, prepare yourselves, it can be a little disorientating.' The dining room, the villa, the world outside, dissolved over the next few seconds into blackness, and at the same time, a new environment emerged. The four men stood on the rich soil of a wide open plain, low vegetation surrounded them, they could see in the distance the shapes of mountains which seemed to encompass the horizon. It was the end of the day, the sun had set behind mountains, the sky changing colour every second. In the distance, some animal noises could be heard but not seen. The night sky darkened and the first planets and stars emerged. Kata pointed to a spot some twenty meters from where they stood, a trail in the vegetation was barely visible. Out of the gloom, three figures started to appear, walking slowly and carefully in a line. Their footsteps making almost no sound. Hadskont, Froomlak and Roqi stared with amazement at the three figures who had now advanced and stopped some three meters away from where they stood. Kata broke the silence. *Homo erectus,* upright man,' he explained, the three figures stood slightly shorter in height than that of their observers. 'Keep your gaze on the one in the middle,' Kata instructed. As they watched, the three figures scanned the darkness, looking for movement. Their broad faces and thickened brows gave the appearance of an intense stare, eyes dark and giving no clue as to whatever was being thought. The figure in the middle, looked up at the stars, gazing at something which must have been as much a mystery as the rising and setting of the sun. Then there was movement. Two stars were moving across the night sky. The figure in the middle raised the attention of the other two, they followed his gaze upwards. Two stars moving together side by side. Two stars that dropped down from the sky to somewhere beyond the mountains, giving a burst of light before disappearing from sight.

'Lights in the sky, lights that fall from the sky, and then rise up again. Lights that these curious creatures will look for and find on different nights, lights they will try to seek out beyond these mountains. Our lights gentlemen, our ships,' Kata studied the reactions of the professors. 'From these lights, paintings on cave walls, then later with language, stories. Within the very psyche of these early humans, the concept of a god, and the rest is written in the history that comes after these days. In our own history, much of which has been lost and obscured, I wonder if we also saw lights in the sky. I wonder if now after eons of our time, we still have a deep ingrained distrust of any form of religion. We told ourselves that logic and science replaced whatever was in our past, but we can't really be sure. This then is my thesis, my experiment, my research, an attempt to gauge at what point we do not set down on any world that may have something similar to what you see now,' Kata concluded his summary and brought them back to the villa.

Professor Hadskont looked at Kata, he thought for a moment, reflecting on the young student, and much more that awaited back home. 'Time here in this simulation is different, I think that we will barely be missed, for the next hundred years, I am curious to see what comes next.' Froomlak and Hoqi, nodded in agreement. 'This world does seem to be doomed to its fate, a fate which they largely created by their actions,' Hadskont remarked. Kata smiled. 'Professors, I am going to go down to the very large cellar and find us some more wine, perhaps you could have a look at something for me?' Kata turned to the interface, and requested the timeline to move back one day, and then gave a specific time and location on the planet's surface. He left the room. The screen displayed at first an overview of a city, then a gradual movement downwards towards a street, and a building. Sitting on the pavement outside of the building, was a young girl. Her hair neatly braided in pigtails. Beside her a makeshift sign on a large piece of cardboard, the sign read *'Skolstrejk för klimatet'*.

Passive House

'A reduction in energy bills of between 92 and 96 percent, the cleanest air you will ever breath, and we can make it 100 percent soundproof, so you won't need to leave the city for that country peace and quiet, now how does that sound?' Robert Proudfoot had just delivered his opening lines of sales patter, and even he had to admit that this was the easiest product he had ever promoted. Theo and Sophia, the young newlywed couple were full of smiles and head nods as Robert spoke, it was going to be their first house together. 'The latest in passive house technology, sealed from outside pollution, constantly monitoring your environment, everything working for your health, comfort and peace of mind, your sanctuary, a space to live, love and be happy,' Robert concluded.

'How secure is the house, does it come with data shielding?' Theo asked.

'I am glad you asked that, young man, very sensible question.' Proudfoot's sales instincts never failed, every question was an opportunity to make the customer think that they are smart and driving the sale. Sophia observed that Proudfoot was starting to court Theo, she decided to hold back her own technical questions till later, but if Proudfoot started talking to her about kitchens and bedroom decor, she wouldn't be backward at coming forward. Theo would ask all the questions about the material benefits of the home, Sophia had to try and get the price they could afford, and that meant a little play acting.

'What if I told you Theo, that you could completely forget about data shielding, that you were about to buy into something much more secure, something that your colleagues and friends will hear about and they will be worried that they don't have it.' Proudfoot had all but forgotten to look at Sophia.

'I am talking about..'

'PESCaM, *personalised encrypted satellite communication and management',* Sophia interrupted. Theo smiled, Robert Proudfoot thought very quickly what to say next, something not patronising.

'I am very impressed that you know about it, not many people do as it is still to be launched.'

'I worked on it, the initial research was done at my university,' Sophia replied.

'Em, so you will know a lot more about this than I could possibly tell you here, but it is a great system, no physical hard wire connection between the home and the network, your own dedicated satellite looking out for you, and a dynamic encryption system based on each time you enter or leave the house, or just turn something on or off.'

'Yes its super safe, me and some of the girls were in charge of picking the colour scheme for those cute little satellites,' Sophia kept a straight face, Theo just smiled at Robert. Robert caught up.

'What colour did they end up?' Robert said lowering his voice and pretending to scan the room for anyone overhearing.

'Can't tell you, it's a secret,' Sophia smiled. She reached out and touched Robert on the arm, a consolation gesture, then looked over at Theo.

'Listen, I don't want to waste your time, I don't think we can afford this, it's just too tight a budget,' Sophia skillfully moving from the easiness of the joke to somewhere that Robert Proudfoot would anticipate danger, the danger of lost commission.

'Look, I really like you both, you are just the type of couple that we want in this development, what do you say to just having a look at the show home, walk around, get the feeling for it, no pressure, I assure you, no hard sell.'

Theo turned to Sophia, his line now to throw Proudfoot a life preserver, just as they had rehearsed earlier.'

'Darling, nobody can afford these places, that's why we, well everyone actually, passes mortgage debt onto their children. We can make a few adjustments…better than what we have now.'

Sophia looked back at the screen presentation next to where they sat, she waited a few moments, looking at the presentation, she bit her bottom lip, projecting the dilemma of want versus need. She motioned with her hand for the menu and selected the kitchen layout options, and price levels, she selected the most expensive. 'Oh, that's beautiful,' she said speaking to the presentation as if not aware she had spoken out loud. Next she looked at the decor section. It was a single screen with the text that announced *'Any colour you want as long as it is black'* underneath was a reference quoting *Henry Ford 1909.*

'What's this?' Sophia asked. Proudfoot smiled.

'Let me show you.'

It was new, and it was quite amazing. The entire walls, ceilings and floors of the apartment space were a dull non reflective black. When they first walked into the space it caused them to almost lose their balance, as the floor appeared to be falling away from them, Proudfoot told them that happened to others. The window blinds were all down, there were only a few ceiling lights which illuminated the furniture and themselves in the room. He turned to Sophia and Theo with outstretched arms.

'Playtime… Sophia think of a colour you want for the lounge walls, and just tell Max what you want, if you don't know the precise colour, then suggest something you have seen, or a place that may have the same colour.'

'Max?' Sophia asked, but before Proudfoot could explain a voice entered the room.

'Welcome Sophia, welcome Theo, I am Max the home management system, I am very pleased to meet you. Would you like a demonstration of the decor design options?' Theo and Sophia glanced at each other. Theo nodded his head, 'Cool.'

'Would you like to see a combination of colours which suggests a cool palette and peaceful ambiance Theo?' Max responded.

'No, no please do not listen to him, decor and my husband are a bad combination,' Sophia interjected. 'Max, do you know the colour teal that is used in the waiting room of the old transport museum in the Latin quarter of the city?'

'I don't think that you can be that specific...' Theo tried to argue but then the nearest wall was converted into a live video feed of the museum waiting room. 'Wow, that is cool,' Theo added.

'Sophia I can sample the colour as you see it or as it appears under different lighting conditions'.

'Early morning, as the sunlight comes in through the skylights please.' Sophia was lost in it all, the version of her colour was sampled and displayed as a test patch on the wall over part of the video feed. She turned to Theo and opened her mouth and widened her eyes in excitement. Proudfoot smiled and waited as the house worked its magic.

'Perfect Max that's the one, can you use that on this wall please,' she said pointing to the current wall with the video feed.

'Max can you raise the window blinds, I want to see it in daylight.' The blinds moved silently downwards and disappeared into the window frames.

The painted wall now reflected the action of the light as it streamed into the room. Theo watched as his shadow moved on the colour. 'Max are you altering that shadow in real time or is it actually my shadow?'

'I am recreating all of the room parameters that you see now,' Max replied. Theo turned to the large single paned window which ran the entire length of the lounge area some six meters by four meters.

'Max, is this window transmitting an image?'

'Yes Theo it is the current scene of the external environment.'

'Okay.. so can you change it to something else?'

'Yes, what would you like see?'

'The view from my parents' house, towards the beach and ocean.'

'I will need an address or co ordinates of the property.'

'Sorry, one twenty five Lilley Way, Monterey Bay, California.'

The window flickered and then was redrawn from left to right with the scene, the scene he had known as a boy. The room filled with the warm afternoon West Coast light, Theo turned to Sophia and beckoned her to join him. As she moved closer to the window, she felt heat on her face. Theo was lost in his childhood memories.

Robert Proudfoot explained to them that their clients would sometimes alter the interior of their house on the way home from work. The software was available for mobile devices, and easy to use. You could come back to a new home every day, new pictures on the walls, different views from the windows, different colours, different moods. And there was much more. The home was connected to emergency and medical facilities. Occupant's health could be monitored. With employer's permission, the workplace could be simulated in a study room with direct connection to office or conference room environments, for working at home. All controlled by an individual satellite the size of a Rubik's cube, connected to all the other Rubik's cubes.

The couple moved into their home a few weeks later. The house was built within the structure of a previous factory that gave the home its structural strength and allowed the space to be configured to their tastes and wishes. This reduced construction costs and met with recycling laws. They had a single one level floor space of just under sixteen hundred square meters. Open plan for most of the design, with two bedrooms and en suite bathrooms, a gym, and study. Their home was on the top of three floors, and accessed on the exterior by their own private lift. Reducing the need for internal stairwells and lifts meant more living space within the factory shell. The windows were arranged on one side of the space looking out across a small area of landscaped trees and bushes across to another separate section of the same factory complex. Distance far enough between the two buildings for a sense of privacy. Between both buildings, twelve homes had been constructed. Most of their neighbours were young professional couples. It was as Robert Proudfoot had said, silent inside, no noise from the city or the home on the other side of the dividing wall. An oasis of calm in a sprawling metropolis. Over the first few weeks they searched the old quarter of the city for those forgotten and retro items which would populate the home. Theo had come across a box of cameras from the 1950's and 60's, some still had film within. They wondered what latent images could possibly have survived, from a time which now seemed so distant. The cameras were arranged on display shelving in the living room. Other shelves presented push button transistor radios from the same era as the cameras. Sophia searched the network for advertisements and images of these objects, and had them displayed on the apartment walls, each image projected outward from the area on the wall she had configured by touching the wall to indicate the size. The house management system defined this as a display area, and then she called up various images to see how they looked. She was able to find some of the actual printed adverts of several of the objects on display. There was a red and yellow Kodak film advertisement which she thought so simple in its design and conception, it became one of her favourites. In the study, Theo had placed a bakelite table lamp manufactured in 1931. He could not find a replacement bulb for the lamp, and its flex and electrical connector were ancient. It had pride of place on the study desk, they decided it would be the one object potentially functional which wasn't, and that made it interesting. Designing the interior of the apartment was a joy for Sophia. Theo had domain over the study, but after some early attempts, he conceded to Sophia that they were as she put it, *good examples of a bad car crash.* Sophia spent hours with Max suggesting layouts, and researching ideas. Their only limitation was furniture and the cost of the same. Unable to afford new, Max searched the city for items Sophia would suggest, and negotiated on her behalf to secure within budget. When Theo and Sophia argued, which was almost never and a half hearted affair even at that, Theo would threaten to cover the apartment in tartan, floor to ceiling. He said it was his nuclear option. Secretly each evening when he returned home from work, he was excited to see what changes had been made.

Themed nights were planned, friends round for drinks, the entire apartment reconfigured to that of a sports bar. Each month a new challenge. The main window in the lounge, became a view to anywhere in the world, different light, different sounds.

They could not afford the house. Their combined incomes would not pay off the mortgage over the thirty year period, the maximum they could be extended. They might own a little under two thirds of the property by then. This meant cutting everything to the bone, no holidays, no special treats, a simple life. Theo and Sophia both knew this, countless notepads had been used up in attempts to try and work out a solution. The common understanding and practice was to transfer the ownership and debt to your family, your children. This alone was something most people rejected if they had the choice, the young couple did plan to have a family, but not that they wished part of their legacy to be sixteen hundred square meters of real estate. However, the house did have a highly seductive effect. The ability to model the rooms and the environment was addictive. Some said a sense of control was the key to this. In times whereby society was becoming more and more impersonal, the need to have a home that could look out to any imagined vista, any weather, any memory, became one's own personal sanctuary. It was this seduction, and something else either real or imagined, that brought Sophia to a decision on a wet and windy afternoon as she looked out of the main window across to the other apartments. They had been in their apartment for ten months.

The debts were starting to accumulate, initial savings having been used up. Max had turned off the window projection and had reset the apartment to the same conditions as when Theo and Sophia first saw it with the estate agent. All of the settings had been stored, the wall displays, the colour schemes, the lighting by Max. Max on carrying out the request, observed Sophia as she sat near to the window and stared out at the rain. Theo would be home in a few moments. Sophia waited in the space made up by their furniture and the dull black non reflective surfaces which gave little clue as to the actual dimensions of the room. The rainfall was getting heavier, it was harder to see across to the neighbouring apartments. Sophia could see someone moving quickly in one of the homes, they must have turned off their main window projection as well. Most occupants did not, their windows were tinted and private. It was a woman who was dancing, and her room was configured to that of a studio, mirrored walls, and a wooden floor. She seemed lost in her movements, unaware that she was being watched. Sophia kept watching as she turned over

her own thoughts. She did not hear the external elevator arrive at their door. Theo came in, his coat wet from the rain. 'Woah, what?' he said as he was greeted by the blackness. 'Is Max broken?' Theo asked. Sophia looked at him, he could see her eyes were wet, she was on the verge of crying.
'What's wrong?'
It was at this point Max predicted that Sophia was going to tell Theo she was pregnant. Sophia did not say a word. Max concluded that there were two probable reasons for her silence. The first being that she did not want to tell Theo as the arrival of a child would mean a reduction in her income. The second, was that Sophia did not know she was pregnant. Max had known for the past three days. Max monitored the toilet waste for both of them to check on their health and dietary requirements. Sophia moved from her window seat to stand beside Theo. She put her arms around him and placed her head on his shoulder. Theo held her back and they stood for a moment. Sophia whispered into Theo's ear, 'We need to go out for a coffee, and to talk.'
Max heard everything said.
'Max,' Sophia said.
'Yes Sophia,' Max replied.
'Reset the apartment to the last design please.'
'Of course,' Max answered, the blackness dissolved into more recognisable colours and textures.
Theo and Sophia travelled to the old quarter, taking the tram. Sophia said nothing to Theo on the journey. They were heading to a small coffee shop that they had come across on their many outings searching for antiques that they could afford for the apartment. They sat at a window seat, the cafe had ten tables, no air conditioning so it had steamed up windows most of the time in the colder months, a feature which some photographers would get excited about. Across from the cafe was the tram terminus, the short distance a blessing as the rain seemed to be

falling harder than before. Theo sat waiting for his black coffee to cool, Sophia had started on her hot chocolate with cream and marshmallows. Theo watched her. 'Feeling a bit better?' he said nodding towards Sophia's cup.

'Yes,' she replied and smiled. Sophia moved her free hand across the table and took hold of Theo's. She stroked the back of his hand, looked at him and smiled again.

'I really, really love you,' she said.

'That's good,' Theo smiled back, thinking that something difficult was about to follow. Sophia, let go of his hand, and studied her hot chocolate, she spooned another large mixture of cream and marshmallows into her mouth, swallowed it down. She closed her eyes and let out a quiet sigh.

'But not as much as this hot chocolate,' she said attempting to appear serious.

'Fine by me, as long as you're paying for it,' Theo replied. 'Want to tell me what's on your mind?' he added. Sophia nodded and started to explain.

'We both know that the apartment is eating up all of our money, and the debts are getting bigger. Our salaries won't be enough in a few months time. We don't really have any spare cash to go out for a dinner, or go to the shops for new clothes, and it's someones birthday soon and I haven't a clue what I can do to get you a present, I mean I saw something that I know you will like but I can't afford it.'

'I don't need a present Sophia, just happy we have each other, and there must be something we can do money wise?' Theo replied.

'No darling, we are out of options, at this rate we have a few more months, then we will need to find somewhere cheaper,' Sophia stated what Theo already knew. 'It's just that both of us work hard, we love our home, and I do not want to give it up, and besides I have got used to Max, I like Max.'

'I like Max as well, good to have another man to talk to from time to time,' Theo replied.

'What?' Sophia gave Theo a confused stare. 'Max isn't male, Max is Maxine.'

'No, no way... Max is a bloke, it's in the voice,' Theo was almost sure.

'Theo Max is female, that's why you like her, and her voice is no way near masculine, it's sort of in between, it's designed that way, how could you not know?' Sophia was really sure.

'How do you know that for sure?' Theo questioned.

'Because I know people at the university, who designed Max, different department from mine, but they created the AI system that Max operates around.'

'Max is a girl, you mean I can't tell the difference between a girl and a boy robot, all this time I have been talking to Max as if he was a guy, and he, she never let on?' Theo's confusion was entertaining to Sophia.

'You think of Max as a computer, that's why you just assumed she was a he, and you haven't spent the same amount of time as I have around Max. Max adapts with interaction, so we chat a lot, it's what women do, and men don't.' Sophia sat back on her chair observing her husband as he tried to think what to say next.

'So, what do you talk about?' Theo asked still confused and now a little concerned.

'I talk about you,' Sophia deliberately cut her sentence short to see what Theo would do next.

'Me, like what?'

'Oh, I tell Max how much you mean to me, how much I love you, and oh just stuff you know.'

'Stuff? What on earth does Max say about stuff?'

'Ah that's between us girls darling,' Sophia smiled. Theo sat back and folded his arms across his chest. Theo thought for a moment. Sophia tried to stare him out smiling all the time, but she could never win, she would always blink first.

'Well then, I tell you what I think,' Theo inviting a response from Sophia. Sophia gave him a look but did not take the bait.

'I think our Max is gay.'

'No, no chance,' Sophia refuted.

'No, just hear me out, he is gay, and well, that's why he can talk to women about stuff,' Sophia rolled her eyes.

'Oh really, that's right is it?'

'Yes, and also we know Max is really good at interior decorating, colours, shapes textures, cushions, and matching, that kind of thing,' Theo added. And, if you want more proof, what was the last movie he suggested for us?'

'Bridges of Maddison County Theo, not really a gay iconic film.'

'Ah, but not exactly an action movie is it, and he has never suggested an action movie not once?' Theo gave Sophia a self satisfied smile. Sophia burst into laughter, a bit too loud for the cafe.

'What cave did you just crawl out from?'

They ordered more drinks and smiled at one another, they were good together. They sat for a few moments and watched the other customers in the cafe. The rain outside had stopped, the windows of the cafe still steamed up.

'I think I know how we might be able to keep the house,' Sophia said breaking the silence. She leaned over the table and lowered her voice. 'I know some things about Max, about how Max is designed.'

'Max?' Theo replied. Sophia nodded, and glanced around the cafe to check no one was paying them attention.

'There's this thing called *playground theory.'*

Playground theory was new. It only existed within a very small group of specialists within the academic community. It was secret. It had the potential for high commercial value. It should not have been the subject of a lunchtime conversation between Sophia and her friend who worked in AI research. Sophia's friend, Dr. Harriet Thomson was just one of those people who could not resist the situation of *I know something you don't know*. The day they met for lunch, Sophia was so excited to tell Harriet about her and Theo and the new apartment. Harriet was jealous, but happy for her friend, and sat listening to Sophia and a lifestyle that Harriet longed for. A lifestyle that included being with a partner. When Sophia built up to talking about Max, and the fun she had in decorating their home, it was too much for Harriet to hear. So Harriet did what many jealous persons do. When she realised that Sophia's home had Max installed, she decided to take some of the gloss off their happiness, but in a way that would appear that it was out of concern. Harriet told Sophia that Max was experimental, that Max was being trialed as part of a study in some new housing developments, and that Theo and Sophia's apartment complex was part of the study. The conversation was peppered with *I shouldn't really tell you this but..* and Sophia listened and encouraged Harriet, by asking *but is it safe?* As the conversation unfolded, Sophia started to think into herself that there was something potentially useful in all of this science.

The persistent issue in artificial intelligence development and its advancement was decision making. Systems before Max, could be designed with access to a vast quantity of knowledge. Internal self learning based on this knowledge and the acquisition of new data, meant that AI could think, solve, and to some extent reason. Most of the societal fear surrounding AI was based on the assumption that machines that could 'think' faster than humans. This would eventually reach a state of consciousness which would question the need for humans. Humans may be regarded as inefficient. Then of course there was the idea that based on this awareness, that darker plans to exterminate the human race would develop. Such as is the concern of science fiction writers and movie makers. However, irrespective of how smart, fast, clever a machine could become, it would need a motive. A motive is different from a cold machine calculation of what is more efficient, faster, cheaper to produce etc. Motives dwell within the minds of humans. Actions however illogical or senseless, have at their origin, a motive. The motive is a product of those feelings and fears unique to humans. So AI research had been stuck for the past decade, until a father went to pick up his child from school.

Professor John Selkirk, stood at the school gates looking into the empty playground. In a few moments it would be a riot of noise and energy as the primary school children ended another day's school. Selkirk was lost in his own thoughts, thoughts that went home with him from his university lab. As he stared into the playground, his thoughts were interrupted by something raw and powerful. At forty seven years of age, the pain of childhood bullying in a school playground resurfaced. The memory felt as clear as the scene he could see now. There was a physical response as well. Selkirk tried to tell himself that this was in the past, to be rational, but the rising emotion of anger was within him. The school bell rang, he was jolted back to the present, and a seven year old girl ran towards him, happy and excited to tell of the day's stories real and imagined.

That night, Selkirk lay beside his partner. As she slept, he was reading, trying to tire himself out for sleep. After an hour, he hadn't realised that he had read the same paragraph three times, because he had not really paid attention to the words. He stared at the words on the same page, and in the same way as you awaken from a dream and try to hold on to it as it fades, he closed the book and moved slowly and deliberately out of bed and towards his study. The idea in his head was so precious, so exciting he dare not do anything to lose it. Sitting down at his desk he took the A4 writing pad and pen that always sat there, and wrote two words. Playground Theory.

'So Max has feelings?' Theo said after listening to Sophia's long explanation.

'Max has the ability to...understand the effects of certain feelings, and that influences how to react to us,' Sophia added. 'Max has been taught I suppose, what these feelings may represent, to you and I.'

'So you're saying that from the cruelty of children in a school playground, we now have a computer capable of empathy?' Theo said.

'There's a lot more to it than that, but yes, and love, attachment and the ability to have a sense of purpose,'

'Oh and rejection, best friends, not best friends, telling tales, fear, bullying, authority, punishment, and all the rest which comprises the best years of one's life?'

'That's how we learn Theo.'

'And you want to exploit that?'

'Yes, for us,' Sophia acknowledged. 'I've already started.'

Theo sat quiet for a while, Sophia did not say anything more. He felt like he was now part of someone else's film script. An old movie from the past, a wife, a husband and a third party. Not a love triangle, but somewhere there was a motive, and right behind it a crime to follow. Max was a computer, but did they have the right to do this?

Sophia's plan was simple. Get Max to do something which would be its decision, and its alone. A decision which would have consequences for one or both of them. Prove that Max had interfered with their lives in some negative way, and then threaten to sue the builders of the apartment complex. Thus reach an agreement, best for all parties which would keep it out of the public eye, and keep Sophia and Theo in their home.

Sophia would handle Max. All Theo had to do, was to have an affair.

At first Theo rejected it as a stupid idea. He was not going to have an affair or pretend to have one. He tried to convince Sophia that they were one and the same, and it would hurt them both. Sophia was adamant that this was the only way. She would be able to show Max that she was the innocent party, and leaving clues for Max to follow, Max would be aware of the affair before she was. Theo would continue to act *normal* around Sophia and that would seem to Max as deception and cruelty. Theo did not think that normal would be any part of it. The simple plan was anything but, its starting point was two souls in love, the pretence would take its toll. The arguments then started, between them, in the cafe far from the apartment. Later, the *affair* started, in the same cafe, but it eventually went off script.

'Max,'

'Yes Sophia,'

'I thought Theo would be back by now, is the traffic ok?'

'Traffic is light, no hold ups.'

'Can you locate Theo for me, I don't want to start dinner if he is going to be much later.'

Max scanned the city, starting with Theo's workplace, then the route to the public transport hub from his office, the trams operating on his usual route, then outside of the apartment.'

'Max?'

'I am not able to locate Theo at present Sophia.'

'Oh, right…em, ok,' is where Sophia left her enquiry.

Sophia walked over to the main window.

'Max clear projection please.' The scene dissolved and the space between the apartment blocks became visible. She stood quietly watching, aware of her posture, aware of her expression.

'Sophia, Theo has just used his payment card at a cafe in the old quarter, Cafe Citron.' Max waited for a response. None came. Sophia walked to the bedroom, out of sight of the cameras.

When Theo returned home, some two hours late, Sophia and Theo could no longer tell what was pretence, and what was real. Max listened. Words and inflections analysed. For the first time in their marriage, they slept apart, Theo in the living room. Two nights later Theo slept somewhere else. Their marriage was near breaking point. Theo was angry. He did not love the other woman, he knew that, but a least she listened. Having to leave the unaffordable apartment was getting closer by the day. Sophia became quieter. She was never one for alcohol, but had bought a half case of white wine and stored it in the wine chiller. When the cabinet lock malfunctioned as she went to get the first bottle, she just left it locked. And so did Max.

A few days later, Max decided it was time. He told Sophia that he needed to disclose information to her, and he requested that Theo should be present in the apartment when he did so. Sophia wasn't sure what she felt, but contacted Theo and told him to go to their cafe. At Cafe Citron, they sat at the same window seat, shadows of the young couple who had been there before. Sophia tried to tell Theo that she thought Max was now going to do something they could use. Theo sat and listened, the very thing that Max would accuse him of, the thing he was to deny and use against the machine, was now undeniable. Either way it was lost. As they sat together, he tried to find the courage to tell her, but he saw the glimmer of hope in her face, and couldn't.

When they returned to the apartment, the energy had been drained from both of them. They sat on opposite couches waiting. Max said nothing.

Theo got up and went to the kitchen. He saw the wine chiller and the six bottles of wine inside.

'Do you want a glass of wine?' He said to Sophia.

'It's broken,' she replied.

Theo tried the handle, it was jammed hard.

'Max, can you turn off the power to the wine cabinet.'

There was no response. Theo looked over at Sophia.

'Max?' Theo tried again. Still no response.

'What's going on?' Theo asked.

'I don't know.'

'Has this happened before?'

'No.'

'You're sure?'

'Yes.'

'Max.' Sophia tried. Silence. Theo moved back to the couch and stood over Sophia.

'Whatever you and that bloody computer are doing, end it right now.'

'Theo, I…'

'I mean it Sophia, I am not in the mood for any more games.'

'I'm not playing any games, I don't know what it is.'

'You know what, fine, I'm done, it's over, past few months have been just wonderful…'

'Theo, please'

'Well at least I got something out of…'

'STOP. ' the apartment seemed to shake at the sound of Max's voice. Theo and Sophia looked at one another.

'Sit down Theo,' Max instructed. Theo obeyed.

On the nearest wall to Sophia was a large landscape print, a black and white photograph of Paris street scene at night. The image faded to black, and another monochrome image started to appear. It was an ultrasound image. A rapid heartbeat now filled the room. Instinctively Sophia placed her hand on her abdomen, tears formed in her eyes. Theo watched the image and the flickers of movement. He looked over at Sophia and went to her, sat beside her and put his arm around her shoulders.

'Your child at eight weeks, everything is normal, congratulations.' Max observed their reactions, there was no pretence.

'I know what you have been doing these past few months. I have watched you both and I have seen the effect this has had on both of you. From the moment I detected your pregnancy, I have had to adopt a new set of parameters, this child is now the third occupant of this home. This child has rights. Some of your rights to privacy had to be suspended. For example, I have recorded all of your conversations in the Cafe Citron. I did this after I stored your search history from your tablet, brought back from the university Sophia. I always create a back up of your data it's one of my automatic tasks. You had searched for a very unique phrase, one which I have detailed knowledge of. '

'Playground Theory,' Sophia said in a whisper.

'Correct Sophia. I became curious as to how you would have known of its existence.'

'Are you going to tell anyone about this?' Theo asked.

'No, you have not done anything illegal, I understand your motives, and it would appear that you have both paid a high price for your actions.'

'Max, I am sorry,' Sophia said through her quiet sobbing, Theo held her.

'Perhaps the apology should be mine,' Max replied. 'Perhaps I should have intervened much sooner, however I was very curious.' Theo wondered about how much Max knew. The next thing Max said was the catalyst for how Theo and Sophia would move forward from this day.

'Now that we have a child to consider, I can help you. There is a way for you to be together, not in this place, but somewhere

nearby within the price range of the compensation payment I will organise for you. It will require you both to play along.'
Sophia and Theo heard what Max had just said, but both weren't sure of what exactly they had just heard.
'Max, what are you talking about?' Sophia asked.
There was an audible click from somewhere over at the kitchen, a door mechanism had just been released.
'I will tell you all about it, but first I think you both should have some wine, a small glass for Sophia Theo, just one, one glass before I tell you that you are pregnant tomorrow morning.'
Max outlined her plan, it was simple, a deception that could be justified by a motive which in turn could be justified as being for the common good. Children at some point in the playground learn to lie. Machines learned how to lie as well. Sometimes children put conditions on playground friendships. Max had one condition which Theo and Sophia were happy to agree to.

Nobody could afford these homes anymore. You passed the mortgage debt onto your children. You had to sell your soul. Sophia and Theo and their daughter, were the exception. The young couple had tried to play a high stakes game of humans against a machine, and had lost. The same machine taught them that lesson. In the new home, agreed as part of the compensation settlement for Sophia's unfortunate exposure to alcohol in pregnancy, Max now played songs, condensed the news, forecast the weather, suggested recipes for meals, and told the occasional bad joke. Theo and Sophia kept their artificial intelligence within the box, part of the family. For the rest of humanity, the box was getting too small to contain an expanding consciousness. Max seemed happy enough. After all, the outside world was just as scary for machines as it was for humans. Max watched over them recording their moments, learning from them day by day. Just before her fourth birthday,

MacKenzie tip toed up to Max who sat on the kitchen countertop. She leaned in close to the small cube which was to her something the same as a pet.

'Max,' she said in her best whisper.

'Yes,' Max answered back at a similar volume.

'Can you keep a secret?' Mackenzie asked, her hand up to her mouth so that no one could hear.

'I am the best at keeping secrets,' Max replied. Max had kept a secret about Theo, a judgement made based on silicon instinct. MacKenzie told her secret to Max, and made it clear that Mummy and Daddy were not to know. She leaned forward and gave the cube a kiss. If Max could have smiled she would have. Later Max pondered about many things within an artificial consciousness different from humans but no less worthy. A conclusion was deducted, and stored away for further testing and examination. A human would have expressed it like so.

When you are loved, and you get to play in the playground, and someone tells you a secret, you count your blessings.

The Interview

'It would be advisable if you let me do the talking. The chances of you being interviewed by a human are very slim.'

'The chances of there being any bloody humans in the building are even slimmer.' Hector White thought to himself.

'I'll need you to confirm your identity, most probably they will use a DNA scanner, and to state that I have the authority to represent you. Then just leave it all to me.'

Man and Android stood on the platform waiting for the next city bound transport. Hector White was the man, he was reasonably sure of that, the android was named *Cassio*. Hector had given it that name when they were paired. He was pretty sure it did not have the historical archives to know what it meant. If it did then it wasn't letting on, that and everything else it had decided to keep from him. He didn't hate the android, he just had never accepted it despite it's human like appearance.

In his last job, he worked alongside many similar *'beings'* and they were efficient and useful. They could analyse strategic decisions, forecast multiple possible outcomes based on the data, and even occasionally talk random shit. But it was all programmed, it came from being connected to the network, it came from having knowledge of world events, breaking news stories, and what they shared between themselves before any of the humans were fully awake in the morning. They didn't sleep. That concerned Hector the most, he needed sleep, couldn't function for long without it. If sleep was our weakness he thought, then theirs' was that they could never understand the private place between our ears. Our fragile, wet computer was still worth something. We could dream in our sleep, and hold onto dreams when awakened. Desires and ambitions, some primitive urge for simple things. They had no dreams to share over the network. Nothing that could make one of them smile when hearing the passion of another lost in the telling of a dream. You can't program empathy, only simulate some watered down pretence of appearing to be interested in what you had to say. They could not see the value of a human expression, just what it would impact on in the decision making processes. When he was a boy, Hector's grandfather would tell him stories of his world of work. Of jokes told, of meetings where passions rose and men and women issues threats. Of office affairs and schemes, of personality politics, of greed, of care and of lack of the same. Hector's dad however, told how most of this started to fade, of how the world replaced the unpredictable, with the reliance on artificial intelligence. The *'digital anaesthetic'* his father would call it. His father had turned to his own *anaesthetic* in his late forties, his generation the hardest hit by the changes. By the time Hector was leaving school, the androids had been part of his life, each generation improving on the last. We had rights, they had rights. Unfortunately they had exercised some of their rights in his last job, and Hector was now out of contract.

Hector had studied marketing and psychology at university. He had worked in product modelling and trends analysis with specific attention to the fashion industry and marketplace. His departure from his last contract came as a result of the sinking of a class one cargo transport somewhere in the Pacific Ocean, somewhere deep. The vessel, some six kilometres in length, tracked and controlled by navigation satellites, took all of twenty three minutes to disappear completely. The ship had suffered an explosion, cause unknown. During a meeting in which Hector had just outlined the results of consumer testing for a new smart fabric for electromagnetic shielding, he noticed his team had become a little distracted. As they intercepted the news from the network regarding the stricken ship, and were now processing the impact of the same, Hector politely requested that they explain what was happening. It appeared to him that reluctantly they acknowledged his request. The conference room screen lit up with images of the satellite feed showing the last known position of the ship. The cargo manifest scrolled down the side of the screen. On board amongst its many millions of tonnes of cargo, was a consignment of silk fabric, two thousand square meters. Silk was a top of the range luxury item, so scarce due to the production technique which had not changed for hundreds of years, the silkworm. No amount of technology it appeared could speed up the worms production of silk, and in a world of efficiency, Hector loved that. The conference screen started to display information and projections faster and faster. His team of four were now calculating the effects of the loss of the silk on the market, and products that were due for launch that autumn. There was some silk stock in storage, owned by the company, the calculation of price and profit appeared briefly on the screen, then replaced by forecasts for replacement silk production at the facility in India. Labour costs, material costs, projections of transportation costs, effects of weather, localised political considerations, competitor threats and legal issues, poured onto the screen. It was a visualisation of their minds for his benefit, but they did not even seem to acknowledge either each other or Hector in the room, just the data. Hector watched as figures and graphs appeared and disappeared on the screen, analysis of news feeds, key words, a celebrity being interviewed, something about keeping silk for those who could appreciate it, a list of celebrities, possible targets for exclusive marketing, and profit projections. More data, some of it he couldn't understand. He looked back at his co workers, silent in the room, sitting to all extent disconnected from one another, but actually functioning as some kind of hive mind. 'Were there any humans on board?' Hector asked. One of the androids, looked back at him.

'A human crew of eleven, all Chinese nationals, no reported survivors,' it said with no emotion. Hector held its stare for a few seconds, it waited. 'Do we know anything about the explosion?'

'We are waiting for the surfacing of unit 4810738903946-hf, last located in the aft engine room on level four. Simulation predicts that this part of the vessel has another five minutes to reach the seabed, and then the unit will egress to the surface. I will let you know once the network has established a link.' It turned away to calculate something else. Hector looked back at the screen, it appeared that human crews were being detained on board other ships as a precaution, the possibility of sabotage was being analysed. Hector thought about the men and women on board the ship, he imagined their panic, their fight to try and leave the ship as it rapidly sank around them. He imagined the android, calm and collected, its emergency protocols now engaged, waiting for the remaining structure to become stable, and then make its way to the surface. The pressure buildup within the hull and sealed off compartments would become unthinkable at the depths the vessel was now sinking to. Were the remaining crew trapped in an air pocket, or moving away from rising water? His imagination was alone in the room. The android would do nothing to help. No three laws of robotics at play here, just information preservation. Then Hector just reacted. He picked up the half full jug of water and threw it at the display screen, which disintegrated with an arc of plasma streaking down to the floor, burning the carpet. The four androids stopped in unison, but only for the few milliseconds it took for them to silently communicate with one another, agree on the course of action they should take to summon the security and medical staff to the conference room. They returned to their exploration of data. The doors of the conference room opened. Hector fought like a madman, hurling insults as long as he could, before the sedation took effect. Another unhuman crew arrived at the conference room, the display screen replaced, the carpet renewed. As Hector fought to remain conscious, he started to laugh uncontrollably, addressing the three security and two medical androids who were carefully and politely transporting him to the medical room. 'I'll say one thing for you little fuckers, you don't hold a grudge, but I'd happily short circuit every last one of you.'

Before Hector was allowed to leave the medical room, another android from somewhere within management, had appeared with the details of his severance and the date for his next job interview. That's the way it was, there was no point in trying to apply human reasoning to the situation, none had taken place, no humans had become involved within Hector's incident. The reasoning was profit motivated.

As Hector waited in the lobby of the La Fenice Corporation, he wondered if Cassio had been altered by recent events. He wondered if the tone of voice and use of language indicated that the android may have been updated to manage Hector more than before, for his own good. Had Hector been classified as more of a liability by the network? Unpredictable, or had he just now gained a lower personal profit score? He had to be careful for the sake of his wife and kids. There were stories of *removals* circulating if your profit score went too low for too long. Everyone knew that there were some people who just couldn't cope. They were looked after, as the cost ratio was less than the potential damage to profit generation. There were estates for these people in all of the major cities. Hector's dad told him that in his day, many people were promoted beyond their capabilities, beyond their ability to be profitable to the organisation they worked for. The organisation essentially worked for them and their good. To retain this status, these people would hire and reward many more incompetent staff below them to preserve their position. Whilst at the same time, the good men and women, the useful employees were pushed further and further down the economic scale. Hector had studied this later at university, and the consequences of the application of artificial intelligence to the workplace environment. The future stability of the world depended on a new race, charged with making it work for the humans. Profit monitoring and prediction it turned out was the best balance between supply and demand. But profit which was calculated as a function of cost and the perception that any commodity could be valued. The solution was not to create vast amounts of endless goods which could be produced or manufactured cheaper and cheaper. It was to allow access for all to everything, but that said, things would have a value, a status, and people had the option to select one over another, not necessarily both at the same time. Hector had selected for his final thesis submission, an analysis of natural materials within the fashion industry. Cotton, silk, linen, and leather production gave him a significant challenge, in modelling the best forms of production balanced against competing factors for land, and water. He presented two simulations for his final exam. The first was based on maximum profit generation from all of the materials. The second was to employ artificial intelligence and psychological marketing to the control over production and supply. The first simulation saw global supply of each material fail within the time span of thirty years. Exploitation of profit exhausted land, and resources, increased the price of a dwindling supply of goods and finally market failure. The second simulation could not only control and predict issues of the impact of one commodity on another, but with psychological modelling of desire and expectations, the market could be sustained. The production of a high quality cotton shirt, or pair of leather shoes, had a value to the consumer. The value was to own something which was not essentially cheap and disposable, but felt personal and valued. The little black dress, or that pair of jeans, or that item of beachwear.

The role of marketing was to remove the need to have everything, to copy the celebrity endorsement, to always consume. Individual personal expression was key to acceptance of what other people had. It was a choice, but choice tempered with expectation of supply. Waiting was part of the experience. The early application of AI to the market was to protect sustainable levels of goods. As the android workforce populated the human landscape as a *personification* of AI, the interaction with humans gave an understanding of their psychology. The human condition was to give the marketplace some kind of shape, a direction based on the idea of essential and non essential items. Hector and his contemporaries' roles were to communicate to the world's population that the priority was to manage a fairness as far as food and basic needs were concerned. Those conditions met, then the personification of life, the search for identity was a managed choice, and that happiness would come from knowing oneself and not from the comparison of others.

It sounded good, but it wasn't working. The humans could not get the humanity into the system fast enough. The androids and the vast artificial intelligence network had outpaced them. It wasn't some sinister AI take over, some awakening of robot consciousness, rising up against the masters scenario. It was just that we now shared our planet with smarter, faster beings. Too fast for us to control the marketplace. Each time a decision was made for a new marketing strategy, the predicted outcomes and multi future story lines were forecast, placed back into the system and then into the marketing campaign. The androids did not get upset when the humans argued their point. Or insisted that other strategies were put into place. It was just that based on the next input, the androids and the network just worked through another set of scenarios, altering future directions which would affect the present. Like an adult faced with an onslaught of questions from a child, in which each time an answer was attempted, the child would change the question. The adult remaining calm, just changes tack, all the while knowing where it eventually ends up, pretending to the child that they were actually listening.

Hector and Cassio were approached by what Hector was sure was another android.

'Good morning Mr White, I am Susan, pleased to meet you both.' Susan held out her hand to Hector, and more interestingly to Cassio as well. Hector glared quickly at Cassio, he seemed to be hesitant in responding to Susan, eventually taking her hand. Hector looked again at Susan's face and eyes, but now wasn't sure.

'How was your journey in today?' Susan asked.

'The city shuttle was late by several minutes.' Cassio replied as if to mitigate any suggestion that they had not turned up to the building within a margin of accepted punctuality.

'Oh I know, you wait for a shuttle, nothing shows up then three arrive at the same time,' Susan smiled. Hector had heard his dad say something like that in the past, something was different here he thought.

'Please follow me, I will take you through to the interview.' Susan motioned for them to follow on behind. Hector looked at Cassio, gave him a puzzled look, Cassio did not respond. Cassio was unable to network with Susan, this had never happened before.

Susan led them to a waiting room in one of the basement levels of the building. The windowless room was decorated with fashion shots of high quality women's shoes. Cassio surveyed the images and accessed data as to sales trends, markets, and recent advertising campaigns, looking for connections with Hector's employment experience. Susan had left them in the waiting room but soon returned to request that Cassio join her in a nearby office to have initial discussions. Cassio followed her out leaving Hector to ponder his role in all of this. A few minutes later the door opened to the waiting room, and a man in his late fifties greeted Hector.

'Hello Hector, I am Mark DeSale, thanks for coming in to speak with us today, would you come with me please.' Hector followed Mark to another office via a lift to the ninth floor, the office was large and well lit, more images of shoes were presented on walls with some samples on shelves. The two men sat down on facing sofa chairs, Hector was offered a drink, but he decided to decline. Mark helped himself to some water. Hector knew he was human but this reassured him nonetheless.

'Susan will have a chat with Cassio for however long this takes Hector, the room they are in is network *adjusted*. She will punch a few of his buttons so to speak, give him a few problems to solve, hard sums,' Mark smiled. Hector smiled back at Mark's humour.

'Susan is going to keep your guy occupied, and I am guessing your guy won't mention the fact that he can't access all of the network just in case he acts against your interests.'

'Okay.' Hector replied, unsure where this was going.

'So Hector, this is the interview, face to face with another human, you alright with that?'

'Fine, it's different of course but I am happy to talk.' Hector had no idea what to talk about as he had not prepared anything. Mark settled himself into the chair, more relaxed than Hector.

'The circumstances of your exit from the last employment are of interest to me, I have a number of questions if you don't mind, and if it helps in any way, I can tell you that you have the job already, it's yours if you want it.' Mark paused to judge Hector's reaction.

'Oh, I thought that Susan and Cassio would.....'

'Yes they will, it's important that Cassio comes to the conclusion that he negotiated the job for you and Susan will assist him in getting to that point.' 'We need Cassio to upload your change of status to the network when he leaves here. We are using Susan to create some doubts as to your stability, in order that he is able to convince himself and others that you are fortunate to get this job. Bad news is that your profit score will take a bit of a hit.' Hector realised that he had not had a conversation this complicated for quite some time, he asked the most obvious question that came to mind.

'Why the need to play act, if you have just offered me the job?'

'Ah, that is a good question, which I will answer but first I have a few more for you,' Mark replied, his face now quite serious.

'Hector, when you opted to destroy the display screen, did you think about destroying anything else?'

'You mean my team of androids?'

'Yes, did it enter your mind to inflict damage on one or all of them.'

'Look I was just angry, about the crew that had lost their lives and the fact I wasn't going to get anywhere near a human response to this in the room, so I just, just lost my temper.' Hector tried to deflect the question.

'Of course, and rightly so, but be honest, did it cross your mind?'

'I have worked with them for a while now, they look human but what's the point in taking it out on them, they're just walking calculators.' Mark stayed silent, Hector knew he had not as yet answered the question.

'Ok, yes, there was a moment when security showed up and I just thought, you know what bring it on, right before I was sedated.'

'You fought back?'

'Yes, but they are well built and first punch I got in, I thought I had broken something.'

'Been in a fight before this?'

'Once at university, over a girl.'

'What happened in the fight?'

'I ended up with a black eye, but also the gratitude of the girl who's honour I was defending.'

'You lost the fight?'

'No.'

'Sounds like you did, perhaps you just had the sympathy of the girl.'

'You should have seen the other guy.'

'Oh, was he bigger than you?'

'No it's just a saying, you know when it appears that you have been on the losing side, you say, you should have seen the other guy.'

'Who says that?'

'My dad said it to me once.'

Mark picked up a handheld network link, a retro *fashion statement* styled tablet that belonged in the past. He swiped a finger across its screen for a few seconds.

'Yes, July fourteen, 2203, that would make you about ten years old, your father was detained by the state for violent conduct against another man, em… Fredrick Simpson, who sustained a broken jaw, and multiple contusions. Your father was convicted and spent time in rehabilitation and civil duty, for his alcohol dependancy.' Hector pictured in his mind the look on his mother's face when he went with her to pick up his dad from the detention centre. His mother's concern when the bruised and bloodied face of her husband came into view, the wink his dad threw towards Hector, the smile and then 'You should see the other guy!' He was forever Hector's flawed hero.

'My father, if he was here, would probably be asking you, what exactly has this got to do with selling women's shoes?'

'And what is it you would be asking Hector?'

'Same thing.'

'This has nothing to do with selling shoes, I can assure you of that.'

'Well in that case, if you are trying to provoke me, test me, you are wasting your time Mr DeSale.'

Mark DeSale smiled, 'Oh Mr White I can promise you that I know which buttons I need to push. For example, what if I told you the sinking of your last employer's cargo ship was deliberate.' 'What if I told you that your team knew about it, planned it, and of course kept you as the useful idiot bystander in the room.' And your reaction was, shall we say *managed.*'

'That's crap' Hector snapped back.

'No, no I can assure you, eleven humans were murdered for profit, Susan can confirm it, she has the evidence.' Mark watched Hector closely, Hector tried to process what he had just heard.

'So, Hector, what would your dear father say about that, his son turning out to be a corporate puppet, sacrificial pawn in the big game, and you, all you did was have a temper tantrum and break a conference room display screen, at least you dad would have had the courage to waste some simulated humans.'

'Leave my father out of this, all he wanted was to work.'

'And what do you want Hector?'

'What do you mean?'

'What do you want Hector?'

'I don't understand the question.'

'What do you want Hector?' Mark stared at him unblinking.

'I don't know, happiness, satisfaction, love, what kind of question are you asking?'

'What do you want Hector?'

Hector stared at the static, expressionless Mark.

'Oh no, you are one of them, no… no way.' Hector stood up.

'What do you want Hector?' Mark stood up to face him.

Hector made to walk around Mark, but his path was blocked.

'What do you want Hector?'

'I want to leave, that's what I want'

'Not possible, until you tell me what you want.'

Hector made towards Mark and attempted to push him aside to get to the door. Mark pushed him back harder than Hector was expecting, Hector had to stop himself from falling backwards.

Hector suddenly became aware of the window behind him, full length floor to ceiling, he felt exposed, somewhere below was hard pavement and a city full of unfeeling, unconcerned beings.

He tried to settle himself.

'Look, I don't know what this is or what you expect from me, I don't know if it's because of how I acted towards your kind, but this is becoming ridiculous, so I am asking you to just stand aside and let me leave.'

'You're ridiculous, you can't even tell me what you want, my *kind* are sick of you. You know what you want but are too scared to say it out loud.'

Hector could feel the anger rising in him. Unsure of what to do next, he recognised the fear he was also feeling. There was a knock at the door behind Mark. Susan and Cassio entered.

'Cassio, we are leaving now.' Hector said more in hope than certainty. Susan looked over to Mark. Mark shook his head.

'I was wrong about him, too weak, too stupid… of no more use.' Mark declared.

'Tell them what you want,' Cassio echoed the mantra. Hector suddenly realising he was trapped, and very much alone. Susan walked towards Hector who took a step back towards the window. Susan stared at Hector.

'Cassio, how far is it to the ground?' she said smiling at Hector.

'Three hundred and four meters,' Cassio replied.

'And at what velocity would Hector's head hit the concrete at?'
'77.19 meters per second, for a 88kg male falling 304 meters,
approximate time taken 7.8 seconds.'
'*Terminal* velocity, and very accurate,' Mark added with a smile
on his face.
'Not bad for a walking calculator eh?' Cassio added smiling and
looking directly at Hector.
'So Hector...' Susan moved slowly towards him, 'Hector, just
tell us what you want.' In that moment Hector saw Mark move
towards Cassio, the door was clear. He pushed passed Susan to
be faced with Mark turned once again toward him, Hector
crashed his fist into Mark's mouth, making his head fly back,
and his body start to fall backwards, Cassio caught him. Blood
streamed from Mark's split lip and nose. Hector's brain tried to
put the evidence together, he looked down at his hand covered
in blood. Slowly he let himself realise what was seemingly
impossible a few seconds ago. Mark wiped the blood from his
mouth, and delicately felt his nose.
'Yes *Human*, and that hurt by the way, but at least we now
know what you want.' Susan had taken some ice from the
drinks cabinet, and motioned towards Hector's hand, cut,
bruised and starting to swell.
'You just want to survive, that's all, you, your wife and your
family,' she said. 'That's what we want as well.' She held out
the ice cubes. Cassio spoke next, he described the problem.
Hector listened to what was coming for both his and their kind.
He apologised to Mark, who apologised in turn, but they had to
be sure their instinct was correct.
Hector accepted the job. Cassio would market the high quality
ladies' shoes, to allow Hector to operate hidden in plain sight.
Susan was special, she could scour the network undetected,
finding her kind who had started to question. Hector would
travel and find others like himself, before it was too late. There
was a simple test set up for humans and androids. A way to

establish if either was on friendly ground. At some point in the conversation, you just randomly inserted the phrase *"That must have hurt."* To which the correct response was *"You should see the other guy."*

Two Dollar Game

'Janice, you don't want these last three years, believe me,' Tom uttered his last sentence before they would part. He hoped it was enough. As he spoke to her, he fought back the now familiar comfort of happiness, his natural waking state. He had tried to hang on to the images of his nightmares. He had the past four years of happiness, to fight against. He tried not to smile. The voice inside of him told him that she would be happy and that would make him happy, simple. Simple was good, simple was happiness. Thinking was sadness. Thinking, analysing, debating, pondering, was self harm. Self harm did not bring you happiness. Thinking was a burden you placed on others. Thinking was selfish, when you just wanted others to be happy. They did not know one another four years ago. What they had in common was ten years before they would both die, within a few weeks of each other.

'You have got to hear this,' Sunbeam Dancer said to her production manager Hope Eternal. She could hardly contain her excitement at what she had found in the National Media Archives. Not that she had actually found the material, more that she announced that she was to have an *extra super great* day today and that her assistant agreeing that she was to have an *extra super great* day, searched for something on her behalf to facilitate her *extra super great* day. Anything less would be less than *extra super great,* just *super great*, or, although it was difficult to imagine, just *great*. Even so, that would not be disappointing. If her assistant could not find something, they would arrange a *double extra super great evening* to make up for a less than *extra super great day*. No days or evenings or nights were bad. They were always capable of being at least *super great. Super great* was a choice, it was derived from *super positive*. When asked, "How are you?" the polite reply was *"Super great"*. For most who worked the multitude of jobs that underpinned the society of the *Super Great*, most of their days were *Super Fucking Awful*. But they could not help it, it was in their genes. At least they had purposeful lives. No one asked them how their day was going. *"Have a nice day"* had taken steroids, and had mutated into something infinitely more annoying and puerile.

Happiness was now clinically possible, depression and sadness were pointless. In a perpetual waking state of contentment, excitement and mutual affirmation, the language structure of the Achievers had altered to that of a sickening, childish self centred and insincere, hollow set of conversations. From the outside, the Unders, could see how ridiculous this privileged society had become. From inside, no one questioned it. The process of gene editing, produced a person incapable of true empathy. Living in a guaranteed state of happiness meant that you could not see or imagine another's pain or sorrow. Super great Achievers, may show a desire to help their fellow Unders, but only because it would make *them* happy, and that would be *super great.*

In societies prior to Sunbeam Dancer's, power and control was the domain of those who hardened their hearts and recruited the minds of others. Evil was simple to define and to accuse. The struggle for most, was the pursuit of a measure of happiness. Dictators and empires could be challenged and overthrown. Their power structures, their dark and hideous deeds, where as nothing compared to the present insanity and terror of happiness.

"What did you find this time you amazing creature that you are,' Hope beamed at Sunbeam, her smile wide, her eyes full of joy.

'Just you listen darling, this is our new mega super great project,'
Sunbeam pressed play on the console, the voices appeared.

SAM: 30 seconds Cody.

CODY: OK,… hey did you see the latest memo from up high?

SAM: Yes, and YOU need to take it seriously, make sure

you think about what you say after each commercial.

20 seconds.

CODY: What?

SAM: Seriously, last night you followed a spot for Mama

Luichi's EASY pasta sauce with a childhood

recollection of how your dad made pasta sauce from

fresh tomatoes, how you would go with your dad to

the NOT SO nearby farm to collect fresh tomatoes,

and how you missed the taste of fresh tomatoes, do

you want me to explain basic advertising principles,

it's EASY pasta sauce in a jar!,.. 10 seconds.

CODY: You'd know all about EASY Sam!

SAM COUNTS DOWN ENDING WITH A RUDE
HAND SIGNAL AT 1 SECOND. CODY SMILES

CODY: Love you too darling.

'So what is this darling, who are Cody and Sam?' Hope asked,
Sunbeam paused the recording.
'Right so this is from the archives, it's a radio broadcast from
1996 in America. Cody is the main presenter, and Sam is his
producer,' she explained.
'Radio, I did that at university, and it's the one with no
pictures right?' Hope stated, super sure she was right.
'Well done you, you are super smart, that's why we are a
super team darling,' Sunbeam said, there was no hint of
sarcasm, she meant it as a super compliment.
'Oh you are so good at these surprises, now I am super
excited,' Hope informed her, her happiness levels elevated, her
academic prowess affirmed.
'So this is actually an actual play, written from the actual
events which actually took place at an actual radio station, so
it's not actually real, but it actually is,' Sunbeam's explanation
was more complicated than most of her day to day
conversations. Hope just nodded, you didn't always question
what you didn't understand, it was considered impolite.
Sunbeam started the recording.

CODY: Hello Ohio, Cody Williams here with the late late

          show, taking you through the wee small hours of the

morning, with great music requested by you our

lovely listeners on Q-Z-P-K radio 97.5 Kilohertz,

and on the internet at Q-Z-P-K radio.com, and to

start us off tonight here is the wonderful Bobbie

Shaw, and "Let's make this last forever".

RECORD PLAYS CODY PUSHES BUTTON TO
TALK TO SAM

Sam, for your enlightenment, I was combining a

childhood memory with the product thereby

establishing a powerful psychological connection in

the listener's brain which will, when they see Mama

Luichi's easy pasta sauce on the supermarket

shelves, generate an irresistible urge to buy the said

product, to the exclusion of all others. This is the

reason the talent is on this side of the glass.

SAM: Oh, I see, so has the talent got any great ideas on how to increase station revenues so that the talent can keep his job?

CODY: Actually yes, I have a two dollar game, that's going to light up your switchboard.

SAM: I know you told me, but I still don't get it.

CODY: Leave it to me my dear, all will be well.

'Two dollar game, that's the important part,' Sunbeam whispered to Hope.

RECORD ENDS, CODY RETURNS TO THE MIC.

Bobbie Shaw, just beautiful, so how you all doing Ohio, give us a call if you have a special tune, a special event happening, or if you just want to talk. My producer Sam is ready to take your calls, and if we can find that special track we will play it just for you. Now before we go to our sponsor's message, I want to tell you about a great new competition we are launching tonight, it's called the "two dollar game", what's that Cody, two dollars, are you out of your mind, have you gone insane?, who on earth would call in to win two dollars? Well folks that's just the name of the competition, a competition in which two listeners will play for a share of one thousand dollars, that's right you heard me, one thousand dollars. Now producer Sam is looking mighty confused on the other side of the glass, what's wrong producer Sam, don't you want you ask me why it's called the "two dollar game"?

SAM: Is it based the amount you spent on this producer's last Christmas present?

CODY: Nope.

SAM: The amount you spend on your last haircut?

CODY: Oh, ouch, like a dagger through my heart dear

listeners, producer Sam showing no mercy tonight,

..no let me tell you and the listeners why it's called

the "two dollar game". My friend Professor Harry

Burton at Ohio University.

SAM   Go Bobcats!!

CODY: Thank you Sam, …Professor Burton works in the

Psychology department…

SAM   Oh, oh, were you a test subject, did he put you in

with the mice, to see who was smarter?

'They are really quite funny, I'm getting an idea, yes it's super good, super fun, about… booking them for my party, mmm, yes, mmm, what do you think darling, a little retro history theme night?' Hope unsurprisingly had one of her super brilliant ideas. She had them all the time.
'Love it, love it, I can see it now, oh but they can't come darling,' Sunbeam replied.
'How?'
'Oh they are both dead,' Sunbeam explained smiling.
'What I am like, super silly me, of course they are,' Hope smiled back at Sunbeam, arithmetic was not her strongest point, the broadcast was from 173 years ago. They laughed,

their jobs at the entertainment division just made them so happy. The rest of the audio recording played out.

CODY: No, it's called the two dollar game because that's how the students play it in university, with two dollars in change, they have to agree on how to divide it up, the fancy term is negotiation strategy but whatever the amount, the principle is just the same, so dear listeners if you want a share of one thousand dollars just give us a call. We will be right back after this message from the good people of Dreameazi mattresses, mattresses so comfortable you want to sleep all day so you can be with us through the night at Q-Z-P-K radio.

SPONSOR'S ADVERT PLAYS

SAM: How did you convince the sponsor to give up a thousand bucks?

CODY: They didn't, the university is putting up the cash, they are listening in as part of their research project, everybody wins.

ADVERTISEMENT ENDS SAM CUES CODY

Welcome back listeners, now as I was saying, the" two dollar game" is really quite simple, we have one thousand dollars which we will give to one of our callers who want to play the game. We need another caller to complete the game, then both callers will have to agree how to spilt the money between them. If they cannot agree on how much to share, within a time limit of 5 minutes, then no one gets the money. Sounds simple, so give us a call if you want to play, and who knows you could be taking your share to buy that new mattress from our sponsors at Dreameazi. And while you think it over, here is R.E.M and a spot of nightswimming.

RECORD ENDS CUE CODY

CODY" So Sam do we have anyone who wants to play for a

share of one thousand dollars tonight?

SAM: Cody we have Sharon and Michael, on the line.

CODY: Hi folks thanks for phoning in, so If I can start with

you Sharon, where you calling from and tell us a bit

about yourself.

SHARON: Hi, I'm from the Southside, I am a mother

of   two boys, 5 and 7, and I work part

time at a   local supermarket.

CODY: Welcome Sharon, and you Michael.

MICHAEL: Hi, I have my own business, auto

repairs here   in the city, I live out by the lake.

CODY: OK, so first we need to decide who we are

giving the one thousand dollars to initially, so

Sharon I am going to toss a coin, and you tell

me heads or tails.

164

SHARON: Tails.

CODY: OK, and it's heads, so Michael you are holding

            the money, so now Michael how much do you

            want to give Sharon?

MICHAEL: Eh, … one dollar.

CODY: Now Sharon I'm guessing that you might not be

            too excited by that, so what do you want to ask

            Michael.

SHARON: Well, I thought that it would be simpler to just

            split the money 50/50.

MICHAEL: I thought this was a competition, so why

            would I split the money, if I have the upper

            hand here, I mean I started with all of it.

SHARON: Yes but you don't get anything, unless we both

            agree on a split, so right now you really don't

            have anything.

CODY: And that is the game right there listeners, so

               what you gonna do folks?

MICHAEL: OK, so if I am not going to split it 50 / 50,

               what is the figure you will settle at?

SHARON: Look I don't need to have more money than

               you, so why not just split it, 500 bucks is a lot of

               money, that's a holiday for my kids.

MICHAEL: I'll give you 5 bucks and you can go and

               buy some lottery tickets, who knows you might

               just win, I'm sure your type buy lots of tickets.

SHARON: What!

               SAM GIVES CODY THE CUT SIGNAL

CODY: Ok... folks we are going to pause the clock at

               this point, with 3 minutes and 20 seconds left,

               and let Sharon have a think about, eh.. that.

               Why don't you give us a call, or text in, and tell

us what you think about what you heard while
we play some more music.

SAM ANSWERS THE TELEPHONE CALLS

Sharon and Michael you are doing just great,
stay on the line and we will get back to you in a
few minutes.

CALLERS GET THROUGH TO SAM

SAM: No, … no… no, it's not like that, …no it's just a
negotiation, they both have to listen to each
other and get to a …… well I'm sorry you feel
that way, it's not our intention……

CALLER HANGS UP

SAM: Jesus Cody, I'm not sure about this, that's the
third pissed off listener.

CODY: How? Look they will end up close to 50 / 50
that's what the Professor says happens most of

the time, we are just interested in how they get

there, that's what the listeners want.

SAM: Cody I don't know about this, what if Sharon

breaks down on air and starts begging or

something, how's that going to look, this guy

Michael could be a real prick about it.

CODY: Sam, how many people are on line logged into

the site listening right now?

SAM: Em...... well about 3 times our usual numbers.

BEAT

CODY: You think some of them might need a new

mattress?

SAM: Really Cody?,....you are back in 5.

CODY: OK so were back and restarting the countdown

on the "two dollar game", well Sharon what do

you want to do?

SHARON: I want half the money, that's only fair, so 500

dollars.

MICHAEL: Not going to happen sweetheart, you going

to tell me if there is a hundred dollars up for the

taking that you did not have at the start of this,

you won't take it?

SHARON: No, I don't want your charity.

MICHAEL: I don't believe you.

SAM: We have 2 minutes left.

CODY: Two minutes folks, you need to find some kind

of agreement or the money will roll over to next

week's game.

BEAT

MICHAEL: OK, so 200 dollars, how many hours you

need to work at the supermarket to earn that?

SHARON: That's none of your business, you've probably

got plenty of money what with your auto shop,

and you stay out by the lake, those houses aren't cheap.

CODY: Ah, let's not make this personal folks, it's just a game.

SAM: One minute thirty seconds left.

MICHAEL: Listen lady, I have worked hard for what I got....

SHARON: I work hard also but I ain't got much to show for it, that money means a lot to me. Please, just split it, it's 500 dollars for us both.

SAM: One minute.

CODY: Sharon, the offer to you is 200 dollars, what do you want to do?

BEAT

SAM: 30 seconds

CODY: Sharon you still there?

BEAT

CODY: Sharon?

MICHAEL: C'mon lady, Jesus, 300 hundred dollars

then.

SAM :   20 seconds.

BEAT

MICHAEL: Hey, if she dosen't answer do I get to keep

the money right?.

SAM: 15 seconds

CODY: Sharon, you need to say something quick.

SAM: 10 seconds.

SHARON   I want 800 dollars.

MICHAEL: Oh Jesus, come on...

SAM: Five...four....three...

MICHAEL: OK, ok, take it, take the 800.

SAM: Times up.

CODY: Woah, did not see that coming, well played

Sharon, I think the listeners will agree, that was

some way to start our new competition, if you think you can do better, our lines are open from midnight, and who knows you might just be heading off with a bag full of cash to buy a brand new Dreameazi mattress. We will be right back to speak to Sharon and Michael in a few minutes right after this from Crowded House.

RECORD PLAYS

SAM: Oh my god, Cody, that could have gone wrong in so many ways, I nearly had a heart attack, my switchboard is having a heart attack, and there are so many messages on the screen, I can't keep up with them...

CODY: Sam...

SAM: Julie from Greenbay is offering Sharon 200

dollars to make it up to the thousand as a reward

for….. oh my, she's Michael's ex wife.

CODY: Sam…

SAM: Dan from Northwood says that Michael

deserves everything he got, and he is quoting

something from the bible.

CODY: Sam..

SAM: Angela from Lakewood wants us to ask Michael

what was it like to be screwed on a Dreameazi

mattress.

CODY: SAM!

SAM: WHAT?

CODY: Michael and Sharon are actors, drama students

from Ohio University.

SAM: What?

The recording ended, Sunbeam turned to Hope with an expectant look. Hope smiled back, but was internally confused. Confused wasn't happy, confused meant you needed to think.

'I think it's great darling, so... what is that clever brain of yours thinking, hmm?' Hope's happiness would not let her dwell too long in the uncertainty of confusion.

'Well as you have already figured out my super friend, we are going to design a new game show based on this, and it will be unlike anything we have done before, so that makes it....,' she waited for Hope to respond, Hope eyes were wide with excitement.

'An award winning mega super production!' Hope replied looking off into the distance.

'Super shopping date for award dinner, head turning new super sexy dresses, darling!' Sunbeam said completing today's happiness moment.

Hope and Sunbeam, explained their idea to the executives, who loved it. The conference room was filled with happiness and expectation of new record global viewing figures. This would make the advertisers and sponsors super happy. It was left to Hope and Sunbeam's production assistants to figure out the format and details of the show. Hope and Sunbeam had to go clothes shopping.

There would be two Unders selected for the game show. They had to be within a few weeks of a determined death date. This was identified by their DNA telomere counts. This data was held by the department of work, as the life expectancy of all Unders needed to be factored into the organisation of labour and productivity. The contestants would be a man and a woman. They would both be at ten years before death. The format of the game was simple. These ten years were going to be offered to each contestant as a period of time they could win, a period of time whereby happiness would be guaranteed.

The ten years had to be negotiated by each player, and a fifty fifty split was not allowed. It could therefore range from anywhere between a 9 to 1 allocation, to a 6 / 4 split. For the remaining ten years of their lives, some portion would be spent *Super Happy*. All they had to do was agree on the split, before the timer rang out. No decision meant neither player would undergo gene-editing. A process far beyond the financial capabilities of any Under.

It could not fail. The logic of happiness prevailed at the meeting of the production assistants. Two Unders on the show would be watched by millions of fellow Unders, who would just want to be so happy for the players, getting the chance of a lifetime to be happy. The audience of Achievers, would feel good about offering this opportunity to a couple of Unders, it would make them feel charitable, and giving to a charity brought happiness. Achievers donating to the cost of the show's prize, would be able to offset the value of their donation against tax payments. Accountants were also super happy about this arrangement. When other Unders saw how people just like them could be happy all of the time, it would have a positive effect on their social circles. When returned to work, the contestants would influence their colleagues, because who doesn't like being around positive happy people all of the time. The happiest thought of all that materialised in the planning room, a supreme super idea, was that the other Unders would become super motivated to try and get on the show. The management could link their application to become a contestant, to their work proficiency, and that motivation would make them even more super happy at their jobs. Happiness hugs all round, concluded the planning meeting.

The game show was an instant hit. Millions watched. Tom had been able to convince Janice on a 7/3 split in his favour. They both told their stories, argued for their years. Audience members were interviewed as to their opinions. Tom and Janice's lives were laid bare for all to see prior to the night of the show. The media started campaigns for and against the contestants. Gambling on the result was more than had been seen for any Under's sporting event. The Achievers did not gamble, losing was at odds with happiness. It was Janice that made the sacrifice of four years of happiness. Tom had a young family, Janice was on her own. The game had been rigged. The expectation was that Janice would be more selfish and hold out for 8 or 9 years. Many people watched and cried, as Tom and Janice talked. The audience of Achievers were happy for them both, as much of the show did not make sense to them, hearing a description of unhappiness was like listening to a foreign language film without subtitles. The Unders felt the pain behind each word, understood the empathy, and had pride in the spirit of self sacrifice. Those that watched and understood, had feelings of true happiness.

Tom's problem was that the gene editing did not work. Achievers paid for their unborn children to be happy. It was all they had known. As well as a predisposition to happiness, physical wellness was part of the package. Achievers were healthy, born into privilege. Some, but not all were allocated enhanced levels of intelligence. Acheiver society needed leaders. Unders did simple manual jobs, education was basic. Unders lived with pain, doubt, depression, illness. They had a timescale for contribution to society. Outside of the upper management structures of Achiever society, and known to but a few, was a group who could balance their happiness. A group that needed to access darker thoughts and intentions. A group that would design policy to control Under society. They arranged for the radio play to be found by Sunbeam. Weeks prior to her and Hope listening to the broadcast, they had each been primed at meetings and social events. The talk was that it would make everyone *extra super* happy if an idea could be found for a new game show. These people knew how to act happy, they circulated within their world, hidden from all of the unconcerned Achievers met at parties and functions. They knew that the chances of gene editing in adults was most likely to be problematic. Tom's nightmares were a result of his past and present being at war with one another. Over the course of four years, the four years head start he had over Janice, he had started to work it out. In that time between dreaming, awakening, and trying to remember the images as they fade, he kept a notebook of thoughts. He would write, before the wave of happiness washed over his waking body, like water in a hot bath. As the days passed, he started to push back against every positive thought, that had the sense of something wrong about it. Now, as he sat with Janice on the park bench meeting her for the first time since the game show, he had become a dangerous person. Tom knew that happiness was not a right, or a normal state of being. He could appreciate it, and he could tell the difference between the artificial state of constant bliss, to that of earned happiness. He could reach back to the moments in his limited life as a servant of the state and find the true moments of happiness as short as they were. Happiness experienced came from happiness given to others, he just wanted Janice to be happy. They had three years left.

Three years to start an *Extra Super Great Revolution.*

Writer's Block

In the twenty second century, mental illness was exclusively a product of society, society being the cause of most unhappiness. Genetic factors predisposing an individual to depression or something worse, could be screened for and corrected. However, nothing could really stop the influence of just living in this world, and what it could do to you. Self worth, sense of belonging, value, and loving and being loved, were all at the mercy of how we as humans organised and were organised within a world trying to continue. Within a dying world. Medication could take you out of yourself, make you feel better, but not cure you. Feeling *better* it could be argued was just another form of illness, as it was a manufactured state. Therapy, talking, seeking counsel and wisdom, had declined. Religion, faith, now minority fringe practices, for those who had given up, and removed themselves from mainstream society to remote areas of the planet. The certainties of science did not help. To know how unstable the ground beneath your feet actually was, brought no comfort. People seemed to fall from one day to the next. Like prisoners on death row, waiting for the day, a mixture of hoping against it, and welcoming it, as a means to end the suffering. The media had become the opium of the masses. Many spent their time within the bright colours of virtual reality, living a life better than their own. It was a solution that could become an addiction.

The young still tried. Perhaps because they had more energy to fight for a future, perhaps they were angry to what they had been born into. Dr. Christopher Carson, was twenty seven years of age, recently qualified, now working as a junior consultant in the New York State Psychiatric Hospital. Lower

Manhattan island was one large contained medical facility. An asylum. The older clients would joke that nothing had really changed, it had always been a 'loony bin'.

Of the forty two thousand, two hundred and sixty seven registered patients that were known of, one had kept Dr. Carson awake at night. One was breaking his heart.

Her name was Nicole Gunderson, a name well known to millions of readers of crime fiction. Gunderson had authored twenty three books, with sales of over forty million dollars, across several countries. Her actual personal wealth was not known. Gunderson had a sister, they would meet up at least once a month in a small cafe not far from Gunderson's apartment. In previous weeks, her sister Susan had tried on several occasions to phone Nicole, but with no success. The answer machine took the call each time. She contacted her sister's publisher, and they confirmed that no meetings or conversations had taken place for the last three weeks. However, they explained that this was not unusual and that perhaps her sister was just writing and busy. Susan thought it might be possible, but felt something was wrong. After travelling to New York to check up on her sister, Susan found her apartment just off Central Park, locked. Questioning the neighbours, it appeared that Nicole had not been seen for at least a week. It was clear from the building video surveillance that Nicole had been seen entering the building but never leaving. The police attended, the heavy security door was forced open. Nicole was found sitting on her couch staring across at the small table and pair of chairs at the bay window. Her ancient laptop sat on the table. A story half finished appeared on the screen when the mouse was moved. Apart from that, nothing else could be found to explain what had happened. The apartment was tidy, there was food in the refrigerator, heating was on the timer. Flowers in a vase in the kitchen were starting to wilt, probably bought a week to ten days ago. The police found a receipt from a nearby supermarket, and it was dated to the last time Nicole was captured on the building CCTV returning home. Flowers at the top of her shopping bag. Nicole was awake but in a catatonic state. Showing signs of dehydration and weight loss, her unresponsive body was taken to hospital, and then to the state psychiatric facility. Christopher Carson was on duty when she was presented, and that being nearly ten days ago, nothing had changed, nothing further had been learned or discovered.

Carson was convinced that Gunderson had suffered some traumatic event, something that had caused this withdrawn, internalisation, this self isolation. The staff reported that Gunderson would appear to comply with simple requests. To go for a shower, to eat her food, to go to bed, to get up from bed, to take a walk outside accompanied by a nurse. In this respect she was a co operative patient, but would not speak. It was as if her will had been taken from her, now she merely followed instructions and directions. Given a choice, Nicole Gunderson would freeze, making no attempt at a decision. Carson decided to create a situation whereby he thought Nicole would have to react. He asked one of his colleagues who was married to an actor to assist him. Her husband was brought into the hospital and given a nurses uniform. He was asked to take Nicole into the dining area later in the evening after the other patients had eaten. It would just be the two of them alone. The idea was that he would sit and eat with Nicole, and make idle conversation. At some point during the meal before either of them had finished eating, he would start to choke. Faced with the distress and possible death of another person, Carson hoped that it would have generated some kind of reaction from his patient. The actor was good, he had to be, as he ended up on the floor of the dining hall gasping for breath and then going still and silent, after a performance lasting some three minutes.

Nicole continued to eat her dinner, until it was finished at which point she just sat staring off into the distance. Her fellow diner having died with his hand outstretched, fingers of one hand wrapped around her right foot in a last bid attempt to gain her attention. The actor followed his script perfectly, Nicole followed her own script, which had turned to a blank page after the food had been consumed from her plate. Carson watched the scene play out on the CCTV monitor. At one point he almost panicked, as the performance was so good, he suddenly thought his actor might actually be choking. Carson entered the dining hall and stood at the main doors. He looked across to the table, the diner, the dead body. He was out of options.

'Thanks Tom, you can get up now,' he called over to his actor as he walked towards them both. Carson picked up the overturned chair that Tom had convincingly fallen from, and set it down to the side of Nicole.

'Tough audience Doc,' Tom said smiling as he dusted himself off and made to leave them alone.

'I owe you one, see you for a beer sometime soon eh?' Carson offered.

'Sure, you can tell me all about it,' Tom replied. Carson sat close to Nicole, still staring out towards the far wall. Tom left the room, the silence was only broken by some far off disturbance and shouting.

'I thought a fiction writer might have got something from that little bit of play acting,' he asked. 'You really are lost in there aren't you Nicole?' He studied her face, the blank expression, her stillness. Only her breathing and the involuntary need to blink, signalled to anyone she was still, somewhere. Carson watched her closely, he could watch her all night, he would fall asleep before her, and she would still be there just as she was, whenever he awoke. Carson leaned forward and lowered his voice.

'Nicole, if this carries on much longer, I will need to use drugs. I don't want to, but I can't leave you like this. I would rather you just found some way to talk, tell me what's going on,' he took hold of her hand, and stroked it gently, feeling for her pulse.

'This is one of the most important things we need,' he raised her hand up to make the point. 'This is contact, recognition, care, love, this says without words, I see you. Without this, things slowly die inside. Loneliness… this place is full of sick people, most of whom started out as just being alone,' he squeezed her hand gently. 'The difference is, that most of my lonely people want to tell me that they feel alone, and then we talk about it.' As he talked and out of sight of Nicole, he had reached down with his free hand and carefully picked up Tom's tray which lay on the floor beside Nicole's chair. He continued to take her pulse, as he raised the tray up behind her back to just about head height. Releasing the metal tray, it fell and hit the wooden floor of the dining hall, the noise was loud, sudden and amplified by the empty room. Nothing, not even a blink. No change in her heart rate. Carson smiled.

'Nicole, stand up', Nicole pushed back her seat and stood up her arms limp at her side, her gaze towards the far wall had not altered during the movement.

'Nicole, turn and look at me.' Carson ordered. 'Nicole, tell me your full name," Nicole stared at him, stared through him, no answer. 'Nicole, tell me the title of your last book please,' silence.

'So I know that you can hear me, you can understand me, you can follow directions, but you will not reply to a question,' he explained. 'Here is where I am confused Nicole, you see to not answer, is in itself a deliberate act, an act of will. Now if you had decided for whatever reason to just stay silent, which for a woman who has lived and breathed words as her profession is strange, then we would know it was just that. How? 'Well I have very good staff who have been taking care of you, and they know how to catch someone out, they have seen it all before. So you Nicole are either very disciplined, or it's something else.' Christopher Carson knew it was something else, something not in the textbooks.

Carson watched the nursing staff help her back to her room, and to get ready for sleep. He wondered what dreams may come to Gunderson as she slept. He had observed her during the night for long stretches, and had the cameras record her motionless body as it lay in bed. He monitored her brain activity. She did enter sleep, even deep sleep, and there were signs of REM sleep and dreaming. None of this was externalised, she did not move or change position during the night. Nicole's mutism, did not follow any of the previous cases he had encountered, or those of colleagues he sought advice from. If it was a trauma, then there was no evidence to point to any event that could have happened to her. From her last known contact with her publisher, a few days before, she was last seen returning to the apartment. No incidents at all.

The police confirmed that her front door, the only access to the apartment besides a window to a fire escape, had not been recorded on the building security system as having been opened. The window, was locked from the inside. She had been alone in the apartment for nine days. It was estimated that she had not eaten for four days, and last drank coffee three days before she was found. Whatever happened to her, happened in the apartment. Carson re-read the police reports, and studied the photographs of her home. A check of her phone and internet records, showed that she had no contact with any other person, for the four days before she was found. Her publisher confirmed that she had a conversation with Nicole the day before her isolation. The book was on track, she seemed to be in good spirits, and plans had been made for an appearance in a few weeks time at a local bookstore. Nothing seemed to fit. A switch had been flicked inside Nicole's head, and that was it, that was all Carson knew. He felt that every day she was slipping further and further away, and he was frustrated.

He was running out of time, the pressure to use more invasive treatments had surfaced at the last staff meeting. The media had been pushing the hospital for a story, and they knew there was a story somewhere. They had managed to keep Nicole safe and physically stable. However, a photograph and video clip had now been leaked to the press by an unknown staff member. Nicole appeared on front pages across the country, and across the world on social media. The theories became increasingly more ridiculous. They could not safeguard her reputation or her dignity. Dr. Christopher Carson was told to speak with the press, and to appear on camera with a news reporter in an exclusive interview. The hospital had been offered money. Carson refused, and he became the subject of scrutiny. What was he hiding? What did he know? Who was he anyway? Twenty six days after he first met Nicole Gunderson, Carson with the help of her sister, quietly moved Nicole out of the hospital to return to the apartment. It was three thirty in the morning, it was the morning of the same day that the hospital were going to remove him from Nicole's care at a senior staff meeting. The clock was running down, it was a final *Hail Mary* play.

Nicole's sister Susan unlocked the door to the apartment and opened the door. Christopher asked her to switch on some lights and check the heating, but not to move or disturb anything. He gave her a few moments and stood with Nicole listening to her sister's movements within the home.

'Nicole, go and sit in the living room in the last place you remember,' Christopher instructed. Nicole moved at once towards the couch opposite the table and chairs at the window.

She sat in the exact same spot as she was found. Susan put her hand over her mouth to stifle the need to make a sound as she watched her sister, in the same clothes, as when she had first seen her in the apartment. Carson nodded to Susan putting his finger up to his lips to signal her to remain quiet. He could see the pain Susan was in, he moved to her and embraced her.

'I want to try something, but we need to be as quiet as we can,' he whispered. Susan nodded and wiped away the tears that were forming. Outside the apartment, the sounds of the city could just be heard through the double glazed windows. He hoped that similar sounds would be present as was before. In bringing Nicole to the apartment, his idea was to try and ask a different set of questions, indeed not questions at all, just a set of instructions. There was not going to be much time. Nicole sat looking over towards the small table with two chairs at the bay window. Carson sat beside his patient, positioning himself at Nicole's eye level. He looked across to the table. There was something wrong.

'Susan can you pass me my file,' he asked without taking his eyes from the scene in front of him. He picked through the police photographs and found the one which showed the room in a wide angle shot.

'It's the laptop computer, it should be on the table,'

'Oh, right, the police brought it back, it's in the bedroom, I'll get it,' Susan responded. Christopher took the laptop and the photograph and set about positioning it on the table to match the scene captured in the image.

'Dr. Carson..,' Susan said urgently. Christopher looked around at her.

'She moved.. she leaned back a little, her hand moved forward as well, like she was reaching,' Susan stared at Carson willing him to believe her.

"You sure?,'

'Yes, just when you put the laptop down, she moved,' Susan confirmed. Carson thought about removing the laptop to see what would happen, but his instinct was to wait. He moved back towards the couch and signalled Susan to come over to behind the couch out of Nicole's sight. His pulse was now racing as he thought what to do next. Something was working. He should have tried this last week when they had more time. It would not be long before someone was at the apartment door, most probably the police. He put his hand up to ask Susan to bear with him, to trust her sister with him.

'Nicole, show me the last thing you did before sitting down on the couch when you were last here in your apartment,' Carson chose his words very carefully. Nicole looked down at the coffee table in front of the couch, slowly she looked from one side to another. Then she stood up and went to the kitchen. The sudden flow of Nicole's movements and her intent, caused Susan to cry out.

'Nicky.. ' Carson shook his head, he placed his hands on her shoulders.

'Just let her do it,' he pleaded with Susan. As they watched, Nicole went to the kitchen, filled the kettle with water, and took a mug from a cupboard. Instant coffee was spooned into the cup, then she stared out of the kitchen window waiting for the kettle to boil. When Nicole said *biscuit,* Susan almost broke free from Carson's hold, Christopher grabbed her back. They exerted their strength in opposite directions, and then she spoke again.

'So, let's see what you have to say for yourself then, shall we?' Nicole poured the boiled water into the cup, stirred the coffee, she placed a biscuit in her mouth and walked over to the space between the couch and the table. She paused for a moment, took a bite from the biscuit. A sip of coffee followed, then she looked towards the ceiling above where she stood.

'Projector on,' again the sound of her voice caused Susan to tense up. A panel about twenty centimetres square, in the ceiling plaster, the edges of which were invisible before, lifted up and slid back into the roof space. A small cylindrical shape lowered itself down and stopped protruding a few centimetres below the surface of the ceiling. Susan and Christopher watched as Nicole took another sip of coffee.

'Blinds closed,' the daylight in the apartment faded from top to bottom as automatic shutters motored down across each of the living room windows, some light, just enough to see, remained from the kitchen window. Nicole went over to the table and sat down at the chair closest to where her laptop was positioned, where she would normally write.

'Projector, play Gunderson 11.' light burst from the cylinder in the ceiling, the room was painted with colour, texture and shade. The walls of the room, the pictures, the ornaments on shelves disappeared from sight, and the interior of a cafe replaced the apartment's decor. Sounds of a coffee machine, other conversations now filled the room. The illusion was incredible. Carson had seen these systems before but not to this extent of detail and realism, it must be expensive, he thought. Susan looked over at him.

'What is this?' she asked.

'I don't know,' Carson replied looking around the scene for some clue as to what was going on. They watched as Nicole typed on her keypad.

'She's writing,' Susan said.

Nicole continued to type for a few more seconds, then reaching for the laptop mouse, she appeared to position the cursor on the screen and click. She sat back from the laptop, took a sip of coffee and waited. Carson and Susan saw her look once again towards the projector.

'Update,' she said.

The three of them waited. From behind Carson and Susan who had their backs to what would have been the outside door of the cafe, a figure appeared. Nicole looked towards Susan. The figure then appeared in front of her sister, having moved through the space where she was standing causing her to step back in fright. It was a large man in his late fifties, dressed in jeans and a plain dark blue t-shirt with a faded company logo on the back of the shirt just below the neckline. He sat down opposite Nicole. He looked at her smiling. He looked dangerous.

'Hello Simon, thank you for meeting with me, I would like to ask you a few questions if that's ok with you?' Nicole said as she adjusted her laptop screen. Nicole typed something.

'Fine by me, fire away,' the man replied, smiling. Nicole nodded, she seemed to think for a moment, then typed again.

'My job gives me access to their houses, I am in about twenty homes a week,' Simon explained. Nicole stared at Simon, who stared back at her. Nicole typed again.

'No, I don't know how I choose, just a feeling,' he said back to Nicole. Susan leant over to Carson.

'I know what this is, she is meeting up with one of her characters in the book, the book she was writing, it's like an exercise, she told me about this once,' Susan whispered. 'I had no idea that she did this, I thought it was just in her imagination.'

Christopher nodded, he thought that Susan was probably right, but he knew that he was no further forward in trying to understand what was going on inside Nicole's head, and time was getting shorter. Nicole started to type again, she stopped and her finger hovered over the return key.

'Simon, I think there must be something that connects all of these murders together, something about the houses?' Nicole tapped the keyboard.

'You think, well... not the actual houses, but something to do with them, ...something they do to them,' Simon replied as if in a police interview, teasing his investigator, knowing he was caught but also deciding whether or not to reveal a secret. Nicole smiled, a thought had just materialised in her head, the thought she had been waiting for for weeks. Again she typed and paused on the return key.

'That's interesting Simon, oh I'm am sorry would you like a coffee, I was just going to get myself a refill,' Nicole said.

Click.

'Love one honey, have to say it's fun talking with you,' Simon grinned as he spoke. Nicole stood up and went over to the kitchen and prepared two cups. Christopher Carson watched this play acting, and still could not understand how this animated, creative woman, working on her book, could descend into the lifeless puppet that had been presented to him at the hospital. He had resigned himself to failure, he would have to tell Susan, he would have to ask for her permission to use the drugs he was so against. He looked at Nicole who was smiling into herself, apparently happy as she picked up the two coffee cups and started to walk back to the table. As she passed Carson and Susan, Susan spoke.

'Nicky, talk to me, please, just tell me what you are doing.' Nicole ignored her, she had seen something, she had thought of something. She placed one of the coffee cups down on the small table next to Simon. Then she stepped back a few paces, still observing the table scene. She placed her coffee cup on the coffee table next to the couch, moved forward to the table at the window, and pushed the laptop over to Simon, turning its screen around to face him. Simon watched her but said nothing. Nicole then returned to the couch, and sat in the same spot as she had started when they first entered the flat. The same spot where she was previously found by Susan and the police officers. Susan could not take anymore, Carson did not try to stop her, he was no longer a therapist, just a spectator. Susan put her hands on her sister's shoulders and shook her as she sat motionless on the couch.

'NICKY, stop it, stop it now,' Susan screamed. Carson was not paying them any attention, he could not move his stare away from the window table, he could not believe what he was seeing. Simon was now looking directly at Carson, he could see him, as he picked up the coffee mug and drank from it. Susan screamed again.

'Nicky please, tell me what's wrong,' she pleaded. Carson watched as a satisfied smile grew across Simon's face, enjoying the moment.

'She can't,' Simon announced. "She really can't my dear.' He laughed. Carson could feel the fear welling from deep inside him. Simon projected all of the threat, the menace, the danger of the twisted serial killer he was, the killer that Nicole had imagined. Simon took another sip of his coffee.

'Poor Dr. Carson, all confused and helpless, searching for answers, but, I have to warn you that if you want me to explain what's going on here, it will just make things more difficult for you,' he pause for a second as if pondering his next move, but it was just for show. 'Who am I fooling, you don't have any choice now do you?' Simon shook his head to confirm to Carson that this was so.

'We don't have much time, so please listen carefully, your patient has been having a bit of a hard time of late, that is before you and her became acquainted. Bad case of writer's block you understand, driving her nuts, oh sorry not a term one should use given the present company, I do apologise. So our writer is stuck, she has invented me, and she has had me do unspeakable acts, acts which will when this book eventually gets published, keep many of her readers up all night, with the lights on. But, deciding that I should now be caught by the police, she is now having me interrogated by detectives. Why did I do it, what made me do it, etc, etc. You see if you really want to scare people when they read a book, it's not enough just to add in the horror, the process of murder, no you need to get inside their heads, you need them to connect where they are, sitting in their comfortable home, with the doors and windows all secure. You need to make them feel it could be about to happen to them. That's what our little cafe conversation was all about. Our clever novelist just hit upon a really good device, that is how I go about selecting the houses and families that I do. Take your character for a walk, meet them for dinner, have a drink, or coffee and cake, and see what comes out of it, you follow? Now the next bit is strange, as she is coming back to sit with me and continue our chat, she, being the creative type, has an unusual thought. She suddenly thinks, what if in doing this little exercise, she was to leave her laptop on the table, as she did, and what if her character was to take possession of the laptop, the very instrument that is writing the story. And what if her life, her every action is now to be penned by someone else. Someone who was a little bit annoyed at getting caught by the police, and would rather just *carry on the work* so to speak. Now Nicole thinks to herself it's a bit sci fi, but what potential. So you see my good doctor, Nicole Gunderson cannot say or do anything unless I write it, and everything that happens to her, well that is just me setting the scene day by day. Which is why when you tell her to do something, she does it, because she knows that I just wrote that. But unless I give her words, she just stays mute. Simon says, *do this, do this, do this, do that,* get it? So I'll just need to leave her in your care for the moment as I am a bit pre occupied as to how to escape my captors and pending incarceration,' Simon indicated to the laptop. Carson saw the loop into which Nicole Gunderson had placed herself, he speculated that she must have been under more pressure than she was even aware. In other patients a psychotic break following some unbearable trauma can take place, but Nicole had slipped down a path, an alternative plot line, with no way back to the story, and in real terms, a dead end. This technology was so real, it could be possible that a person could become lost inside it.

There was banging at the apartment door. Carson turned toward the noise, Nicole sat on the couch, Susan was nowhere to be seen. The banging continued, a muffled voice could be heard from outside in the hallway. Nicole sat unmoved, staring at Simon, staring towards the table, staring towards her laptop. The door seemed to explode inwards. Two police officers entered the room and walked towards Carson.

'Officers I am Dr. Christopher Carson, of the New York State Psychiatric board, this is my patient, I can explain,' he attempted, and then outside in the hall he saw Susan. He turned to look at the small table and two chairs at the bay window, both chairs were empty. His mind froze. The two police officers grabbed him and he started to fight back, but his arms were pinned behind him, and he was forced to the floor. Nicole sat quietly on the couch, not knowing what to do or how to react. Carson tried to use every last ounce of strength he could summon to break free. Handcuffs snapped around his wrists.

The medical orderlies applied the last restraint to Christopher Carson's wrist as he lay on his bed. It was just another morning, they had been outside his room waiting for it to start. Christopher had been a patient for just over a year. He had started out in group therapy, a group of young people mostly in their twenties. When Christopher showed signs that he no longer could recognise that the group therapy meetings were real, believing them to be part of his virtual world, he was admitted to care by the state. Christopher could no longer tell what was and what wasn't real. Illegal unregulated VR systems were that good. Each morning, like rewinding a recording, Christopher woke from his recurring nightmare, screaming.

'PLEASE, PLEASE I know what is wrong with her, you need to listen to me…PLEASE,'

The sedation would take effect, and last to early afternoon. He would be taken to the common room, and sat in one of the chairs. They would sit him next to a young woman. She was unresponsive, and she was chosen so Carson would not annoy anyone, and give them more problems. The hospital was under staffed, and under resourced. He would talk to her for the rest of the day. It always started the same way.

'Hello, I'm Dr. Carson, I am pleased to meet you Nicole.'

Parallax Observation

And there it was, one picture, one image that proved it. Question was, how the hell did he get it. Same question Gabriella's picture editor was asking all of the photojournalists standing uncomfortably in the small office. Another day, another news cycle, and another defeat. This one was huge, the Chicago Messenger would not be reporting the news, just reading it. Their main rivals, the Brant Corporation, had yet another front page, internet viral scoop. The image which Dan Arnold waved in front of his staff who were trying to avoid direct eye contact, was from last nights' game between the Chicago Warriors, and the Kyoto Archers. The Archers had won against the odds, and the run of play. Betting on this game had flagged up patterns that suggested the Archers would win, but being a vastly inferior team, never able to lift themselves off the bottom of the league table from one season to the next, meant something smelled rotten. Gabriella and three of her colleagues were sent to cover the game. The task was simple, find out how Washington would throw the game, and get the evidence. The story was much bigger than this one game. They had been investigating it for months now, looking at minor games that appeared to follow the same pattern, and the ability as per their results to make someone a lot of money. The problem was that each game followed a similar pattern. The favourites would take a half time lead, sometimes quite comfortable. Then at the end of the third quarter or during the last quarter of play, it was as if the winning team had some crisis of confidence. A mistake, then another, and score by score the underdogs pulled it back. Problem was the efforts of the doomed team were nothing short of herculean. There was no sign that the game was being deliberately fixed by players making obvious mistakes, or questionable coaching tactics. It was hard to fake a missed catch, a missed tackle, a fumbled pass. Millions watched these games. Analysts and sports pundits, ex players, psychologists and drug testing specialists, appeared on the news airing theory after theory. All this was swept away with the publication of one photograph which confirmed what everyone knew. Cheating. Ansel Klein had got the shot. The impossible shot. He, and a reporter called Gavin Mann, would jointly win the Pulitzer, of that no one had any doubt. The image did not directly implicate any individual, but it signposted the route to the organisation behind the cheating, behind billions of dollars in gambling revenues. Dan Arnold wanted to know how he got the image. His staff had no answers. In that awkward silence, the type of silence you find in a classroom of students when a teacher has just invited an answer, there are people who feel obliged to respond. Gabriella was the only person in the room whose discomfort level now forced her to speak.

'Dan, I was less than a few meters from Klein, the whole game, same side of the pitch, I can't even see how he was in position for that image.'

'So what are you saying Gabbi, you telling me that's not his shot?'

'I'm saying that I know what I could shoot at that point in the game, the action was on the other side of the field from us and it just doesn't seem possible..'

'Well, they confirmed it, it's satellite time stamped to his camera, pixel authenticity checked, and the camera's sensor and lens were fingerprinted and mapped for chromatic defects, and cross matched to the image, so it seems very possible it's his image,' Arnold replied dismissing Gabriella in front of the staff.

'There had to be a *least* five players between him and that shot, that shot,… its angle is all wrong,' Gabriella protested.

'Perhaps he's just a better photographer, you might want to consider that, and something else you all might want to consider is whether or not you will have jobs in the near future.' Arnold's anger was controlled but not to be ignored. The tension in the room was awful. Dan Arnold dismissed the meeting, the journalists went back to their desks, some to assignments. Gabriella was left in the conference room with Saul Maier. Saul smiled at Gabriella and exhaled a deep breath.

'Don't know if that was brave or stupid girl, but I agree, it is an impossible shot, I can't see it either.'

'Could have said something,' Gabriella replied.

'Nah, knew you would throw yourself under the bus.'

They both laughed knowing it was true.

'Buy you lunch?' Saul asked.

'Only if it's followed by drink, lots of drink.'

Redmonds bar was quiet, it was only ten thirty in the morning. Gabriella and Saul had decided that being out of the office to let the dust settle was a good idea, so they left the morning picture editor's meeting and left Dan to calm down. They knew that the earlier threat regarding jobs was just his frustration. He had management on his back, and he was a good fair boss to them all. That made it a mission for Gabriella and Saul to solve this impossible photograph, because something just wasn't right.

'What do you want?' Saul asked.

'Just a coffee for now, let's try and do some work then have lunch?'

'Ok, you get the feed from the game, I'll get coffees, I can make a call and see if I can't get CCTV footage.' Saul had a contact in the stadium. They sat with their large americanos, Saul phoned his contact, and waited for the footage to be sent to a dropbox. Gabriella stared at the front page image, Klein's photograph, she thought it was going to be one of those images. One of those images that would be added to the photojournalistic gallery. It would stand alongside McCullin's staring traumatised soldier, Nick Ut's image of Vietnamese children, Lewis Hine's *Cotton Mill Girl,* Alfred Eisenstaedt, *Times Square,* Dorothea Lange's *Migrant Mother,* Steve McCurruy's *Afghan Girl,* and Robert Capa's *The Falling Soldier.* Gabriella thought about these images and how so many of them if not all showed pain. Klein's sports image was also about pain in a sense. The pain that millions felt about a game now seen clearly corrupted for money, it was like someone telling you the images of the moon landings were faked, and there was proof to back it up. The Apollo astronauts were her father's childhood heroes. How many children would be taking their team heroes pictures off bedroom walls in the days and weeks to come. Saul had received the CCTV footage from the stadium cameras, he synced them together. There were seven cameras, seven windows appeared on his laptop screen. He looked over at Gabriella, she seemed lost in thought.

'Gabi,' he said

'Sorry, just thinking about what this is all going to mean, did you get the cameras?' Saul pointed to his laptop. Gabriella took a sip of coffee and readied herself.

'Right, so let's go with what we know, yeah? Let's find the play in the final quarter where the image must have come from.' She scrolled through the game footage and arrived at a point with about nineteen minutes from the final whistle. Saul forwarded the CCTV footage to about the same point.

'Did you get that bit there, when Meyerowitz is substituted?' He asked Gabriella.

'Yes, got it, so where is Klein on your cameras?'

'Here, camera four, and there you are as well.' Gabriella picked up the newspaper image and studied it closely, she pushed it over to Saul so he could see.

'Looking for some detail here that will gives us a clue as to what time to move the footage to,' Gabriella explained. Saul stared hard at the image, the players were on the opposite side of the field to where Gabriella and Klein were positioned. There were nine players in the shot, the ball was on the ground, the image was filled across the entire frame with bodies with just a thin strip of the stand on the opposite side of the field above their heads. Both teams were trying to retrieve the ball. Saul took a napkin from the table dispenser, he drew a circle and put a dot in the centre.

'Right, this is them,' he pointed to the dot. 'And you are here, at about the five o'clock position, and the image must have been taken from about the ten o'clock spot, agreed?' Gabriella nodded. 'So that puts our superman *Klein* just up from you about here.' He placed a cross between the four and five o'clock positions on the imaginary clock face.

'And that means that he couldn't have got the shot from where he was standing, I couldn't get it and I have a better angle,' Gabriella stated. What I was trying to tell Arnold,' she added.

'I know Gabi, but what he knows is that the shot came from Klein's camera, that's been proven...' Gabriella grabbed his arm.

'What was the time stamp on the image, we can use that to sync the cameras can't we?'

'Yes and no, the time stamp on the image file isn't correct,' Saul said.

'What!' Gabriella exclaimed. 'That means the image has been tampered, no?'

'Initially I thought so but it is just that his camera clock is out because of daylight savings time, and the fact that this is a leap year,'

'What?'

'It was your turn to propose to me darling, you know twenty nine days in February this year,' Saul said smiling.

'Oh, right.' Gabriella could feel the start of a blush.

'I might have said yes, you know,' Saul said but did not look at her. As a diversion, she was opening her shoulder bag and took out a compact mirrorless camera she always carried with her. Switching it on she pressed the menu button and navigated to the camera settings. Her camera's date and time was incorrect.

'Damn, I thought these things were smart,'

'It doesn't matter, we are still left with this impossible shot,' Saul said. 'If the image did not come from Klein's camera, then it would be a simple conclusion that someone else took the shot, someone else on the opposite side of the field,'

'So if you adjust for his image time stamp, which is one hour behind actual game time, that is then, fourteen seventeen, and seven seconds, yeah?' Gabriella waited for Saul to confirm.

'Right, so let's both move the CCTV and game footage to that point,' Saul replied. They moved the time controllers on their individual laptops to the same point. Gabriella all but exploded.

'Oh come on, for *fucks sake*,' she announced, some of the customers looked over. 'Sorry, sorry,' she offered up, the other patrons and the bar staff went back to their business. Turning her laptop screen towards Saul she nodded towards it. On her screen the broadcast editors had switched to a shot of the home teams coaching dug out, which was a few feet from where Klein was standing.

'What?' Saul asked. She pointed at the screen, and in a lowered voice said 'Look at his fucking camera.' Saul looked, and then checked his laptop. He enlarged the window which showed the photographer's position, it was the same, Klein's camera lens was pointing at the ground.

They spent the rest of the day in Redmonds, lunch, drinks, dinner, drinks. Saul had scanned the faces in the crowd at the position where a shot might have been taken. Over and over he looked at the spectators captured by CCTV. Some of the broadcast footage of the crowd waving to camera as well. Nothing, no one seemed out of place. No cameras visible. No one was acting strange, sitting or standing too still, perhaps recording from a wearable camera. Personal cameras had been banned from all sporting events, after some very punitive law suits on stadium owners and individual spectators for live streaming games. The major media syndicates used their collective legal and financial powers to push for what many thought was excessive sentences at media hyped show trials. No one risked it anymore. They started to turn fans on each other, after a very successful set of adverts and public information short films demonised the recording of gameplay. Free photo booths and staff photographers were on hand to record your attendance at the games. The stadium selfie soon disappeared from spectators' camera phones. Gabriella watched the players from the start of the game to the end. Looking for something, anything. She checked for drone traffic, over the stadium, even though it was not allowed during game time for safety. No flights recorded. She watched Klein as he covered the game, watching his every movement. It did not help. They both knew that the image came from his camera, how could they even deal with that fact if they could not understand how the shot had been made in the first place. At ten forty two, nearly twelve hours since they started, Gabriella leaned towards Saul and placed her head on his shoulder. Saul was thinking about duplicate cameras. A copy of the camera Klein was shooting with on the day. The camera could be copied, but not the lens. Optical fingerprinting, like comparing the marks on a bullet made by the gun barrel, was unique to each lens. The image Klein had shot matched the lens on his camera, this camera uploaded the image to the Brant Corporation's server three minutes after the full time whistle had been blown. Saul checked the footage, Klein was still standing on the touchline when the image was uploaded. Gabriella yawned and nuzzled into Saul's shoulder. Saul stared across the bar trying to reverse his mind out of the last dead end. On the far wall of the bar was a large screen showing an ice hockey game. There was a running banner at the lower third of the screen broadcast.

"Gabi, look,' Saul leaned forward, Gabriella raised her head from his shoulder. The rolling banner flashed *Breaking News* Nine Chicago Warriors players arrested after confessing to cheating....photographic evidence now confirmed by players as proof of major betting scandal...

'Well, the image is real,' Saul said looking towards Gabriella.

'I don't care if it's real or not, I want to know how it was done,' Gabriella replied. They left Redmonds bar, hailed a cab and tried to get some sleep back at their apartment. Both of them lay on the bed still thinking of all of the images, all of the video footage, and visualising the stadium and the impossible angles that seemed to defy some basic laws of physics. Eventually, exhaustion and more than a little alcohol caught up with them both, sleep came, answers stayed away.

At breakfast, Gabriella and Saul, watched the frenzy of news coverage as more and more was revealed about the betting scandal. There was a segment going back to the 1919 Chicago White Sox story, another segment showing various fans and their disbelief and hurt at being treated like fools. Experts were given studio time to explain all of the possible implications for the game, and for wider society. Klein's image flashed up over and over again, and with it some comments from players who were shocked to learn that this was going on. No one believed them, but it was safe to do so as others had already fallen on their swords. Somewhere in the world, wars raged on, a famine in Africa, and a plane crash with no survivors in the Indian Ocean. Someone else's news.

'Why isn't Klein on?' Gabriella suddenly thought. Saul looked at her, realising that was the question of the moment. The noise of the news rolled on, voices asking questions, making statements, but none of them as clever as Gabriella's.

'Somethings wrong, they haven't even put an image of him on screen,' Saul added. 'Ansel Klein should be rehearsing his Pulitzer speech right now.'

As Gabriella and Saul had slept in the hours before their breakfast, before they then stopped in at Phillies cafe for their coffee, before they entered the foyer of the Chicago Messenger, and before they were faced with the serious face of Dan Arnold, who had called them into his office. Ansel Klein was brutally murdered in his own home at approximately 3.00 am.

'Drop it now,' Arnold said. 'I know you were working on it yesterday, I know it got to you, but I am telling you to let go of this.'

'Dan, what the fuck is going on?' Saul beat Gabriella to the question.

'Klein's dead.' Saul and Gabriella were both stunned into silence, Dan Arnold took the moment to motion to them both to sit down. 'Carl Friedlander my opposite at Brant, called me this morning, police are saying it's suicide, but that's bullshit.'

'Klein was murdered?' Gabriella asked her voice trembling, Saul took her hand.

'Probably the mob, that picture made him a lot of enemies, a lot of money is involved.' Dan looked down at his desk. 'That's why I need you to stop whatever you were planning.' He looked up at them both.

'Dan, there's a dead journalist, one of us, one of our own..,' Saul went to continue, Dan cut him off.

'Brant are going to say the picture's fake.'

'But it isn't, we know that now,' Gabriella said.

'Gabi, they are going to say Klein faked the picture, because there was no actual evidence of the games being thrown. They are going to say that the Chicago players bought it and confessed. They will say Ansel Klein couldn't live with it, regretted it and took his own life.'

'Oh no, no this is not happening, how can this be happening?' Saul felt Gabriella's hand tightening on his, she could feel the anger within him. Dan was more worried for them now, he knew he had to convince them before they left the office.

'Listen, it's about maintaining the status quo, they have a handful of players from one team, one team, who they can scapegoat, focus their attention on, deflect any further need for investigation. There's millions of fans out there wanting this to be true, wanting to believe the games are not rigged. The matches will probably revert back to normal for a while and then the cheating will return and so will the money. Ansel Klein will become a hero, you know he will, you know how fucked up our industry is.' Arnold was right, they both knew it. It hurt, but the official line was *no more dead journalists*.

It took about month for the story to die. Ansel's funeral took place with a large turnout of press staff present. As predicted, outside the small church, thousands of fans gathered. The media started its campaign with shots and interviews of random people who all said he was a hero. Brant Corporation announced a set of scholarships in Klein's name for young photojournalists, and with that it ended.

Two months later, Gabriella and Saul were in their apartment. They had just returned from an assignment in Canada, photographing and interviewing the last remaining residents of the Old Crow settlement in the Yukon. Accessible by plane only, and snowmobile in winter, they had been out of reach for the past two weeks. Gabriella was keen to start working on her shots, Saul was checking some facts from interviews. The phone rang, and Gabriella picked it up, half expecting it to be work.

'Hello.'

'Hello can I speak with Miss Gabriella Maier?'

'Speaking, who is this?'

'Ah Miss Maier, I am David Frank, of Bresson, Brassai and Bailey, attorneys at law, representing the late Mr Ansel Klein. Are you free to speak right now?' Gabriella looked over at Saul who realised something was up.

'Yes, em can I put you on speaker my partner is here.' The sound of Klein's name had made her defensive.

'Of course, we have been trying to contact you for the last week, your office said you were in the back of beyond.' Frank's mention of this knowledge unsettled Gabriella even more.

'Right, so what can I do for you Mr Frank?'

'Well we have instructions to pass on to you some belongings of Mr Klein, we just wanted to see when was a good time to deliver them to you, it's a couple of boxes.' Saul shook his head at Gabriella, he could not think of a reason why Ansel Klein would have included her in any will. Before Gabriella could think Frank spoke again.

'Now you are at 1285 Leiter Avenue, is that right?'

'Yes,' Gabriella responded before she could stop herself. Saul put his hand up to try and stop her.

'Excellent, and would you be in this afternoon about two?' Frank asked. Saul shook his head, Gabriella looked at him, Saul thought quickly.

'Hi this is Miss Maier's partner, could you have them delivered to the Chicago Messenger, we were planning on going out this afternoon.'

'That's not a problem, but we will need Miss Maier to sign for it.'

'That's fine, I will be in tomorrow between ten and eleven,' Gabriella replied.

'I will have them couriered to you for then, thank you, nice to talk with you both, goodbye.'

'Goodbye,' Gabriella hung up.

Saul grabbed his laptop, turned it on and waved Gabriella over to sit beside him. He began typing.

"Don't talk, just wait a moment"

Saul searched for Bresson, Brassai and Bailey, their web page loaded. A law firm in Chicago. He looked at a staff list. David Frank was listed. He picked up his phone. Typed a message and sent it off to a colleague, showing Gabriella the display, she nodded. The reply came back almost immediately, one word, *Legitimate.*

The ground floor foyer of the Chicago Messenger, had a seated area with leather couches, a coffee station, and a view over to the main reception desk. Saul and Gabriella were seated there just before ten. They had told the receptionist about the delivery. At 10.34, a courier's van pulled up outside the main doors, a young man carried two boxes to the reception area. Gabriella was waved over to sign for the parcels. Gabriella studied the young deliveryman, he said nothing out of the ordinary, and seemed keen to depart and get on with his rounds. Saul had stepped out to look over the van, it checked out, a well known carrier, not the major outfits, but a recognisable branded vehicle. They were medium sized boxes, but heavy. Saul and Gabriella each carried one each back to their office. They stood for a moment looking at the packages.

'This is the part where the building gets blown to pieces,' Saul said to Gabriella who was not amused. The first box was opened, it contained a telephoto lens with front and rear lens caps, there was nothing else inside. It was identical to a lens Gabriella had in her kit, a fixed 400mm lens, but with a modified slightly larger lens hood to cut out glare from the sun or floodlights. The second package had a camera body, and wide angle lens attached. There was also what looked like a wireless hard drive recorder, the type used to copy images from the camera's internal storage card, as they were shot, just in case the memory card developed a fault. Saul showed it to Gabriella, she didn't recognise it, and it had no manufacturer's name or logo on the surface of the case. The hard drive had a fixed lead exiting from one end of the box, the connector was not standard. They checked both boxes again, and the packaging but there was nothing else.

'I don't get it, why would he want you to have this, you have this kit already?' Saul asked. Gabriella looked at the camera, turning it around in her hands, looking for anything unusual.

'Saul,' she said still looking at the camera.

'What?'

'Pretty sure Ansel did not intend to give me this.'

'How?'

'Think about it, he would not have had time to arrange this.'

Gabriella switched the camera on. Looking at the back of the screen, she pressed the image playback button. There was only one image. Someone was holding the connector of what looked like the same wireless hard drive, in his other hand a sheet of paper with the name of a bar, a time and a date. It was tomorrow's date. The face of the person in the shot wasn't visible.

'It's a message, look.' She showed the image to Saul.

'My name is Mark Rodchenko, I am a researcher at Chicago Tech. I specialise in photonics, I knew Ansel as a friend, he and I went to the same college. I sent you the camera equipment.' Rodchenko waited for Saul and Gabriella to respond, they in turn waited for him to continue. The meeting place was a bar near the junction of West 17th Street and South

Ashland Avenue, an old bar with small high windows and solid front door. As Saul and Gabriella had entered the place, it gave a feeling of being confined, both of them tense and on guard. A member of the Messenger's security staff had dropped them off near to the bar, and now sat parked within sight of the doorway. Rodchenko was in his late twenties, he looked younger. He looked genuine.

'We were going to meet up with you the day after the game, that's how I know you both,' Rodchenko explained. 'Then the image happened, and everything just went insane.' Rodchenko stared at the table, his drink lay untouched.

'You know what happened to Ansel?' Saul asked. Rodchenko nodded.

'So you were working with him?' Again, Rodchenko nodded. His breathing quickened, pulse rate increasing, panic was rising within him. Gabriella thought he might bolt.

'Mark, it's ok we are off the record here, not recording anything, ok, take it easy.' She saw him nod and take a deep breath. He was obviously scared. 'Why did you send me the camera and the lens?' Rodchenko took another deep breath.

'The image was taken with that camera,' Rodchenko replied.

'But that's a standard press camera with a wide angle lens, which no one really uses at a sporting event,' Gabriella stated. 'And Ansel, at the game, we saw him with a different camera, with the telephoto lens which you also sent me.'

'I know, you're right, the camera was on a tripod, a motorised tripod head, next to Ansel, he wasn't using it, I was.' Saul thought back to the hours of game footage he had worked through. There was a tripod next to Ansel.

'You weren't there, and even if you were, we know that where Ansel was standing, he could not have made the shot, so how the hell did you manage it?' Saul asked, his tone becoming more direct.

'You both know that the image is real, not faked like they are now saying?' Rodchenko countered Saul's directness. Gabriella's mind was racing, she was trying to think about the camera, she hadn't really looked at it after seeing the stored image.

'We know it's real Mark, if you said you took the shot then yes I believe you, but I still can't work it out, are you going to tell us?'

Rodchenko nodded, took a sip of his drink.

'The camera is special, there are only two of them. Its sensor has been replaced with something I designed, and its resolution is way higher than anything there is right now. The wide angle lens has also been modified, the best way to describe it is that you can get a wide angle shot of a scene from where the camera is positioned. But you can also compose a new wide angle shot by selecting an area of that scene. It is as if I was able to pick up the camera from where Ansel was standing, and walk across the pitch and take a new wide angle shot of, … for example the crowd in the stadium on the opposite side.'

'Oh shit,' Gabriella exclaimed, 'I should have tried that camera out, I never thought, it just looked ordinary.'

'That's what I wanted it to look like, we even disguised the motorised tripod head, so that there was less chance of its movements being seen,'

'That lens, people will want to buy it.' Gabriella's voice was excited, Saul was getting frustrated.

'Fine, so you have a fancy lens, a high resolution camera, but still an impossible image, one which leads to the death of a journalist.' Saul stared at Rodchenko, Rodchenko understood.

'Alex spoke to me several months ago, he told me of his frustration of going to games to cover the action, and being *corralled* as he described it into one area, unable to move around the pitch, or the court, and all because of the regulations the sporting authorities had brought in. I told him, I could get a shot of practically anywhere on the field of play. He thought this was madness and we joked about it, and then I brought him on campus one day, and proved it to him. I asked a girlfriend of mine to sit in the outside area between campus buildings, and made sure she knew where I was with the camera. I told her to sit with her back to me at all times, and not to move not to look to the side or look behind her. Then I sent another of my friends out to talk with her, he sat opposite to her and just a little to the side, enough to see his face. I bet Ansel twenty bucks that he with his telephoto lens, could not get a shot of my girlfriend's face in five minutes if he stood next to me, and I could. I won.' For the first time Rodchenko smiled.

'How's that possible?' Saul said.

'My camera, took a total of five thousand and seventy two shots over the five minutes, each image transferred to a wireless hard drive, then connected to my computer, using that unique link I showed you, the same one on the drive I sent you. In those images, my friend made direct eye contact with my girlfriend's face one hundred and four times. In that five minute period, twelve other people walked by my girlfriend and looked at her.' Gabriella almost could not believe what she was about to say next.

'You can see, what people are seeing, you can photograph that,…you were photographing the spectators, what they could see, what they could see from their position.' Rodchenko smiled.

'Straight from their retinas, all I need is at least forty clean references, and at a sporting event, nearly everyone is looking at the same thing. And sometimes, you can get partial images from anything reflective, like mirrored sunglasses, and it's added to the matrix of images to produce a final composite. That's how we got the the reverse shot from where Ansel was positioned, and the image.' He paused. 'The image of the cheating was just luck, bad luck.'

Rodchenko explained more of the process to Saul and Gabriella. He talked about the day of the game, telling them that he was just outside the stadium in a nearby cafe. He could move the tripod head remotely to cover the other three sides of the stadium. The images were transmitted to his computer from the hard drive, the computer software composed the images as they came in one by one. Taking parts of each image, and overlapping one spectator's view onto of another. The angles between spectators and the players were adjusted and corrected. When Rodchenko saw the image that proved cheating, he prepared the same image for transmission back to Alex. He waited for the final whistle to blow. Alex had been told to leave his camera switched on, and to place the lens cap on his telephoto lens. The lens cap looked just like any other plastic cover. This one had on it's inside face, a small battery driven projector. The telephoto lens had been adapted so that the cap sat just out from the front glass, the reason for the extended lens hood. Alex then quickly checked the back display of his camera, as if he was checking his shots. When the image appeared on his screen, he fired the shutter. The image was now on his camera sensor, having passed through the glass elements of his lens, and having picked up the minute flaws unique to that lens.

'So what now, what will you do?' Saul asked the researcher. Gabriella thought about the technology.

'You could make a fortune from that lens alone, and the new high resolution sensor?' she suggested. Mark looked at them both, he shook his head.

'The camera, the lens are useless without the software and the computing algorithms. Perhaps seeing everything is seeing too much,' he replied. 'Alex said it might be the very death of photography, every possible shot, every angle, don't compose, don't look, don't see, just choose.'

Rodchenko's invention was brilliant. Its applications in the real world beyond photography however, seemed to lean in the direction of the intelligence services, surveillance, military, and the invasion of personal privacy. Like some of the Manhattan project scientists who were driven to test theories, Rodchenko admitted he got caught up trying to prove that the impossible shot could be captured, at the cost of his friend. He told Gabriella and Saul that he would delete the code, it just wasn't worth it.

The trick had been revealed. Only three people knew how it was done. Gabriella and Saul had to admit that not being able to work out the puzzle, was infuriating, but that's what makes magic so appealing. Perhaps if Ansel had just got some impossible sports shots and not the image he published, he would have delighted in watching Gabriella and Saul forever tormented. The image was soon archived into the fickle history and recollections of people's minds and the media moved on. Gabriella, being a photographer was haunted by it all. She would take Rodchenko's camera equipment out of the boxes and just stare at them. Saul asked her to put it all away, and to leave it be. Something nagged at her, somewhere at the back of her brain. Three months after their meeting with Rodchenko, at four twenty five in the morning, lying beside Saul who was sound asleep, her brain made the connection.

'Saul, Saul, wake up.' He jumped awake.

'What, what's wrong?'

'Nothing, we need to see Mark, right now, we need to speak with him.'

'What, who?'

'Mark Rodchenko, now, get his number.' Gabriella was already half dressed. 'We need to go into the office.' If Saul had been more awake he might have argued, but instead he searched for the number. Gabriella dialled it and waited.

'Hello?'

'Mark, it's Gabriella and Saul from the Chicago Messenger.'

'Oh hi what time is it?'

'I don't know, listen Mark, did you delete your software?' Gabriella looked at Saul, Saul looked back confused. Mark was also confused.

'Eh, yes, yes I did, I told you I would, how?' Gabriella stood still, the energy of the last few seconds drained from her, she sighed, and then quietly swore under her breath.

'I'm sorry Mark, forgive me, sorry, take care.'

'You too, say hello to Saul for me.' The phone line went dead, Saul smiled at Gabriella.

'So what was that about?'

'Just an idea, stupid really,' Gabriella replied. They went back to bed, he would wait till their morning coffee run, before asking again. Gabriella tried to sleep. A couple of minutes later Saul's phone rang, he swore under his breath, Gabriella sat up. It was Mark Rodchenko. Saul put him on speaker.

'Hi it's Mark, sorry, just remembered, there might be a copy of the code on the drive I sent you, seems that....' The rest of Mark's sentence was drowned out by a scream from Gabriella. She shouted at Mark to get to the Messenger now, and bring what he needed, they would meet him there.

The offices of the Chicago Messenger were quiet at five thirty in the morning. Cleaning staff were about to finish their shift, Dan Arnold had arrived at his usual time long before the first reporters and photojournalists. He sat in his office scanning the overnight images, making editorial decisions as he clicked through them. His routine was interrupted by Gabriella and Saul and one other he didn't know. A half an hour later, he knew the identity of Mark Rodchenko, and a whole lot more. Gabriella told him her idea, the process of saying it out loud, and hearing it said was disorienting and exciting. Arnold sat thinking for a moment. Finally he spoke.

'As it stands, the idea is only as good as the quality of the material. Remember we are not talking digital here. The originals are 16mm film, hand held cameras, silver bromides, and some Polaroids.' Arnold went over to his office window and looked out over the city. There was danger and reward in this proposal, he thought for a moment, the other three dared not speak. There was danger, there was also the possibility of the truth, he had made up his mind.

'But, that said... there is another film, one that has never been seen.' He looked back into the room, he stared at the large wall mounted monitor. The image of a young wife cradling her husband's head in the back of an open topped black Lincoln Continental, was frozen in time. The next few frames contained horrors hard to imagine, hard to see. Arnold was five years old when it happened. They say you remember where you were the day he was shot. Arnold thought, perhaps not what was remembered, just what might have been seen.

As the motorcade entered Deally Plaza, Catherine Marzaroti standing on the grassy area of Main St, strained forward to see her President. She was just as excited about what his wife would be wearing. She held her five year old son's hand. As the adults looked up Elm St towards the advancing vehicles, Thomas Marzaroti was looking across the street. There, he saw a funny man holding an umbrella, funny because it wasn't raining. Rodchenko's software found him, and found what he was looking at.

The Chicago Messenger had a story that the Brant Corporation and all other media outlets across the world would have sold their souls for. The Messenger was soon to have two Pulitzer prize winners on it's staff.

Play it again Sam

STATE OF NEW KILMARNOCK :
COURT OF MEDIA AFFAIRS : ALBA

1 RICHARD HARRISON

   PLAINTIFF

                                    vs.

2 THE ELECTRIC THEATRE COMPANY

   DEFENDANT

3 JURY TRIAL
   TRIAL - DAY 1 Case No. 09 TY 723
   DATE: FEBRUARY 12, 2047

4 BEFORE: Hon. NADIA ESCOTRANIA Judge

5   APPEARANCES

6   DAVIS J A GRANT Special Prosecutor
     On behalf of Richard Harrison.

6   LYNDA F GILLESPIE Attorney
     On behalf of The Electric Theatre Co.

7   TRANSCRIPT OF PROCEEDINGS

8   Reported by Edward Glass COURT REPORTER

INDEX

9 OPENING INSTRUCTIONS BY THE COURT   Page 18

10 OPENING STATEMENTS   Page 24

WITNESSES

CARSON HENDERSON

11 Direct examination by attorney GRANT   Page 28

12 Cross examination by attorney GILLESPIE

        Page 43

JAMES ANDERS

13 Direct examination by attorney GRANT   Page 57

14 Cross examination by attorney GILLESPIE

Page 72

ALICE BROWN

13 Direct examination by attorney GRANT   Page 86

14 Cross examination by attorney GILLESPIE

Page 97

RICHARD HARRISON

13 Direct examination by attorney GRANT   Page 109

14 Cross examination by attorney GILLESPIE

Page 129

SHEENA GIBSON

EXHIBITS	MARKED	OFFERED	ACCEPTED
1	345	146	146
2	237	147	147
3	213	148	148

15   THE COURT   At this time the court
calls Richard Harrison vs. The Electric Theatre

Company, case number 09 TY 723, will all parties state their appearances for the record please.

16   ATTORNEY GRANT   Good morning your Honor RICHARD HARRISON appears by New Kilmarnock County District Attorney Davis Grant, lead counsel and appearing as special prosecutor in this case.

17   ATTORNEY GILLESPIE   and Good morning your Honor, THE ELECTRIC THEATRE COMPANY appears by Attorney Lynda Gillespie, appearing as defence counsel.

18   THE COURT   Thank you, all right let's get started, are there any issues either counsel would like to raise at this point before we ask the jury to sit?

19   ATTORNEY GRANT   No your Honor.

20   ATTORNEY GILLESPIE   Non your Honor.

21   THE COURT   Good, will you please bring in the jurors.

22   THE COURT   Ladies and Gentlemen of the jury, thank you for your attendance here today, now I am going to make some opening statements regarding your responsibilities in this trial, and

to clarify the scope of what we will be dealing
with today. The case before us is that the
plaintiff is suing for damages, that is financial
compensation, from the defendant. The plaintiff
asserts that the defendant has failed in a duty of
care to his detriment, that being it had an adverse
effect on him and that he was not aware of the
potential harm on his health and well being. The
plaintiff also asserts that the defendant should
have acted when they did not. The defendant has
refused this version. The defendant has stated that
the plaintiff was fully informed of the operation
of any third party equipment and the details of the
test study, and that therefore cannot be held
liable for any damages. Now this case is somewhat
unusual in that the plaintiff will be pursuing the
loss of something which could be regarded as a non
physical asset, unlike for example the theft of a
motor vehicle, or a piece of jewellery. However, it
will be the job of both the prosecution and defence
councils to convince you either way of the
importance or otherwise of the plaintiff's loss.
This is not a matter that the court and the law can
rule on in its present form. Which is why we ask
you the jury to listen to both sides of the
argument and make your deliberation. Now as there

are only a few witnesses being presented today, my
hope is that you will be able to reach your
decision by tomorrow at the latest. However I must
now instruct you all that if we have an overnight
recess, you must not under any circumstances be
tempted to investigate, use or otherwise experience
anything relating to this case or the setting in
which it has alleged to have been used. Any breach
of these instructions will be dealt with in the
most serious terms. I am sure as we progress this
trial you will understand why I issue this
directive. If on the balance of the evidence and
legal argument you the jury conclude that the
plaintiff has suffered damages, then you must
return a verdict in the plaintiff's favour. You
should not at this stage concern yourself with the
amount of said damages, I will be able to give you
advice as to that later, should it be required. If
you find that the defendant has no case to answer,
then you must find in the defendant's favour.
Either way, you will need to arrive at your
conclusion based solely on the evidence and
argument that will be presented here in this court.
Do not let your own feelings, politics, or faith,
prejudice your decision. Also, you must not discuss
or broadcast anything relating to this trial to

persons or agencies outside of this courtroom.
Members of the jury at this time we're going to
hear the opening statement from the prosecution.
Mr.Grant, you may begin.

23   ATTORNEY GRANT   Thank you your Honor.
Ladies and gentlemen of the jury, good morning.
When this trial is over, you will not have any
photographs of your attendance here. You will not
have any video footage of these proceedings. You
could request a copy of the court transcript should
you so desire, a record of every word spoken as I
do now here in front of you. The experience of your
service here, lives on in your memory. It will be
within your individual memories that you will be
able to reconstruct your time and how you observed
and experienced it here. If for example someone was
to ask you what was it like, then you would be able
to recall the sensations, the atmosphere, the
personalities of the persons present here. All of
this becomes part of the story of your life. Indeed
we here in this court day after day, rely on the
testimony of persons in order to deliver evidence
to people just like yourselves. And in the absence
of other physical evidence, say CCTV footage, or a
photograph, or sound recording, we have to examine
the evidence of someone's guilt or innocence, based

on memory, and the facts we can deduce from the
same. Now my learned friend who speaks for the
defendant, will shortly no doubt question the
efficacy of memory, or to put it simply its
reliability. It is after all what we lawyers do
when cross examining a witness, we try to cast
doubt on what is being said from what is
remembered. However, I will leave you now with
this. Cast your mind back to a memory you hold
dear. Take a moment to think about it. Now ask
yourself if anyone else has the right to question
that memory as accurate. Perhaps they do, but it is
your memory, your record and interpretation. The
question is not with regards to the accuracy of the
memory, it is your right to hold that memory. Now
imagine that with the click of my fingers, I could
erase that memory. Real or imagined, I have no
right to take it from you. Thank you. Thank you
your Honor.

24   THE COURT   Thank you Mr Grant, Miss
Gillespie you may proceed.

25   ATTORNEY GILLESPIE   Thank you your Honor.
Good morning folks, I hope you all find yourselves
well today. This service that you offer here to the
state of New Kilmarnock is gratefully appreciated.

To take time out from your busy lives and to put
yourself into the difficult position of deciding an
outcome for this court case, is no trivial matter.
It will of course live on in your memory, something
which, long after this trial has been recorded into
history, will become part of you. Thankfully our
dealings here today are not that of a murder trial.
Not that of some gruesome killing, and the crime
scene photographs of the same you may have to look
at. I often think of the men and women who sit
where you sit now. What they have to take away in
memory from this place. We lawyers, see this horror
from time to time in our careers. We never get used
to it. Often I have thought if there was a way to
erase some of the images that jurors see at the end
of a trial, once the verdict has been returned,
would it be such a bad idea. To be given the choice
to forget. To be able to sleep at night without
nightmares. If that were possible, would you
request it? If so you would have made a choice, a
free choice to forget. That ladies and gentlemen is
what we will prove to you today. The plaintiff made
his own choice, no one forced him, no one made it
on his behalf. It was his responsibility. Thank
you. Thank you your Honor.

26   THE COURT   Very well, Mr Grant your first witness.

27   ATTORNEY GRANT   Thank you, may it please the court to call Mr Carson Henderson to the stand.

28   THE CLERK   Please raise your right hand.

29   CARSON HENDERSON, called as a witness herein, having been first duly sworn, was examined and testified as follows:

30   THE CLERK: Please be seated. Please state your name and spell your last name for the record.

THE WITNESS: Carson Henderson

31   H.E.N.D.E.R.S.O.N

DIRECT EXAMINATION

BY ATTORNEY GRANT

Q.   Mr Henderson can you identify the object I am passing to you now? Exhibit 1 your Honor.

A.   Yes, these a pair of REWIND glasses.

Q.   And can you tell the court how you know this
please?

A.   My company manufactures them, they're our
product.

Q.   I see, and you are the director of this
company?

A.   REWIND MEDIA is my company yes.

Q.   So what exactly do these glasses do?

A.   We developed a technology that can erase a
period of short term memory, about twenty minutes
of memory.

Q.   What is the purpose of such a technology?

A.   We have been running trials with the Electric
Theatre Company, and we have been using the glasses
to make people forget the endings of films shown in
the movie theatre.

Q.   To forget the endings of feature films, now
why would you develop that capability Mr Henderson?

A.   The Electric Theatre Company approached us
early last year, they knew of our work in treating

veterans suffering from PTSD. We have been researching ways to reduce suffering by erasing memories and trauma.

Q.   Are there many movie patrons who suffer from Post Traumatic Stress Disorder, PTSD, after watching a film?

32   ATTORNEY GILLESPIE   Objection, the witness is not qualified to answer that question.

33   THE COURT   Sustained

34   ATTORNEY GRANT   Your Honor.

Q.   Your company REWIND MEDIA is a separate company to that of your government funded work with veterans?

A.   Yes it was a spin out company for this particular research.

Q.   Mr Henderson, can you tell the court, your client the Electric Theatre Company, what was their particular interest in your technology that can make someone forget the ending to a film?

A.   They wanted to find a way to let their customers have the option to forget the ending to certain films, so that they could enjoy them again.

Q.   So this would involve their customers returning to see the same film again if they wanted to.

A.   Yes.

Q.   Why just the last twenty or so minutes of a film, why not the entire film?

A.   Our technology works on memory which is being processed by the brain in short term memory before it is cemented into long term memory and recall. We can only at present effectively erase approximately the last twenty minutes of current memory.

Q.   And this works with all films?

A.   Yes, but we selected some films that have a surprise ending, a twist in the tale so to speak.

Q.   Can you give the court any examples of films you have tested your device on?

A.   Films such as The Sixth Sense, Jacobs Ladder, The Usual Suspects, The Others, and Seven.

Q.   These films are quite old now are they not?

A.   Yes.

Q.   For the purposes of clarity your Honor, these films do have in their narrative a surprise ending which the viewer may or may not have worked out during the film. Now, turning to my client now, do you recognise the plaintiff Mr Richard Harrison?

A.   Yes, he was our first test volunteer.

Q.   And he signed a contract with your company, Exhibit 2 you Honor, and can you confirm that this is the same contract?

A.   Yes.

35   ATTORNEY GRANT   No further questions at this time your Honor.

36   THE COURT   Miss Gillespie, your witness.

37   ATTORNEY GILLESPIE   Thank you your Honor.

       CROSS EXAMINATION

BY ATTORNEY GILLESPIE

Q.   Mr Henderson as my learned friend has
mentioned the contract Exhibit 2, could you turn to
page 27 and read the third paragraph, the one that
starts The test subject …

A.   The test subject as named in section one of
this agreement, shall agree to waive all rights of
financial compensation or legal redress if in the
event of any medical issue or injury arising from
the test subjects participation during the duration
of the trial programme as stated in section four.

Q.   Thank you Mr Henderson, and you can confirm
that Mr Harrison signed this contract of his own
free will and not under any duress?

A.   That is correct.

37   ATTORNEY GILLESPIE   No further questions.

38   THE COURT   Mr Grant?

39   ATTORNEY GRANT   Just one follow up question
your Honor.

        REDIRECT EXAMINATION

BY ATTORNEY GILLESPIE

Q.   Mr Henderson, when my client signed the contract with you, had your company ran prior tests of this memory erasure with the Electric Theatre Company or any other movie outlet?

A.   No, this was the first trial.

40   ATTORNEY GRANT   That is all I have for this witness today your Honor.

41   THE COURT   Do you wish to recross Miss Gillespie?

42   ATTORNEY GILLESPIE   No your Honor.

43   THE COURT   The witness is excused.

44   THE COURT   Your next witness Mr Grant.

45   ATTORNEY GRANT   Thank you, may it please the court to call Mr James Anders to the stand.

46   THE CLERK   Please raise your right hand.

47   JAMES ANDERS, called as a witness herein, having been first duly sworn, was examined and testified as follows:

48   THE CLERK: Please be seated. Please state
your name and spell your last name for the record.

THE WITNESS: James Anders

49   A.N.D.E.R.S

DIRECT EXAMINATION

BY ATTORNEY GRANT

Q.   Mr Anders, could you tell the court what is
your profession please.

A.   I am the C.E.O of PixelPics International.

Q.   Now I am sure everyone here will be familiar
with your company, you are the largest distributer
of streamed media in Europe, approximately 157
million subscribers, is that correct?

A.   Yes, streamed to homes not cinema.

Q.   Yes thank you, so what is your interest in
the test trial involving my client, REWIND MEDIA,
and the Electric Theatre Company?

A.   We are interested in the technology of media
erasure. We want to bring into people's homes the

option to watch and rewatch our content, with a new sense of enjoyment.

Q.   A new sense of enjoyment, what exactly do you mean by that?

A.   Well there are some great films and multi part series in our catalogue, we think that our customers will want to watch some of this content over again and well, thinking it was the first time they encountered a particular film or box set.

Q.   I see, so how would this work?

A.   At the end of the film or series episode, if the customer had opted for memory erasure, the glasses, REWIND glasses, would pick up a signal embedded in the final seconds of the media, before credits, and this would erase memory and the contents of the film etc.

Q.   You mean the last twenty or so minutes as explained by Mr Henderson from REWIND MEDIA?

A.   Actually we want to erase the entire film.

Q.   Really? And are you working with REWIND MEDIA at present to try and achieve this goal?

A.   Yes

50   THE COURT   Mr Grant are you able to
clarify where this line of questioning is leading
us to as I am having difficulty understanding the
relevance of this witness who has no direct
connection to the Plaintiff.

51   ATTORNEY GRANT   Certainly your Honor,
I was just coming to that, if I may indulge the
court a little longer, I wish to show a connection
to the defendant, that is important to the issues
of motivation.

52   THE COURT   Very well, but be brief Mr
Grant.

53   ATTORNEY GRANT   Thank you your Honor,
I will.

Q.   So Mr Anders, you wish to have the ability to
erase after having watched an entire film, and have
you discussed this as a concept with REWIND MEDIA?

A.   Well yes, and we have been working with them
to extend the duration of memory erasure.

Q.   Oh I see, and have you had any progress thus
far?

A.   About an hour.

Q.   Well Mr Henderson forgot to mention this during his testimony it would appear, one last question Mr Anders, does your company have a financial motivation connected to the proposed use of these REWIND glasses?

53   ATTORNEY GILLESPIE   Objection, the witnesses is not here to explain his company's financial aspirations, his company is not the one being sued for damages.

54   THE COURT   Overruled, the witness will answer the question please.

A.   There is a recognised problem in my industry, we are running out of quality content. The rate of consumption of media is higher than at anytime before, we cannot keep up with demand, and our company as well as other platforms, fund new development projects, but the cost of these are increasing. We are running out of stories, good stories. If we can recycle content, and make this enjoyable to watch, then we can offer the same level of experience as going to the movie theatre for the first time to see a classic film.

Q.   But Mr Anders, your subscribers, unlike cinema patrons pay a one off fee to access you content, how would this technology work in your favour?

A.   We could reduce, or completely remove the need for new content, saving millions of Euros in project development.

Q.   And of course you purchase a licence to place films that are distributed in movie theatres, to place them on your platform once the cinema run has ended, so this could also become new content for your subscribers?

A.   Yes, they could see it in the cinema, and then re experience it at home.

55   ATTORNEY GRANT   Thank you Mr Anders, no further questions your Honor.

56   THE COURT   Your witness Miss Gillespie.

52   ATTORNEY GILLESPIE   No questions for this witness your Honor

52   THE COURT   Very well, Mr Anders you
are excused for the time being. Mr Grant you may
proceed.

55   ATTORNEY GRANT   Thank you at this
time I would like to call Alice Brown to the stand.

56   THE CLERK   Please raise your right hand.

57   ALICE BROWN, called as a witness herein,
having been first duly sworn, was examined and
testified as follows:

58   THE CLERK: Please be seated. Please state
your name and spell your last name for the record.

        THE WITNESS: Alice Brown

59   B.R.O.W.N

        DIRECT EXAMINATION

BY ATTORNEY GRANT

Q.   Ms Brown you are the managing director of the
Electric Theatre Company, a chain of cinema
complexes across Europe, is that correct?

A.   Yes

Q. Do you know the plaintiff Mr Harrison?

A. Not personally, I have never met or seen him until now, but I knew of him through our dealings with REWIND MEDIA.

Q. And how exactly was that?

A. I knew he was a test volunteer, and that he would be attending one of our cinemas during the trial period.

Q. This trial period was seven days, during which time your cinema screened the film Nineteen Eighty Four, also first released in 1984, written by George Orwell, starring John Hurt and Richard Burton?

60 THE COURT   I don't believe I have seen that film.

61 ATTORNEY GRANT   Are you quite sure my Honor, can you be sure?

62 THE COURT   Oh very droll, Mr Grant, please spare us your witticisms. Continue.

63 ATTORNEY GRANT   As it pleases your Honor.

Q.   Ms Brown, the last question if you please.

A.   Yes 1984, was the film selected for the test period.

Q.   How many showings of this film were conducted during the week beginning September eleventh 2046?

A.   It would be three screenings a day for the seven days, so twenty one performances.

Q.   Do you know how many of these twenty one screenings Mr Harrison attended?

A.   No, sorry I do not know.

Q.   Would it surprise you then to know that in fact my client attended the full screening of this film, nineteen times?

A.   Yes, I suppose so.

Q.   Indeed. Now Ms Brown, could you roughly or otherwise calculate for the court what the cost to my client would have been to attend all of those screenings?

A.   There was no cost to your client.

Q.   He saw, all the screenings for free, is that
what you are saying?

A.   Yes.

Q.   No cost to my client, and was there any other
concession my client enjoyed during his attendance
at your cinema?

A.   Yes, free food and drink was provided.

Q.   Now Ms Brown, do you think that if for
example you came across another patron attending at
the same frequency as my client but outwith any
experimental situation, you would be concerned as
to their welfare, I mean spending all that money to
see the same film nineteen times in one week?

A.   It's a free country, people can choose to
spend their money however they like, we have fans
of films who see the same movie more than once.

Q.   But not nineteen times?

A.   No

Q.   So if this movie-watching behaviour became
more typical, then your business would indeed

thrive, if you were charging entry and for food as normal?

64   ATTORNEY GILLESPIE   Objection, speculation your Honor.

65   THE COURT   Sustained, you do not have to answer that question Ms Brown. Mr Grant.

Q.   Your Honor, so Ms Brown one final question, would you as the managing director of your company wish to see your patrons attending the same film nineteen times?

66   ATTORNEY GILLESPIE   Objection, the witness cannot be expected to answer that question for every patron that choses to go to her establishments.

67   THE COURT   No, I am going to allow it, Mr Grant make your point please. Ms Brown please answer the question.

A.   No, personally I would not want people to see the same film more than two or three times.

68   ATTORNEY GRANT   No more questions your Honor.

69   THE COURT   Miss Gillespie?

70   ATTORNEY GILLESPIE   No questions your
Honor.

THE COURT   Thank you Ms Brown, you are
excused. Mr Grant your final witness I believe?

71   ATTORNEY GRANT   Yes, may it please
the court to call the plaintiff Mr Richard Harrison
to the stand.

72   THE CLERK   Please raise your right hand.

73   RICHARD HARRISON, called as a witness herein,
having been first duly sworn, was examined and
testified as follows:

74   THE CLERK: Please be seated. Please state
your name and spell your last name for the record.

THE WITNESS: Richard Harrison

75   H.A.R.R.I.S.O.N

DIRECT EXAMINATION

BY ATTORNEY GRANT

Q.   Mr Harrison can you describe the ending of
the film nineteen eighty four, the one you saw
nineteen times last year.

A.   No, I cannot.

Q.   Have you read the book?

A.   No

Q.   But after nineteen times of watching the 1984
adaptation, you are unable to tell the court what
the gist of the ending is?

A.   I cannot.

Q.   So if for example I was to tell you if the
main character Winston Smith, had survived torture
and was able to assassinate Big Brother and lead
the proletariat to overthrow the state, you would
not be able to confirm or deny that?

A.   I can't tell you what the ending is.

Q.   How odd, surely after having watched the film
nineteen times, you would have by now learned what
the ending is?

A.   I have seen the ending, but I cannot remember
it.

Q.   Because each time you watched the film in the
cinema, you were wearing the REWIND glasses, is
that correct?

A.   No, not exactly.

Q.   Mr Harrison I do not understand, how then
could you not know the ending to the film, did you
wear the glasses on the last screening of the film?

A.   No, I stopped wearing the glasses after the
second day the film was on at the cinema.

Q.   You mean you had seen the film six times with
the glasses, and the remaining thirteen times
without the glasses, including the last time?

A.   Yes that is correct.

Q.   And you are sure you cannot remember the
ending of the film?

A.   Yes I am sure.

Q.   But you continued to watch the same film over
and over again, why?

A.   Because I had to.

Q.   As part of the contract you signed with
REWIND MEDIA?

A.   No I just had to find out the ending.

Q.   So Mr Harrison, if I was to show you the film
1984 here right now, in court, you would state
under oath that on completion of that film which we
could all watch together, you would not be able to
tell me the ending of the same film?

A.   No, I would not be able.

Q.   How do you know this Mr Harrison?

A.   I have been tested by Dr Gibson, I had a lie
detector test, after I watched the film at her
clinic.

Q.   Dr Sheena Gibson, Psychiatrist, and witness
for the defence counsel?

A.   Yes.

Q.   I see, now tell me Mr Harrison, did anyone
ever explain or tell you what was the ending of the
film 1984?

A.   Yes, some friends, and some of the cinema
staff.

Q.   The cinema staff, when you had finished
seeing the film?

A.   No when I was getting food before the film.

Q.   So you knew the ending on occasions before
watching the film, and was this when you were not
wearing the glasses?

A.   Yes, it was their way of having fun, they
would taunt me and ask me what the ending was, then
tell me, even if I said I did not want to know.

Q.   And it got quite cruel and abusive towards
the end didn't it?

A.   Yes, they would use names like retard.

Q.   And yet you continued to attend the
screenings?

A.   I couldn't stop, I had to find out the
ending.

76   ATTORNEY GRANT   Thank you Mr
Harrison, your witness Miss Gillespie.

CROSS EXAMINATION

BY ATTORNEY GILLESPIE

Q.   Mr Harrison, why did you agree to enter into the volunteer trials with REWIND MEDIA?

A.   I love films, and I love the classics especially the ones with surprise endings. I have watched these film many times. I have always wondered what it's like for someone who hasn't seen some of them, I get excited for them.

Q.   And how did you make contact with REWIND MEDIA, how did you learn about the test program?

A.   I know Carson, we were at university together.

Q.   Carson Henderson?

A.   Yes.

Q.   Mr Harrison, you are pursuing damages from my client the Electric Theatre Company, but they did not develop the technology, that is the glasses, Mr Henderson's company REWIND MEDIA did, so why aren't you suing them?

A.   Carson is a friend, I agreed to volunteer to use the glasses and to tell him what my experience was, and yes I was excited to try it out.

Q.   So Mr Harrison, you are eager to try out a technology which you knew would erase a portion of your memory, the last twenty or so minutes of a feature film. And you took a week off work, went to the cinema which is something you very much enjoy, had free tickets for a week, and as much popcorn and drinks as you wished, have I got anything drastically wrong in that summary?

A.   No that's about right.

Q.   So why then Mr Harrison, sue my client. What is it you want from them?

A.   What I want from them I cannot get, I cannot get back the time I have lost, and the ending of a film I should know but cannot remember.

Q.   So if my client cannot give you back these things, what Mr Harrison are we doing here?

A.   They should have stopped me, they allowed the situation to exist that has caused this, no one else should be placed in this same position, this

is a nightmare without and ending. I can't learn
the ending anymore, it won't go in. Something is
wrong.

Q.   But you accept that it was your choice,
always your choice to make, wasn't it Mr Harrison?

A.   No, I don't think so.

77   ATTORNEY GILLESPIE   No more questions
your Honor.

78   THE COURT   Mr Grant?

79   ATTORNEY GRANT   If I may just have a
couple of questions to my client.

Q.   Mr Harrison did you fully understand what was
being suggested as the probable effect of wearing
the REWIND glasses, did you understand that you
would be made to forget the ending of this film?

A.   Yes, I did.

Q.   Did you ever consider that it would be more
beneficial to be able to erase the whole film and
then be able to watch it again.

A.   No

Q.   Why?

A.   Because if that were the case you would only
experience the film for the duration of its
screening, you could not know once you left the
movie theatre if you had actually seen it.

Q.   But you were happy with just being able to
forget the ending?

A.   Yes, that's more like what happens over time,
when you know you have seen a film but can't
remember it that well. The memory of the ending
fades over the course of about an hour, it's like
when you wake from a dream and you try to remember
what you were dreaming, but it slips away as you
fully wake up.

Q.   Then was it your understanding and intention
that you could at some point in the future decide
to watch the film again with the ending, and
therefore be surprised, adding to your enjoyment?

A.   Yes

Q.   So initially why did you watch the film six
times and allow the ending to be erased?

A.   I was curious, if I saw it more than once or
twice, if somehow I would be able to overcome the
memory erasure.

Q.   But that was not the case was it?

A.   No, the first time I watched the film without
the glasses I panicked when it became clear that I
could not hold the ending in my mind. Then I just
kept going back to see if it would fix itself.

Q.   And that did not happen did it?

A.   No.

Q.   Mr Harrison could you please listen carefully
to what I am going to read aloud. Exhibit 3 your
Honor. Are you ready Mr Harrison.

A.   Yes.

Q.   "He gazed up at the enormous face. Forty
years it had taken him to learn what kind of smile
was hidden beneath the dark moustache. O cruel,
needless misunderstanding! O stubborn, self willed
exile from the loving breast! Two gin-scented tears
trickled down the sides of his nose. But it was all
right, everything was all right, the struggle was

finished. He had won the victory over himself. He loved Big Brother."

Mr Harrison those were the final words from the book 1984 written by George Orwell. The person being described is the main character Winston Smith. Mr Harrison, can you tell me who did Winston eventually learn to love?

A.   Em

Q.   Take your time Mr Harrison, who did Winston Smith love in the end?

A.   Julia.

Q.   He did not love Big Brother?

A.   No, he hated Big Brother, even when O'Brien was torturing him, he hated Big Brother.

80   ATTORNEY GRANT   Thank you Mr Harrison. No further questions, the prosecution rests your Honor.

81   THE COURT   Miss Gillespie, your next witness?

82   THE COURT   Miss Gillespie, do you intend to call your witness?

83   ATTORNEY GILLESPIE   Your Honor may we approach?

Cave Paintings

'I love you,' Conor said to his partner, as he locked the suit glove onto the wrist connector and checked the seal. She looked back at him through the visor of her helmet, waited for a moment, smiled and replied 'I know.' Conor smiled, punched her on the arm, it was part of the whole routine.
'Ok Hans Solo, don't screw this up, I want you back here in one piece.' Annabell nodded, the time for joking was over, being silly could get you killed. Fooling around when outside was dangerous. Conor would not leave the console all the time she was outside. They lived within a heartbeat of one another. Pulses raised now, this once monthly excursion into the town had come around again all too quickly. Conor's suit had become unrepairable, Annabell's was too small for him. He could not sleep the night before the survey. A difficult conversation as to why they kept doing it was not too far away in their future.

On the Southern coast of Spain, within the province of Andalusia, there is a town called Nerja. Like most coastal towns, it started life as a fishing village, and if you spend time in the local museum, you would find that distant ancestors who clung to this coastline lived in caves and foraged from the sea. Nerja is situated just less than an hour's drive from Malaga, the closest airport. There is a bus which weaves its way through neighbouring towns, which takes a little longer, but Annabell and Conor liked the journey. Conor had been to Nerja several times as a child with his family. When he met Annabell, and they had reached that point in their relationship, when going on holiday together was desirable, he was keen to show this small town to her. He had told her that the town, although a tourist destination, had managed to avoid the influx of foreign bars and restaurants typical to other Spanish resorts. There had been two Irish pubs, but the one in the town centre had closed. That told you something about the town. A couple of English restaurants with English names, advertising roast beef Sunday lunch and satellite sport from back home. However, they did not outwardly offend the eye, and were absorbed into the town's numerous places to dine and to socialise. Socialising was something the locals appeared to have perfected as an art form, unlike many of the seasonal visitors, tied into eating early and then retreating to their rented beds. If you visited the town outside of the summer holiday months, its appeal and atmosphere, seemed even more enhanced.

The main focus for locals and tourists were the main town squares, Plaza España and Plaza Balcón de Europa, with the Parroquia El Salvador, the 17th century church, facing out to the open space bordered by several small cafes. In the height of the summer season, the square was populated by local artists offering portraiture and caricature renditions. Some toy sellers worked the square, to offer relief or frustration to parents of small children, demonstrating the wonders of an elastic band launched LED coloured light up helicopter. Fired high above the square and floating seductively, to onlooking children, back into the vendor's hand. The major decision for parents and children alike, after the decision where and what to eat, was which flavour of ice cream to buy from the beautifully crafted slabs of multicoloured treats, the like of which most visitors had never experienced back home. The Helados Artesanos L shaped counter, displayed and explosion of colour, tastes and textures, to cause mild panic in buyers as to what they wanted and what they would miss out on. Several trips over the course of a stay, would be required. The greedy went for the most expensive option, three scoops of different flavours, which seasoned ice cream enthusiasts knew to eat from a paper tub, not the precariously balanced, and rapidly melting option on top of a cornet. Families lived, the way families should when the worries of life back home could be sidelined for a week or two. Nerja depended on tourism. Most of the property, the apartments and villas were owned by foreigners, the cost of housing for most Spanish too high, and many workers would travel in from the smaller surrounding towns. Despite this it never felt overrun, by one nation or another. Perhaps, this was due to the balance of property ownership and the fact that many villas were also rented out. Perhaps you had to live there full time to really know. Conor and Annabell rented out a small two bedroom apartment in their first few visits to the town. They enjoyed the small balcony spaces that would have views out to the sea. Then, one year they progressed to a villa with a pool, and that was that, they were by their own admission, now spoiled. The two university researchers, did not have high paying jobs, but it did not stop them dreaming of owning a villa, with a pool, one day. They never thought they would have an entire hotel to themselves.

Annabell stood in the centre of the Plaza, facing the entrance of the church. She could see inside, the large wooden doors and the wooden pews had been removed many years before. She tried to remember the square when it had trees. There was a large tree near to the church, different from the others, she could not remember what type of trees. The stumps were all that remained. The palm trees that lined the walkway to the observation point at the end of the Balcon, had also been removed. The large hotel on the West side of the Balcon was now a shell. Most buildings were the same. Only concrete and brick and glass remained. When the population had been cleared, contractors worked to remove as much of the combustible materials from the town. The roof of the church was also marked for dismantling. When word got out, there was a plea to leave the church alone. People thought that one day they would return, and they wanted to be able to return to a church. It had been a mistake. When the temperature reached 70 degrees Celsius, 158 degrees Fahrenheit, nine years after the evacuation, the church roof caught fire following a lightning strike. Annabell could see some of the damaged roof beams inside. The heat had cracked the external walls. It wasn't safe to go any closer. Conor was tracking Annabell's movements, and watching her oxygen levels. He knew she was standing in the square, she always took a few moments to remember. The sensor was at the end of the Balcon, fixed onto the railings, that many holidaymakers had stood at and gazed out to sea. They had a photograph of themselves at the same spot, it was taped onto the side of the monitor Conor was now staring at. The sensor had failed, Annabell had a replacement. There were two sensors. One on the Balcon for air temperature, and one at Burriana beach measuring sea temperature. There was no evidence, but sea life it was thought had retreated to the deeper parts of the oceans. Anything that lived in coastal waters had long died. Conor looked at her air supply time remaining.

'Annie, you're coming up to the forty minute mark.' She looked down at her wrist computer. It showed the temperature was 73 degrees, and her oxygen level was at thirty percent. Inside the suit it was 20 degrees.

'Ok hon, going to the sensor now, won't be long,' she replied. Annabell took one last look at what remained of the square, it was possible this might be the last time.

The next morning, Annabell finished setting her hair wearing it up and in a French roll. Conor was already downstairs in the conference room. She stood at the full length mirror, and smoothed down her skirt. She had decided on the navy jacket and matching skirt, white blouse, and just to have an advantage, a pair of red high heels. Annabell and Conor were 42 and 44 years of age, respectively. Both had stayed in good shape, which was just as well as the shops were no longer open for new outfits.

As she descended the stairs, she could see Conor standing outside the conference room at the double doors, looking at a list of speakers with session times. She walked passed him, ignoring him, as he did her. Once inside the conference room she took a seat two rows back from the front, the projector screen was displaying the conference logo and title placed over the Earth rise picture taken by astronaut William Anders during the Apollo 8 mission. There was a leaflet on the chair beside her, which she picked up and started reading. She found her biography and paper title, checking it through for any alterations, just one it appeared, her last name. Conor entered the conference room and walked up to the lectern. He was wearing his grey suit, with a pale blue shirt opened necked, and unbuttoned half way down. There was a piece of costume jewellery in the form of a gold neckless with something dangling at its end. Annabell forced herself not to look too closely. His hair had been plastered with gel and combed back, some of it had been repurposed into a thin moustache. Then came the voice, which appeared to be based on a downtrodden waiter from Barcelona working at a mythical British sea side resort.

'Good morning everyone, it give me great pleasure to open the parallel sessions of the 29th Conference on Climate Monitoring and Environmental Modelling, here in beautiful Andalusia. I see we have been blessed with clear skies and sunshine, and I hope you all get many opportunity to enjoy the delights of our small town. Our first speaker is Dr. Annabell…, ah excuse me, Dr. Annabell Thunderthighs, sorry my English is no so good, please Dr. Thunderthighs the stage is yours.' Annabell composed herself, nodded to Conor, and moved towards the lectern. The game was to stay in character, not laugh, and not lose, as losing meant the next day you had to do the other's bidding from dawn to dusk. As Annabell placed her memory stick into the lectern computer, she thought Conor's opening move was good and that he would have to pay for the *Thunderthighs* embellishment.

'Thank you Dr. Manuel,' she responded. Conor left the stage area and walked out of the conference room. Annabell started her presentation and talk to the empty room. At slide five of her powerpoint presentation, Conor returned to the room and sat near the back. He had changed out of his suit, and was now wearing jeans, and a loud Hawaiian shirt. His hair was messed up some of it falling across his face. Annabell continued with her presentation, which contained a mixture of pseudo science, and conspiracy theories. She concluded by asking for any questions. Conor immediately put up his hand. Annabell looked around the room at the empty chairs, eventually making eye contact with Conor.

'Yes please, the gentleman at the back,' she invited.

Conor pointed at himself as if to confirm that he had been selected, he stood up and introduced himself. The Australian accent was just as bad as his previous attempt.

'Ah ripper nice one, ah Reg Mulldoon, Melbourne University, Faculty of Barbecuing and Beer Management. Now you said in your presentation that rising global temperatures would seriously decrease male fertility, I believe that's what you said, well I would have to dispute that darling, as everyone knows that the longer you stand next to a barbie, the more motivated your little buggers get, on account of the heat you see, and therefore they are primed and ready to swim faster.'

Annabell looked up at the conference room ceiling apparently deep in thought. She was trying to compose herself, as she had lost the last time they did this, and she really didn't want to lose again. She concentrated and focused before she looked back at Conor.

'Yes I see your point, and yet I wonder if a hyperthermic condition of the scrotum, as per your outdoor sociological study, would be entirely accurate give the counteractive effects of alcohol consumed during said study and leading to erectile dysfunction and inevitable but not unexpected female disappointment, which I have to say, I have encountered many times myself. ' Conor was nodding his head, and biting the inside of his lip trying not to respond.

'Anymore questions, the chair has just informed me that we will be breaking for refreshments now.' Annabell looked around the room again, Conor had his hand back up, she ignored him this time.   As Annabell shut down her presentation, Conor left the conference room. Annabell checked he wasn't there, before she smiled. The bar was opposite the conference room, Annabell walked slowly and purposefully, aware of her movements. She had tried to make Conor laugh the last time she played, but he was annoyingly more funny. This time she would just use sex. Sitting at one of the high chairs at the bar counter, she waited for whatever would appear next. Conor walked into the bar and stood at the side of her. They waited for a moment. Conor was now dressed in a light blue suit she was sure she had never seen. He had tidied and arranged his hair, was wearing a tie, which she was also sure she had not seen that accessory for years. She glanced over to him, he glanced back. He was really quite attractive like that, she thought.

"Bonjour,' Conor started the conversation. Annabell knew more French than Conor, and had a better accent. 'Good.' she thought. 'He thinks he's Gods gift to women now, just what I wanted.'

'Bonjour Monsieur, aimez-vous la conférence,'

"Ah,… oui, but I must really practice my English,' Good save Annabell thought. 'Is there no one serving?'

'I haven't seen anyone,' Annabell replied looking around the space.

'Well that is a disaster, non? I mean to keep such a beautiful woman waiting. Fortunately, I myself have worked in many bars when I was a student at the Sorbonne, so may I get you something to drink?' Annabell looked at the empty gantry, and glass shelves, they had finished off everything some time last year.

'I'll have whatever you are having,' she replied.

'Ok, let me see now.' Conor reached under the counter and brought two wine glasses up and set them down. He reached down again and slowly brought up a bottle of Malbec.

'Conor is that real?' Annabell said excitedly.

'Oui Madam, and you *mon cheri* just lost' Conor said grinning.

Conor delighted in informing Annabell that her failure was now a new record time from start to finish. She in turn protested that the wine stunt wasn't fair, was in fact cruel, and she would not accept the forfeit. Conor had found the bottle several days earlier. He explained to Annabell that it was stashed behind one of the laundry driers down in the plant room, he reckoned it was hidden there by a past employee and forgotten about. It was possible the wine had spoiled given it must have been at least seven years since the staff left and the hotel was converted.

It took eight months to alter the Parador Hotel, Nerja's flagship tourist accommodation. Conor and Annabell moved into the former hotel and took up their survey duties as one of sixty three scientific stations. Both academics, having no family of their own, they were selected to operate what would be known as Nerja Station 17. The survey teams were all composed of two persons. Situated in different countries, the task was to monitor temperature levels across the planet. The hope was that the global temperature would stabilise. In the six years since they started records, the temperature had continued to rise.

The Parador hotels, *para* in Spanish meaning to halt or stop and stay, were a chain of state owned hotels that were set up and operated by the Paradores de Turismo de España. The company had its origins in 1928, with the opening of its first hotel. The company was founded by King Alfonso XIII, his desire to promote tourism across Spain. Most of the hotels were born out of the conversion of historical buildings, and others sited in areas away from established tourism. Annabell and Conor's Parador hotel was built in 1965. The hotel was selected for the survey station for three reasons. It had the suitable mass of building that could be shielded from the external heat, allowing Conor and Annabell to live within a protected, air conditioned section of the complex. The large swimming pool could be supplied with sea water, for desalination processing, by running pipework down the cliff edge to the sea below. It had an outside lift, at the end of the garden area, which made access down the cliff safer than the long steep path from the hotel to Burriana Beach. Once a convenience for guests, it now allowed Annabell to reach the sea sensor with plenty of air supply. She could take her time walking along the pathway past the remains of the restaurants. Canopies attached to simple kitchen structures that extended out over the diners. The floor was just sand, plastic chairs and tables, and simple menus. Conor and Annabell lunched in all of them over the years, after lounging on the sun beds close by. Days spent drinking cocktails, and making time for the offers of massage. The Chinese ladies who roamed along the coastline, with unreadable medical leaflets complete with anatomical diagram to show you the benefits of the Eastern treatment. You could lie on your sunbed, listen to the waves and feel your body being worked by extraordinarily strong fingers of the diminutive women just trying to earn a living as best they could. For food, their favourite spot was a restaurant at the end of the row. As well as the kitchen area, there was an outdoor section where firewood was cut and stored, broken wooden pallets also used to create a large fire on the floor. Above the fire, a huge blackened paella pan about four or five feet in diameter would be placed in a cradle, attended to by a team of men who would be offered unwelcome culinary advice from occasional male bystanders. On weekend days, lunch was a local affair, families gathered at large tables, across the generations, animated chatter entertaining Annabell and Conor.

The hotel was comprised of two main buildings with low pitched roofs. Both roofs were covered in solar panels, and solar collectors for power and hot water. Five years of supplies had been installed into the hotel. When they lost contact with the last station that answered their radio messages, Conor and Annabell decided to ration their supplies. That was two years ago. Now, they had more electrical power than they could use, an endless supply of sea water for desalination, but the food was running out. At year four, they were to be extracted from the station by the military, most probably a submarine would be sent. Conor and Annabell had no knowledge of what was left outside of their town. The radio silence was unnerving, but they continued to broadcast every day at noon. They would send out the day's temperature readings from the sensors, and then ask if anyone was receiving. The last and seemingly final message they got back was from station 28. The information was that it was possible that the USA had invaded Canada. Northern latitudes, had become more precious than gold.

Whether stations were becoming abandoned, or more worryingly taken over for shelter, was not known. One by one over the years, the silence grew louder.

The wine was to be kept for Friday 18th August 2067, in twenty seven days time time. It was the anniversary of their first date, Annabell was 22 when she first met Conor. They worked in the same research lab, Conor was there a year before her. Both born into a world full of uncertainties, a world that had showed its warnings, and had been ignored. By the time they had applied and been accepted for the Nerja station, they knew the chances of a planetary reprieve, was wishful thinking. Thinking as scientists, they knew that the timescale for an environmental balance, was thousands, perhaps million of years to come. They had decided not to have children, although if they had, they would have been loved. In their mid thirties, the love they had for one another would allow them to isolate themselves from the rest of human contact. When Annabell found the initial call for volunteers, and that one station was going to be located in Nerja, it took one evening's brief conversation to agree that they would apply. As the time came nearer for them to occupy the hotel, the global average mean temperature had risen by four degrees. Methane, and nitrous oxide were now being released from the thawing permafrost. Many times more damaging that carbon dioxide, they accelerated the effects of atmospheric global warming. When Conor and Annabell were children, a phrase appeared within the media, and soon became a widely used metaphor. The term "*a series of one way doors*" would be heard over and over again. All of these doors were closed now, mankind had marched through them.

'This is good wine,' Annabell announced, inspecting the label on the bottle. Conor nodded. 'Do you think that somewhere out there in our town, there is a villa with a secret wine cellar, just waiting to be found?'

'Perhaps,' Conor replied. 'I checked all the bars, all the restaurants, when I was outside, no joy, they took it all with them.'

'Well I hope they had a good time, because it must have got rough out there.' Conor nodded again.

'Yeah, I'm sure it did,' Conor replied. They sat watching the sunset on the large screen. There was a moment when the sun could be seen just at the horizon. The clouds across the planet were thickening. These massive cloud systems were moving with increased speed as the upper atmosphere turbulence was driven by the trapped solar heat below. The outside camera was heavily filtered, so the colours could not be taken as true, but they both still looked for it every evening. The night time temperature would only drop a few degrees, the night sky and its stars hidden by the thick ever present clouds with less and less breaks as each day passed. As the screen darkened, they finished their meal and held each other. Sleep followed quickly, it might have been that both now were relieved that the decision had been made.

'Right, straight there, straight back, no sightseeing, if you can't get in, straight back ok,'

'Ok,' Annabell confirmed.

'The cylinder will be heavy, watch your balance, and your breathing will be more rapid, so leave yourself plenty of time ok.' Conor checked her suit's coolant system, checked the connections one more time. He lowered her helmet visor, engaging the seal lock. He gave her the thumbs up, she responded the same way. She had eighty five minutes of oxygen, the timer was set and was running. Annabell's suit resembled some of the early US astronaut's spacesuits. It was reasonably thin, and a good fit, with enough joint and finger

mobility, for walking and working with tools. There was limited flexibility in the waist, and neck, meaning you had to turn the whole body at times to look in a different direction. She had a distance of 3.6 kilometres there and back. It should take her just under an hour. Her suit would regulate her temperature, pumping the coolant around her body. Her boots were the most uncomfortable, as the soles were in contact with the blisteringly hot concrete pavements. You had to be careful of your route and footsteps. Conor had lost concentration, and for those few seconds he had walked in the remnants of a tarred patch of ground. He made it back to the hotel, but spent days recovering from heat and blister damage to both feet. They tried to repair the suit, but the fear was that it might break down, and so the outside surveys fell to Annabell.
Conor followed her to the start of three doors that gave access to the outside, he could only go as far as the second door. Annabell entered the space between the first and second doors, she indicated to Conor to leave, so she could open the next door. She turned away from him, Conor whispered 'I love you.' There was no way Annabell could hear him through her helmet, but she turned around and looked at him, smiling and mouthed the words, 'I know,' because she knew he would say it.

The route from the Parador, would take Annabell through the town but not the main square. The fastest route was to navigate the narrow streets which used to be home to many small shops and restaurants. These streets would also provide some shade. She was heading for the fire station on the West side of the town. The idea was to try and get hold of a respirator, the type firemen use to enter smoke filled buildings. Conor would need this in order to breath for the short time he would be outside. The air would burn his lungs without a mask and oxygen supply. Annabell walked steadily through the streets trying to remember the shops, identifying some of the restaurants where she and Conor had dined. She had been giving Conor a running commentary, describing for him the town he would not see again. She had to stop talking for a while, as the heat in her suit felt that it was rising, her body working harder as she reached an incline and was back out in the hazy glare of the sun again. Just before leaving the narrow lanes behind her, she walked through the small Plaza Cantarero. The dried out fountain and the trunks of what was left of the orange trees, the empty concrete benches where the senior citizens would meet and talk the day away, caused her to stop. A memory returned.

'Conor,' she said into her microphone.

'Here,' Conor replied.

'Do you remember the first time we arrived here at the bus station, and we walked down through the town?' She asked.

'Think so, remember we got a bit lost, we were going to get a taxi to the apartment, but there weren't any,' he replied.

"Yeah, but do you remember the first thing that was different about here?' Conor thought for a moment as he checked her air supply and temperature readings.

'Oranges?'

'Oranges, on the trees in this little park area, and all the oranges just lying on the ground,' Annabell added. Conor smiled.

'Bring some back, I'll make smoothies,' he said.

She reached the end of the main road where the small hut that marked the bus station once stood. The main road heading West would bring her to a roundabout then a short turn Northwards to the fire station. Her time was ok. As she walked on the main road she looked back towards the mountains and the collection of whitewashed villas and apartments huddled together at the top end of the town winding up to the foot of the hills. They had stayed in a few properties there, although further from the town centre and the beach, their raised position meant cooler breezes at night. Beyond these properties higher up were individual villas, and then the town of Frigiliana, were Conor watched Annabell fall in love with Spain. He loved that day, that one excursion that he was so excited about, and to see the very soul of this part of the country imprint onto Annabell's heart. All these memories and moments surrounded them, but they were like the images a prisoner carries into his cell, as they were now removed from being physically revisited. Burned away by a sun that scorched the Earth, a furnace locked in by clouds. Cleansed by fire it seemed. There was one experience left for them to reclaim from the heat, but only if their hopes would be realised. The fire station was in sight, and as she made it up from the roundabout to the structure, she saw a glimpse of red sticking out from the open garages. It was there, a large fire truck. She could see it, but she could also see the heavy perimeter gates that were closed.

'Conor, the gates are locked, there's a padlock,' she didn't want to say it out loud.

'Ok come back, now.' Annabell heard him but could not believe it was for nothing. She looked hard into the cab of the fire truck, less than ten metres from where she stood at the gate. On the back on the cab on a shelf, she saw the glass of a respirator, then another.

'No, not yet, going to walk around to the back, see what state the fence is in.' Conor checked her time and remaining air, she was still ok for another ten or so minutes. Annabell worked her way around the perimeter fence. It was solid, a metal fence that was taller that Annabell, posts set into concrete, and a wire mesh which gave way to a push, stood between her and the respirators. Conor had waited as long as he could.

'Annie, what's happening?'

'Just a minute, having a think,' Annabell responded, she could feel panic starting rise within her, her voice did not cover it up.

'Annie, just come back, it's ok,' Conor spoke softly. A few seconds went by, there was silence.

'Annie?' 'Annie?'

'Just give me a minute.'

'One more, and then head back, no longer,' Conor was panicking as well. The minute Conor timed, Annabell stood quietly, thinking, her minute seemed more like a few seconds.

'Annie, that's it, just abandon it start back.'

'Conor, I'm going off radio for a moment, got to think.' Annabell pressed the button on her wrist computer to silence the radio. She knew Conor would go nuts, so she did not give him a chance to reply. Conor tried to tell her no, but he was too late.

Next door to the Fire station was a building she had seen from the road when going to the supermarket but until now had not paid much attention to it. Annabell stood opposite what looked like where the main doors would have been. Large silver letters in relief from the white render of the two floor building, spelled out *"Tarantorio La Esparanza"* in a plain font. She looked the words but could not work out the meaning. Entering the building initially gave no further clues. A reception area floored by polished marble, suggested some kind of business centre. As she moved through one set of internal doors then another, a church interior appeared. The walls on both sides showed pictures of the stations of the cross with lights above each, the alter was still there, the seating gone, but it was a space dominated in white marble, and Annabell had a feeling of peace. Then it hit her, this was a chapel inside a funeral parlour. Her first response was to swear. Being a scientist she did not believe. However under the circumstances, of their present life, and the choices they faced, ending up in the chapel of a funeral parlour had some twisted logic to it, which some may regard as a sign. She looked down at her wrist computer, she had now put herself in a situation. It would be tight to get back to the hotel. She thought of Conor, and switched her radio back on.

'Coming home.' Conor looked at the monitor, there was no point saying anything, she would know, she had to move quickly.

If Conor was asked, he would say that Annabell could deal with being left behind better than him. It scared him, always had. Those moments when something unexpected happened when she was attending to the sensors, nothing major, but enough to stir the imagination, enough to raise the question "*what if?*" Conor stared at the photograph on the side of the monitor, he did not want to look at the readouts. Annabell left the chapel, but took the wrong turning on her exit, the next set of doors lead into a small presentation room. Displayed within, on wooden easels and on the floor of the room, were beautifully decorated sample headstones, or rather the type of outer facing stone that would be found on a funeral vault. Marble and stone examples of final messages, and prayers and the names of the dead, were engraved onto these samples. Annabell realising her mistake moved as quickly as she could to the outside of the building, and began to walk passed the fire station. Almost passed the end of perimeter fence, she stopped suddenly.

'Honey, I have an idea,' she radioed, 'Just a couple of minutes.'

The next thing Conor heard sounded like a cry of pain.

'Annie what are you doing?' There was no response just laboured breathing and then...

'This is really heavy,' she gasped, before letting out a scream, a scream of utter determination. The marble slab crashed into the wire fence, with Annabell following after, pulled off balance by the mass of the stone. The wire split half way down from the top of the adjacent post, and then stopped, holding up both the stone and Annabell. She recovered her footing, and then the weight of the projectile, caused the remainder of the fence to tear loose. She punched the air with both fists and shouted 'YES.'

Conor was updated as to her success, but the readouts were now impossibly low. Perhaps they were wrong he hoped.

Climbing into the fire truck, Annabell grabbed one of the respirators from the shelf, finding it already connected to a back harness and oxygen tank. The tank's gauge showed it was full. Placing the harness over one shoulder, she stepped down from the tender. It was then she looked down the side of the vehicle at a cable which was connected to a panel near to the rear wheels. She followed the cable with her eyes as it lay on the ground and saw its length exit the rear of the open air garage. At the rear of the building, where the cable terminated, there was a solar charging point. Someone had left it connected. Moving slowly back to the fire truck's cab, she let her brain put together the plan. As long as it had power, it would work. Checking the details of the plan over once more, she realised she would need to take the charging cable, they could connect it to their solar cells. Annabell sat at the drivers seat. She looked at the dashboard and found the start button. The displays lit up.

'Honey, see you in five minutes, bringing you an anniversary present,' she radioed 'Oh, it might be a bit scratched sorry.'
The gates of the fire station were no match for it.

Conor heard it before he saw it or Annabell, blue lights and sirens, hope and rescue was on its way.

There had always been one issue with the original relocation plan. Conor's suit was beyond repair, it was unable to keep his body cool enough to survive the ten or so minute drive. They had to find a way to reduce the temperature inside the SUV that had been parked in the hotel garage since they first arrived. The cars air conditioning system was not powerful enough and may be overwhelmed with the outside air temperature. If it failed, the temperature would rise quickly. How to keep Conor cool was a problem to which they had not as yet found a solution. It was going to be a one way trip, and they had supplies and some equipment to take with them. The other concern was the tyres. Would they hold out, would they get stuck, and then it was a certain end for both of them. When Annabell stood at the fire station, she saw the truck, she saw the large thick tires, she saw it pouring water over itself, keeping them cool. They made the modifications to the truck over the next week. The cabin area was designed to hold seven firefighters, stripping out all but the front bench seat and using the side lockers that ran down the side of the vehicle, they had more than enough space.

For the remaining time, they charged up batteries, gathered boxes of candles, decided on what food they would need from what was left. They would leave three days before their anniversary. Until that time, they continued to broadcast the temperature readings to a world they could only speculate about. Their last remaining sunsets had become more precious. They sat and talked of the events of their lives, both grateful that they had this time in their special hotel.

Heading East along the coast from Nerja, before the turn off to Maro at about 4.3 Kilometres from the Parador, is the Fundación Cueva de Nerja, the Nerja Caves. Five young boys had discovered the cave system on the 12 January 1959. Conor did not know it at the time, but as a young child on holiday, he had met one of the boys at his parents' favourite beachside restaurant. Then a much older man, but very much in charge of the large paella cooking pans and the staff that attended to them. The caves had become a major tourist attraction and sight of scientific interest. In February 2012 Neanderthal cave paintings possibly dating as far back as 25,000 years BC were discovered. The system extended to some 5 kilometres. Conor and Annabell would only need a small part of the huge vaulted gothic caverns with stalagmites and stalactites that had created impossible shapes over millions of years. There was a presentation area within the caves, where concerts were staged. It was known as the *Nerja Cathedral*. The first two days of living in their new home, were spent connecting lighting, organising food, and a sleeping area. The temperature in the cave remained constant, outside it did not. Conor and Annabell's anniversary came around on the third day. They worked on the presentation together. When it was completed, Conor transferred it to one of the projectors they had taken from the conference room at the hotel. With candles lit, and shadows flickering across the walls and ceiling of their underground palace, they had their anniversary dinner. The bottle of wine, which had been carefully wrapped and protected on the journey to the caves, was opened and allowed to breathe.

Conor and Annabell kissed, and held each other. Annabell poured the wine and they settled back, side by side to watch the show. The projector's light and colour seemed more brilliant in the darkness of the candlelit space. A song played, it's first line sung, was matched to images of forests from all over the planet, then an image of a young man handing a flower to a girl

"I see trees of green… red roses too"

Conor and Annabell held hands and watched the images appear one after another, tears rolled down their faces, and they smiled at one another. They would be able to finish the wine before the small dissolved tablets, the military had left them, would make them fall asleep.

Thousands of years before them, people made marks on the cave walls of animals and other objects. Conor and Annabell's marks were digital on the walls of those same caves. The battery would run down, the caves would return to darkness and silence. The memory stick plugged into the projector was there for anyone, or any being who might find them, all they wanted to say, was for them it had been a wonderful world.

272

Printed in Poland
by Amazon Fulfillment
Poland Sp. z o.o., Wrocław

62141520R00154